A joy of reading (and writin̪
much we learn about tim
cocooned in a compelling ....,.
Wangard found a time machine that dropped her on the eastern shores of Brazil during World War II. If an invisibility cloak allowed her to fly with the pilots who made the supply runs from the Natal base to Ascension Island. The choice of a rarely-used setting for a WWII novel and the realism provided by historic details gives Ms. Wangard's characters—a Brazilian and an American whose German families were affected by the events of WWI—an amazing stage on which to find love in the midst of intrigue. I truly enjoyed and highly recommend this story.

— Johnnie Alexander, best-selling, award-winning author of *Where Treasure Hides* and *The Cryptographer's Dilemma*

Unsung Stories of World War II – Book One

SEASHELLS IN MY POCKET

TERRI WANGARD

Scrivenings
PRESS
Quench your thirst for story.
www.ScriveningsPress.com

Published by Scrivenings Press LLC
15 Lucky Lane
Morrilton, Arkansas 72110
https://ScriveningsPress.com

Printed in the United States of America

Paperback ISBN 978-1-64917-368-3

eBook ISBN 978-1-64917-369-0

Editors: Amy R. Anguish and Susan Page Davis

Cover design by Linda Fulkerson (bookmarketinggraphics.com)

All characters are fictional, and any resemblance to real people, either factual or historical, is purely coincidental.

Yea, though I walk through the valley of the shadow of death, I will fear no evil: for thou art with me; thy rod and thy staff they comfort me.

~ Psalm 23: 4

Chapter One

Recife, Brazil
1942

Mollusks possessed such incredible artistic ability. Amazing that soft, slimy creatures could secrete the right elements to create such intricate, tough beauty as this.

Isabel Neumann twirled the seashell between her finger and thumb, examining it in a shaft of sunlight. Streaks of blue circled the shell, unlike any coloring she'd seen in an *anachis*. A tiny hole marred its perfection, no doubt why the dove snail inhabitant had abandoned its home.

She considered her design and positioned the shell. No. Maybe a dried daisy amid the circle of pink striated scallop seashells? No again. No flowers for this design either. Maybe not even seashells.

Her customer for this commission, with a rough-and-tumble family of four boys, would want a grittier montage.

Isabel cleared her workspace and rummaged in her box of beach debris. Lots of driftwood and cork. Even an oar lock.

Dozens of broken sand dollars. She fingered a large piece as an idea percolated. "What do you think, Mamãe? I could design a little shop with a sign that reads *Sand Dollar Repair*. A little corn husk figure could patch pieces together. Wouldn't that be appealing?"

Mamãe looked up from her mending and smiled. "Sounds very whimsical, and I think you should create that. But would Mrs. Santos appreciate a charming scene like that?"

"No, she would not. She wants an assortment of shore flotsam like I made for Mrs. Gama." Isabel picked up the oar lock and turned it around and around, her thumb rubbing the rusted shaft. "I know. Everything will represent a fisherman's shipwreck."

Several long pieces of driftwood would serve as shelves or dividers within the three-by-two-foot frame. She positioned the lock, an old bottle, a small block and tackle, and a ratty old fishing lure.

The collage needed seashells for a touch of prettiness. She added a long spiraling *coronium elegans* rock snail shell and a deep orange *conasprella*, another sea snail shell, from a mollusk in the cone snail family. Maybe she'd even spare a sand dollar or two. And a crab's pincer.

What a blessing that people paid her to create artwork from the treasures she found washed up on the beach. Working with shells held far more interest for Isabel than her job at the dry goods store. She loved walking along the shore, listening to the surf, watching sandpipers chase the waves, feeling the surf wash over her toes. Seashells were her preferred finds, and several local homes displayed her delicate shell and pressed flower designs.

So what if her twin brother Marcos referred to her scavenging as cleaning up the beach?

"Time for some coffee." Mamãe rose from the sofa, laying aside her work. She studied Isabel's layout and nodded. "Mrs. Santos will be pleased. What about this tiny pair of sandals? They could dangle from fishing line."

"Ooh, good idea." Isabel grabbed some line and threaded it through the straps. A noise from outside distracted her. She leaned back from her worktable to peer through the living room window. *Oh, no.* "Marcos is home with that friend of his."

At first glance, Uwe Schneider was handsome, with wavy white-blond hair and chiseled features. His cold gray eyes, however, lacked a speck of warmth. His utterances all took the tone of demands, and he expected everyone to jump to do his bidding. Especially Isabel. She suppressed a shudder. Why did he act like he owned her?

Mamãe smiled. "I'm glad Marcos found a good friend. He's seemed so restless since returning from Germany."

"Good friend?" Isabel sputtered. They never should have sent Marcos to Germany for university. Not while the Nazis were in control. "I'm sure he intends to corrupt Marcos. Why would a young man of military age be allowed to leave Germany unless he's a spy or a"—her voice dropped to a whisper—"a saboteur."

"Darling, you have such an imagination. He's a sweet boy." Mamãe laughed, patting Isabel's shoulder. "I'll put the coffee on."

They hadn't realized in 1937 the true state of affairs when Papai's sister invited Marcos to stay with her family in Heidelberg. The Germans tried to draft him into their army a year later, and the family barely got him out of the country. Once home, he'd confided the Germans let him go because they wanted him to send information about Brazil. They wanted him to spy. Now Uwe had followed him across the Atlantic to work on him. Isabel was sure of that.

The men entered the room as Mamãe returned with the refreshments.

"*Guten tag, Frau Neumann. Wie geht es Ihnen?*" Isabel suppressed a *hmphf* at Uwe's obvious ingratiating crooning.

Even worse was Mamãe's simpering, "I'm fine, Uwe. So nice to see you."

Isabel refused to look up from her work.

"*Guten tag*, Isabel." Uwe planted himself at her side, his hand sliding onto her shoulder.

A long moment passed as she dropped her shoulder and leaned away from him.

"*Olá*." She kept her voice flat.

Uwe's hand clenched, pinching her. "You will speak to me in German."

"This is Brazil. We speak Portuguese." She still didn't look at him.

"You will show me respect." He grabbed her arm and yanked her up toward him.

Her leg hit the table hard enough to leave a bruise. The jarring caused several pieces of her artwork to slide out of place. Some fell to the floor. A perfect sand dollar shattered into five pieces.

"My design." She wrenched free of his grip.

"Hey, take it easy." At least her brother made an effort to defend her.

"Uwe, leave her be." Mamãe tried to step between them.

"Don't tell me what to do, frau." Uwe shoved Mamãe out of the way.

Marcos leaped forward and caught Mamãe before she fell.

Papai appeared in the doorway, his eyes ablaze. "Leave our home, *Herr Schneider*. You no longer are welcome here."

Isabel hadn't realized Papai had come in. Last she knew, he'd been helping their neighbor construct a stone patio overlooking the beach. He must have seen Uwe arrive with Marcos and suspected trouble. At least he believed Uwe was a Nazi spy sent to bend Marcos to do his will. Isabel had heard Papai and Marcos argue more than once about Uwe's merits.

Now Uwe's chest heaved like he would fight Papai until, eyes scowling, he spun around. "Come on, Marcos."

Marcos hesitated, glancing at both parents, before following him out.

Mamãe stood wide-eyed, a hand at her throat. Maybe now her image of Uwe as a sweet boy had changed.

Isabel fled to her room. Sounds of a heated disagreement in the drive floated through the open window.

"Will you just forget about her?" Exasperation rang in Marcos's voice.

"She will come around."

"You do realize she doesn't like you."

"Doesn't matter. I will make her mine." Uwe's arrogance repulsed her, but then his words registered.

No, no, no. Isabel twisted a lock of hair round and round her finger. Here in Brazil, they'd heard the Nazis were bullies, and Uwe certainly lived up to the rumor. She agreed with Papai that he must be a spy and wanted to entangle Marcos in his misdeeds, but why did he fixate on her?

Grabbing her Bible from the bedside table, she pulled out the postcards of Cypress Gardens tucked within the cover. Her cousin Huberto had sent them from the United States.

She recalled the day he'd shown up at their door. They had still lived in Florianópolis then, in southern Brazil.

Huberto had been a sailor in the German navy and escaped when his ship limped into port in Montevideo. He detested the Nazis and what they were doing to Germany, and he resolved to thwart their evil purposes. Papai paid his way to America, where he now worked for U.S. military intelligence. He'd sent these postcards to inform them of his safe arrival.

Isabel studied the cards. Cypress Gardens looked beautiful. Lots of lush, colorful flowers. Pretty girls wearing bathing suits, sitting in small boats. Moss hanging from trees. A gazebo overlooking a lagoon. How she wished she could join him there.

Marcos appeared in her doorway, leaning against the frame. "German women are proud to serve the Reich in every way they can. A woman's most joyous task is to care for her family." His mouth twisted. "Uwe believes Papai totally failed in bringing you up properly. He is determined to bring you to heel and train you into his perfect wife."

Isabel shuddered. "Never. I absolutely will not marry such an arrogant creep." She dropped the postcards on the table before she ended up wrinkling them. "And why would I serve the Reich? I've never been there. I'm Brazilian, not German."

"Doesn't matter. In the Germans' eyes, you are a German because of your heritage." He knocked twice on the doorframe. "The Nazis' arrogance makes them confident bullies who don't hesitate to demand their way. They have the German people intimidated into looking the other way from their nasty deeds. Uwe expects you to behave the same way. Don't ever let him catch you alone."

Marcos sauntered down the hall and Isabel stared out the window. Palm fronds swayed in the ocean breeze. Close by, a bird sang a cheerful tune, and in the background, waves crashed onto the shore. She sighed. Her joy in the day had been tarnished.

True, southern Brazil was filled with Germans. Mamãe's family had immigrated after the 1848 revolutions in Germany had failed. Papai, a pilot in the Great War, left Germany in 1919.

He promptly met and married Mamãe. A year later, Isabel and Marcos joined them.

Life in Florianópolis had been idyllic, and Papai said it was like living in Germany. Hundreds of thousands of Germans had settled here. Maybe even a million. She and Marcos attended German schools, their minister came from Germany, buildings boasted German architecture, and everyone spoke German. Mamãe told them there'd been tension and a few incidents during the Great War twenty-five years ago, but their good life continued.

And now another war, much worse. The Brazilian government prohibited the German language. German pilots in Brazil lost their jobs with German or Italian airlines. Papai wisely remained independent, operating his own air cargo business with three planes. They'd moved to Recife to avoid the German enclave.

They lived in a beachfront house where she could indulge her passion for collecting seashells. She'd made a few friends. Anyone would say they'd assimilated with their Brazilian neighbors.

But she didn't feel at home here. She didn't want to return to the German community in Florianópolis either. What did she want?

She fingered the postcards. Of course, Huberto wasn't in Cypress Gardens anymore. He lived in Washington, D.C. She'd seen pictures of monuments surrounded by cherry blossoms. She'd like to see that too. Unfortunately, she didn't have any intelligence to share with the Americans.

She sat up straight as an idea struck her. Maybe she could still work for them.

The Americans were building an air base in Natal as part of their South Atlantic ferry route. Natal had been chosen because it stood on the tip of Brazil's bulge into the Atlantic, the closest point to Africa. Maybe she could get a job at Parnamirim Field. Did they hire Brazilian civilians? According to the news, hundreds of Brazilians had been hired to construct the base, but surely they'd still need local help for their operations.

Mamãe and Papai wouldn't like her going so far from home. Not one little bit. But she was twenty-two years old. Time to be on her own. Natal lay over one hundred fifty miles north, and the roads were horrible. But Papai could fly her there in his airplane. Perfect. No reason in the world why her fantasy couldn't come true.

Chapter Two

Ascension Island, South Atlantic
1943

The very long night was nearly over. Dawn broke and spilled sunlight onto Ascension Island as the cargo plane lined up with the runway and settled gently on the pavement. The small island held dozens of aircraft, many of them belonging to the Air Transport Command. Waging war required a lot of equipment, and it was more difficult when the fighting took place on the opposite side of the world from the United States.

Daniel Lambert eased his C-47 Douglas Skytrain into the designated spot and went through the parking checklist with Reggie Wendt, his co-pilot. "Parking brake."

"On."

"Tailwheel."

"Locked."

"Fuel selectors."

"Off."

Daniel stifled a yawn. He could do this in his sleep, but it wasn't recommended. By the time he reached the pitot cover, which protected the sensors acting as flow meters, he couldn't hold back. His yawn nearly unhinged his jaw. "As soon as we get checked in, I'm going to hibernate."

Reggie nodded to a jeep pulling up to their nose. "First things first. My guess is that the general down there is the guy expecting his fancy fridge."

"Oh, bother."

Trust the problems to crop up immediately upon landing. It made sense, of course. The high brass wanted their luxuries on foreign battlefields and didn't hesitate to commandeer cargo space. Never mind that the men under them desperately needed the weapons and medicine the cargo planes ought to be hauling. And if the big man didn't show up to grab his indulgences right away, someone else might see them and help himself. But why was he here on Ascension? Had he left the African battlefield to escort his refrigerator? Or maybe he was delaying his arrival over there until he had all his luggage in tow. Either way, he didn't seem like the kind of commanding officer Daniel would care to serve under.

Easing out of the cramped cockpit, he snatched up the manifest clipboard. "All right. Time to disappoint the guy."

A truck had been positioned at the tiny forward door. Daniel slid through and jumped into the truck bed, searching for a loadmaster. The base was as busy as Natal. They'd have to wait their turn. Too bad. He'd have to deal with this pompous general on his own.

The man didn't waste words. "Lieutenant, did you come from Brazil? Do you have a special package to be forwarded to Khartoum?"

Daniel held back a snort of derision. Clever of the man to offer a destination in Africa instead of his name. Made it sound official. He studied his clipboard, knowing he'd refused to allow it on his plane in Natal. *Package*. Like the fridge was something he could have tucked under his seat.

"No, sir. We're full of high priority refrigerated whole blood for transfusions and crates of grenades urgently needed in Africa." He didn't bother to mention the five sacks of mail squeezed into the spot that could have held the fridge.

The general slapped the truck. "This delay is insufferable. It's delaying our departure."

His aide spoke up. "Maybe they can pack the refrigerator with blood so that it pays its way, so to speak."

Daniel kept a poker face with difficulty. Brazen of the aide to admit the general wanted his personal comforts.

The general practiced no restraint. His face mottled with red splotches, and he snapped at the poor man. "Enough, Smythe. See to the jeep before those bozos take it."

He stomped off, and a wave of sighs tickled Daniel's ears. He glanced back to watch his crew wilt in the doorway. A glimpse of the hapless aide prompted a tired smile. "Do you like working for the general?"

The man stiffened. "There are worse jobs."

"Right." Daniel nodded. "Latrine duty." He spun around before he laughed in the guy's face. "Okay, fellas. You know the drill. See that the cargo is claimed. Stay out of trouble. Get some rest. Reggie, it's your show. I have to get some shuteye."

He'd barely closed his eyes in a transient crew tent, it seemed, when Reggie shook him awake. "Rise and shine. Wheels up in sixty minutes."

"What?"

Daniel lay bathed in sweat, the tent was so hot. The flap hadn't been left open to allow a bit of ocean breeze. A cacophony of sound assaulted him—men yelling, machines

11

clanking, and engines revving. Through bleary eyes, he spotted the purple sky. "What time is it?"

"It's 0400."

"What?"

"You slept around the clock, Daniel. Come on, they're serving something that passes for breakfast. That ought to wake you up."

Daniel scrubbed his eyes with his palms. "Do we have a load to take back?"

"Yep. Wounded from the North African battlefields."

"Lovely. They'll want a smooth flight." Daniel swayed as he worked himself into a sitting position.

"See you at chow." Reggie whistled his way out.

A rustling—and was that a faint snicker?—behind him brought his head around. Bill Nelson, his navigator, packed his duffel, a smirk on his face and his uniform appearing freshly ironed. Daniel gritted his teeth. Billy Boy's superior attitude rankled him, but he couldn't let on. Nelson would feel empowered. All because he was four years older.

Daniel gathered his gear. "Time for a bath."

Surprise flashed across Nelson's face. "Didn't you hear Wendt? We're scheduled to take off in an hour."

"Probably more like fifty-five minutes now." Stepping out of the tent, Daniel spotted the bathing facility and set off whistling Reggie's tune. He needed to be clean more than having a full belly to feel human. All his life he'd been sensitive to smells, and right now? He wasn't daisy fresh, that was for sure. The island was a dry place and water was rationed, but he'd manage with a spit bath.

As the eastern horizon lightened, he made out the cloud-shrouded Green Mountain, the only place where vegetation grew on these thirty-four square miles of British-owned lava rock. Sharp reefs and tidal currents made swimming dangerous along much of the coast, or he'd take a dip in the surf. Strange, forbidding place here, midway between Africa and South America.

He made it to the plane with ten minutes to spare, his stomach satisfied with powdered eggs, dry toast, and canned peaches. He'd even smuggled out two canteens filled with water, into which he dumped lemonade powder. It wasn't the tastiest, but neither was the water.

Both cargo doors at the rear remained open, allowing a view of the wounded occupying every seat and stretcher. Daniel trotted up the steps and did a quick count. Twelve sat in the uncomfortable sling seats and ten lay on stretchers, plus a little red-haired nurse and a pudgy orderly. As he walked up the narrow sloping aisle, he noted the aircraft appeared well cleaned and the luggage was securely stowed, but then he noticed a loose stretcher bracket.

"Kenny? Bring a screwdriver."

Exuberant crew chief Kenny Wright appeared at Daniel's elbow with the requested tool and tightened the proud screw. "We may have a problem patient." He nodded toward one of the sitting passengers. "That colonel must be a friend of the refrigerator general. He asked where the VIP accommodations are."

Daniel winced. "Great. Just great." He cast another glance around the airplane. "Looks like Nelson's getting the latest weather dope. Are we fueled up?"

"Eight hundred gallons. We're ready to go."

A feathery touch on Daniel's leg gained his attention. He looked down into the pain-glazed eyes of a patient. "How long till we get home?"

Daniel crouched down. "It'll be a few days yet. There are no nonstop flights from Africa to the U.S., so you're hopscotching all over. From here we'll fly to Brazil, then on to Trinidad and

Miami Maybe a few more stops. This flight from Ascension to Natal, Brazil, will take nine hours."

The boy groaned. "I feel like I'm about to slide out of here." He twitched a shoulder. "But I can stand it. I'm going home. That's the main thing."

Daniel patted his shoulder. "We're at a steep angle now because the nose is so much higher than the tail, but once we're airborne, we'll be level."

He found his way to the nurse, peering at her name badge. "Lieutenant Fromm, I'm Lieutenant Lambert, the pilot."

"Well, hello." The sultry voice didn't match her petite size. "What may I do for you?"

He jerked his gaze from his readiness inspection to her. Did she think she was a stewardess? "Nothing for me." He pointed with his pen. "That patient seems to be in bad shape."

"Maybe he could use a shot of morphine." She gave Daniel a sidelong flirty smile. "I'll check him out." The lieutenant sashayed away.

"Zowie. She's got it bad for you, sir." Kenny's eyebrows shimmied like a speeding caterpillar.

"Oh, hush." All Daniel needed was his crew teasing him about a little gal who was too forward for her own good. He hoped Nelson, standing in front of his station with a sour expression, hadn't noticed. "Was the weather report full of glad tidings?"

"Same old. Look for a tailwind at nine thousand."

"All right then." Daniel touched the shoulder of Hal Busch, his radio operator, a serious young man who rarely smiled. His radios occupied a small space on the right, directly behind the cockpit and across from the navigator. "Call the controller. Tell him we're ready to go."

He hadn't told the pain-ridden patient that he wouldn't be taking them all the way to the States. Another crew would take over in Natal, but not right away. First they'd have a rest in the base hospital with a full medical staff caring for them until the next leg of their journey.

For himself, Daniel anticipated a day of lounging on the town's sandy beach.

But first, those nine hours of flying over open ocean. Once they had reached their cruising altitude of ten thousand feet, he fumbled for his sunglasses. They flew ahead of the sun, but its glare bounced off the sparkling ocean.

At the midway point of the monotonous flight, he left the controls in Reggie's capable hands and walked through the cargo hold. The wounded on stretchers appeared to be sleeping, including the boy eager to reach home. Those in the sling seats slumped in uncomfortable repose, except for one man. He sprawled half off the seat, his legs stretched out in the walkway.

Daniel checked his tag. Abdominal surgery less than two weeks ago. He glanced around for the medical staff. They sat in back, the orderly with his chin planted on his chest, the nurse filing her nails. With a huff of exasperation, he strode back and shook the orderly awake. "One of your surgical patients needs to be put back properly in his seat. Come on."

Lieutenant Fromm followed on their heels and didn't stop chattering as the men eased the patient back into a healthier position. "I checked the men just a minute ago and everyone was fine. I don't understand how he could have gotten out of his seat like that."

The colonel beckoned Daniel. "Don't you have a more comfortable chair?"

Seriously? Daniel strove to keep his irritation out of his voice. "No, sir, not on a military aircraft."

The colonel grumbled about the lack of courtesy for a field officer.

Kenny leaned close when Daniel returned to the cockpit. "I bet he wasn't wounded in combat. He probably broke his ankle when he tripped over a communications cable while trying to save his neck."

Daniel chuckled under his breath. Maybe he should suggest practicing the courtesy the colonel felt was his due, but he wouldn't be surprised if Kenny was right.

As the plane approached the Brazilian coast on an unusually cloudy day, a pink cloud rose.

Reggie leaned closer to the windshield. "What's with the pink fog?"

It didn't look like fog. Whatever it was, they were about to fly through it. Too late, Daniel recognized it.

"Flamingos."

Flying at one hundred twenty miles per hour, they were on them in an instant.

Multiple thumps impacted the plane. Two birds struck the windshield. The glass broke and a bird flopped on the copilot's instruments. Reggie yelled as the engine pitch changed. Daniel scanned his instruments before trying to view the left engine. "Engine one off and feathered."

"No kidding. There are feathers all over."

"Shut off the fuel to one and the fuel cross-feed valve."

"Done."

Over their headphones, Nelson demanded, "What's going on?"

Daniel ignored him. "Hal, radio Parnamirim. Tell them we've had multiple bird strikes, lost one engine and the other is running ragged. We need to land immediately."

Nelson muttered something about their carelessness.

Reggie dropped the dead bird on the floor. "Evasive action at this altitude means a crash, Nelson. Would you prefer that?"

They didn't hear another peep out of the navigator, but they did hear Kenny reassuring their passengers. "We're coming into Parnamirim Air Base in Natal, Brazil. A flock of flamingos greeted us by knocking out one engine, but don't you worry. We've got the best pilot in the air force at the controls."

Maybe this would keep the patients from objecting to a stay at the hospital instead of continuing on to Trinidad immediately. Too often, the wounded became upset at the delay. Daniel didn't blame them. He wouldn't care to take the tour of military hospitals around the world either.

He increased the rpm on engine two. "Lower the landing gear and lock the tail wheel, but hold off on the flaps until ... okay, now. Flaps down."

He normally made beautiful three-point landings, but now he opted for the novice's approach and landed on the main wheels. They chirped on contact with the runway and he applied the brakes. Their working engine hiccupped as he turned off the runway, but it powered them to the tarmac.

Not until they had parked the plane did he take a look at Reggie. "Were you injured by glass or bird?"

"My heart did the jitterbug, but no blood was drawn." He looked down at their uninvited guest. "I should look for a taxidermist. This can be our mascot."

"Oh, please." Daniel eased out of his cramped seat and stretched. "As soon as we're disinfected, I'll head over to operations and report our damaged bird."

"Do you mean the airplane or the feathered mess?"

As the Brazilian malaria patrol came aboard with their pyrethrum spray, Daniel contemplated taking the flamingo along as proof. Nope, it could have lice, although the spray might take care of that. It was definitely on the gory side.

One of the health officials came to the cockpit and gaped at the bird He raised his gaze to the windshield and frowned. "Broken glass will not seal in the spray."

"I haven't heard any mosquitoes buzz my ears." Reggie grinned before pointing to the carcass. "No telling what hitchhikers this intruder may have brought in, though."

He lifted the flamingo by a leg and the official doused it with spray. He also took extra care spraying the cockpit and them. Daniel kept his hands over his face, leaning toward the broken windshield in hopes of a bit of fresh air. The health team finally left with their usual warning to keep the plane door closed for ten minutes to allow the spray to do its work.

As the time ticked away, Daniel moved back into the cargo hold and called to Kenny. "Would you mind cleaning up the blood in the cockpit? I need to report in about the damage."

Jaws dropped throughout the plane, including the colonel's, and Daniel snickered under his breath. He caught a ride to the operations building and hurried inside. Rounding a corner, he nearly collided with a vision clad in a flamingo pink dress. He stepped aside to his right as she stepped to her left. They both slid the other way.

Grinning, he grabbed her hand. "May I have this dance?" He twirled her around, released her, and bowed. Her cheeks glowed as pink as her dress, although humor sparkled in her eyes.

He wouldn't mind running into her again.

Chapter Three

Isabel grinned all the way outside to the picnic table set up in the afternoon shade of the office building. She glanced skyward at the rumble of an airplane winging overhead. Four engines, twin tail fins. Her grin widened. A B-24 bomber, probably the navy's. She'd quickly acquired the skill of aircraft recognition.

Sandra Pennock, one of her housemates, watched with narrowed eyes. "You look like the cat that lapped up all the cream."

Isabel laughed. "I just ran into a gorgeous pilot. He has thick brown hair and light brown eyes that probably turn green in the sun. And he's this tall." She held her hand six inches over her head. "We needed to pass each other in the hallway, but we kept moving in the same direction. So he took my hands and danced me around so I was clear to go my way and he his way."

"Uh-huh." The willowy brunette drummed her fingers on the table. "What's his name?"

Isabel plopped down on the wooden bench seat and

nibbled her lip. Sandra doused her giddiness the way an ocean roller sucked the prettiest shells back into the deep before she could snatch them up. How could she have forgotten Sandra's propensity for one-upmanship?

"I don't know, except it ends with a t."

Sandra's laughter rang out. "That narrows down the possibilities among the thousands of men passing through Parnamirim each day. You say he's a pilot?"

"He wore wings. And he has a deep voice. He's probably asked to read the Scriptures at church, but everyone concentrates on his tone, not the words, so they totally miss the meaning."

"I'll have to watch for him." Sandra laughed again. "Are all the girls swooning, like you're doing now?"

Isabel straightened. "I'm not swooning. Isn't that like fainting?"

Shaking her head, Sandra pushed a flyer across the table. "Do you know where this leather shop is? My mother heard about the Natal cowboy boots and she wants me to send a pair for my brother."

"Sure, it's not far off the Bonde route, near the Grande Hotel. Do you want me to go with you?"

Sandra set her jaw. "No, thanks. I think we've gone about in the town often enough that I can manage the trolley on my own." She thumped her fist on the table. "I am a woman on a mission. I will succeed." She slouched. "I hope. Here I do fine, but out there, I feel like a foreigner."

"I wonder why." Isabel traced circles on the flyer. "There are sure to be lots of servicemen around who can help you."

"They don't speak Portuguese, which is where I would need help."

"Oh, there he is." Isabel's gaze riveted to the office. "He just came out with Captain Carter."

Lloyd Carter served as the weight and balance officer in charge of loading cargo onto the planes. He was also Isabel's boss. She had never seen anyone so covered with freckles, and he wasn't even a redhead. Right now, he had a full head of steam.

"I can't get it through his thick skull that packing a plane with wounded just won't do. His line is that ambulatory patients would appreciate the chance to stand up and stretch, but he's ignoring the fact that planes experience turbulence. Toppling over isn't going to do the wounded any good. Hello, ladies." Lloyd switched gears faster than anyone she'd ever met.

"Is someone not valuing your learned opinion on how to stuff airplanes?" Sandra's patronizing comment caused the handsome pilot's eyes to balloon, but Isabel, used to her needling, offered the man a minute shrug.

The captain's mouth quirked, but he got right back into his soliloquy. "When fuel is consumed and the cargo's weight needs to be redistributed, you want to shove around inanimate objects, not broken bodies."

He turned to the pilot without missing a beat. "Have you met Sandra Pennock and Isabel Neumann? Sandra gets her kicks by pretending I know nothing about my job. And Isabel makes my job easier by calculating load distribution. She's a genius." He waved at the pilot when he addressed the women. "Lieutenant Daniel Lambert here flies C-47s to Ascension Island and back."

Daniel Lambert. A tingle zipped through Isabel all the way down to her toes. "You are based here in Natal?"

His brows jerked upward. "Yes, I am."

She understood his surprise. Her accent gave her away. All the Americans she met were astonished to find a foreigner in such an important position. Native civilians worked in the mess hall or on the janitorial staff. She had started in the mess hall, wiping tables, until she glanced at a load chart beside the captain's plate and pointed out a mathematical error. Next thing she knew, he'd transferred her to his staff.

She worked six days a week in the office or on the tarmac, overseeing the loading of the airplanes. On her first day in his office, Captain Carter had shown her a film about loading. If too much weight was placed forward, the plane could nosedive. Too much weight in the rear caused the nose to pull up, and the airplane stalled and fell to earth. If the cargo shifted in-flight, same results. Or if the cargo wasn't shifted as the fuel load burned off, the plane would unbalance.

Correctly loading an aircraft didn't require a genius, just a bit of mathematical prowess. Calculating a load was like putting together a jigsaw puzzle.

"Isabel here swallowed a calculator. Rattle off any equation, and she'll give you the answer like that." Carter snapped his fingers.

Daniel crossed his arms and gazed skyward for a moment. "Twelve plus three minus one times two."

"Twenty-eight." Isabel's cheeks heated when he winked at her instant response.

He grinned at her boss. "She is good."

"Even I knew that one." Sandra tended to pout if left out of a conversation for long.

"And what do you do?" Daniel's question was polite, but his eyes didn't gleam with the humor he'd offered Isabel.

"I work with the U.S. Engineering Department."

"Ah. A USED girl."

Sandra raised a hand. "No jokes, please. I've heard them all."

A closed-lipped smile stretched across his face, but it appeared forced. He shifted his gaze between Lloyd and Isabel.

"Has a general asked to have his personal refrigerator shipped to Africa?"

Lloyd shook his head, but Isabel nodded. "A cute little red Frigidaire? Yes, someone was trying to get it onboard an eastbound plane."

She would have loved to have that refrigerator. The ancient unit at home wheezed like an old man. Just yesterday, her roommate Graziela had used a chisel to remove ice built up in the freezer. Even milk in the refrigerator section rattled with ice. The diminutive contraband Frigidaire couldn't hold as much, but it had to be more efficient.

"*Was* trying?" Lloyd's brows bunched up over his nose. "Did anyone take it?"

She nodded. "I saw him pay a pilot." When Lloyd's face darkened, she hurried on. "I told the pilot he had a full load already, and the refrigerator weighed fifty pounds according to its crate. He told his crew to remove mail sacks, but I kept watching him."

The pilot expected to charm her into looking the other way. She'd had a lifetime of experience of watching Marcos wheedle his way out of mischief, however, and now she followed Mamãe's method of one eyebrow raised and one foot tapping.

"I heard about that." Sandra jumped in. "Isabel said, 'The soldiers look forward to their mail. You'd rather grease your hands?'" With a peal of condescending laughter, she patted Isabel's shoulder. "Issy does well with English, but she doesn't get all the expressions right."

Daniel's eyes narrowed at Sandra before returning his attention to Isabel. She straightened and shrugged off Sandra's outburst. "One of his crewmen understood he'd been paid and refused to remove the mail. Instead, they took off two cases of their own, and the pilot had to share his grease money with them."

"Good for them." Daniel paused. "I think. What was in the cases they left behind?"

"Bootleg bourbon, I heard it was."

"Kentucky bourbon?" Lloyd planted his hands on his hips. "Did they buy it in Puerto Rico, by any chance?"

"Yes. The pilot said something like fifths for a dollar fifty? They claim they can sell them for twenty-five dollars in England." Isabel's eyes widened as a storm cloud brewed across Lloyd's face. "They say bootlegs are an acceptable part of military transportation as long as you're discreet."

"Sure, they are. Do you know if this is a crew who comes through here regularly?"

"They were a ferrying crew taking the plane all the way to England."

Shaking his head, Lloyd turned away, then swung back around. "What happened to the cases left behind?"

"They disappeared very quickly." Isabel grinned. "And the trash was full of bottles this morning."

"Serves the bums right. We can't police every plane from start to take off." Lloyd's words lingered in the air as he strode off.

"Ladies." Daniel nodded to them before heading in the direction of the officers' barracks.

Isabel stood. "Good luck finding those boots, Sandra. I'm heading home to do some laundry. Tomorrow, I'm going to the beach."

She bit her lip as Sandra grumbled about the injustice of having to do her mother's bidding and finding those blasted boots. Relief coursed through Isabel. She would have accompanied Sandra on her errand, but while the woman usually sounded polite, most of her comments belittled Isabel. Besides, finishing chores so she could spend time at the beach was far preferable. Her toes itched to splash in the waves.

She noticed Daniel Lambert didn't appear to be in a hurry to reach his destination. He watched a gull fly overhead. Someone hailed him, and he waved in acknowledgment. A small dog gamboled to him, and he reached down to ruffle its ears.

He was based here. She'd watch for his name on the manifests. They'd meet again. Oh yes. She'd see to that.

Chapter Four

After catching a ride from Parnamirim Field to the navy's seaplane base early the next morning, Daniel hastened to the shoreline before his steps faltered.

"Tomorrow, I'm going to the beach," he'd heard Isabel say.

Excellent. The best part of being based here in Natal was the quick access to the beach. The ocean was nothing like being at the shoreline of Lake Michigan. He'd miss it when the war ended and he returned home. The lake would be a disappointment without the crash of waves swooshing up onto the shore.

And now here he was. Like Parnamirim, the seaplane base stood south of Natal. He searched north along the coast, then south. Where might Isabel be? Most likely, she'd be to the north, but what if he hiked in that direction and she'd gone south? Surely she wouldn't go to the USO Beach Club.

Face it, Lambert. You're acting like a lovesick teenager.

His sister Theresa would fall over laughing. She and cousin Gloria would never let him forget his rush to the beach to find a girl. Or would they? They weren't kids anymore. They were young women who might find his efforts romantic.

Great. Now he was a romantic fool.

He couldn't help it. She stirred his blood like no woman ever had. Not because of her great packaging—and it was great. He envisioned her ocean blue eyes, golden hair curling on her shoulders. She was on the tall side, but that meant he wouldn't need to lean down far to kiss her.

Her choice of friends was regrettable. Actually, she'd seemed embarrassed by the brassy Sandra. She was kind-hearted, and the other woman would likely run roughshod over her.

The steady splash of waves upon the shore drew him to the water's edge. A wave murmured its pleasure to deposit tiny shells on the beach before sliding back into the ocean. The shells tumbled about, creating tinkling music.

Daniel removed his shoes and socks and stepped closer. The next wave lapped over his feet, coating them with sand.

Bother. He'd rushed off so fast, he'd forgotten to bring a towel. Now he'd have to shove sandy toes back into his socks.

He knotted his laces together, slung his shoes over his shoulder, and rolled up his trousers. The waves delighted in tossing sea spray onto his pants as he trod farther into the surf. He heaved a contented sigh and tucked his hands in his pockets.

Just fourteen hundred miles away, Ascension Island grew out of the Atlantic. He, who had never left Wisconsin before the war, flew to that tiny speck several times a month. Satisfaction welled up within him. His mother had emigrated from Germany, his paternal grandparents from Belgium, and Uncle Peter, his godfather, had fought in France during the last war. Now he lived in the Southern Hemisphere. Amazing.

Travel was truly an education. He hadn't realized he had wanderlust. Too bad war was the cause of his gadding about.

Splashing to his right drew his attention. His heart skipped a beat. It was her. He shook his head with a snort of disbelief. Why should he be surprised? He'd known she planned to come to the beach. He'd planned to as well, but the chance to see her again was a definite bonus.

She kept her head down, watching her steps. Necessary, apparently, since she was farther out than he was. She'd pass right by him without noticing.

"Isabel."

Her head jerked up. A smile bloomed. "Daniel. After flying yesterday, you are not, um, hitting the sack?"

He grinned at her effort to use American sayings. "He who snoozes, loses. Walking the beach is a great way to unwind. Put all thoughts of work out of my mind. Commune with nature. Bask in the sound of the waves. Get away from all the other flyboys." He took a deep breath. What had gotten into him, babbling away like this?

To his relief, her grin indicated approval rather than scorn. "This is my favorite place in the world." She shrugged as her cheeks turned rosy. "Not that I've been anywhere besides Brazil and a few neighboring countries."

"This whole scene reminds me of my grandmother singing, 'All nature sings, and round me rings the music of the spheres.'"

A wave of homesickness washed over him. He finally met a pretty, intriguing lady and he was pining for family. *Snap out of it, Lambert.*

"That's a church song." Isabel's bright blue eyes regarded him with ... approval?

He nodded. "It's her favorite. She always encouraged us to

29

memorize hymns and sing them in our minds, if not out loud. They are guaranteed to raise wilting spirits."

Isabel ran her fingers through the crest of a passing wave. "Has she had a difficult life?"

"Not really. The last war was hard on her. That's when she made an effort to fill her mind with honest, pure, lovely thoughts. She'd sing her way out of the doldrums."

Isabel's head tilted. "Did your grandfather have to fight? Or, her son?"

"Uncle Albert joined the navy. He served on a destroyer hunting submarines." Daniel hunched his shoulders. "Not as dangerous, maybe, as the fighting in France."

A flock of seagulls soared overhead, hoping for handouts. They epitomized the freedom of flight.

"And my grandfather didn't fight," he added. "He was arrested and sent to an internment camp."

Daniel had been a baby, too young to understand the turmoil his family had endured. All his memories of Gramps were of a laughing, compassionate, intelligent man who delighted in playing with his grandkids. Even now, Daniel's fingers itched to write to his family, knowing how tickled Gramps would be by the fried flamingos.

Isabel stumbled against him as a wave knocked her off balance. "Arrested? Why? Did he do something?"

He grasped her arm until she regained her footing, wishing he could take her hand. "No, that was the problem. He hadn't completed the naturalization process, so he was classified as an enemy alien. Worse, he taught at the German high school. Science and mathematics, mind you. Hardly subversive. But an anti-German hysteria had swept the country." He gazed out to sea. "Hard to fathom, really. How could America be so afraid of Germany? Of course, a high number of Germans live in the U.S."

Isabel paused to watch the waves too. "I wonder if my father knew about that. If that's why he moved to Brazil instead of the United States. We lived in a German city in the south, but he moved us to Recife because he suspected problems would come."

"And did they?"

"Yes." She raised her hands and let them drop. "German schools were closed, and we were required to speak Portuguese."

"Ah. Yes, that happened in America. Well, not Portuguese." He shook his fist as he said, "'No speaking in German.' And the schools stopped teaching it. Short-sighted to my way of thinking. It's best to study your enemy's ways. You don't want to depend on their interpreters. How do you know they're honest? The German communities were forced into assimilation. That's helped them avoid undue attention with this war. Now, the rage is directed at the Japanese."

Daniel spoke fluent German. As war loomed for the U.S., he'd considered applying for an intelligence or interpretation post. That would have been interesting, but he wanted to fly.

They resumed walking. He racked his brain for something else to talk about. Something unrelated to war, this one or the past.

"My cousin works for U.S. intelligence as a German interpreter."

Isabel's words nearly caused him to stumble on the uneven sand. Had he voiced his thoughts out loud?

"Is he German or American?"

"Oh, he's German." Isabel studied Daniel, like she was taking his measure. She inhaled sharply and glanced around the empty beach. "He was a sailor in the Kriegsmarine. The more he learned of Hitler's work, the more he condemned it. He saw a chance to leave, and he grabbed it."

31

Daniel glanced over his shoulder too. "Did he desert?"

"Yes." Her answer floated to him in a whisper. "He was aboard the *Graf Spee*."

"The *Graf* ..." Daniel sucked in his breath and stopped. "Isn't that the cruiser that sank after a battle with British ships?"

She nodded. "December, 1939. They were off the coast of Uruguay. The *Graf Spee* was badly damaged and entered the harbor at Montevideo. They weren't allowed to stay more than three days, not nearly enough time for repairs, so the Germans scuttled it rather than allow the British to capture it. The sailors were to be taken to Argentina to be interned for the rest of the war, but Huberto escaped and came to us in Florianópolis. If the Germans caught him, he'd be tried for treason and executed."

Daniel whistled. "To have the strength to follow your convictions like that. Do the Germans know he's in America?"

"Officially, he's dead. A lot of men died in the battle, and I don't suppose they took time to record the dead. My father wrote to my uncle, telling him in a roundabout way that someone is alive and well."

"Reading between the lines, hmm? Have you spent time in the States? Your English is so good."

"Languages come easy to me. I know Portuguese, German, English, and French."

"Amazing." His foot came down on something sharp. "Yowch."

His thoughts spun toward a jellyfish or even a crab pincer, but when he yanked off the offending object, relief swept through him. "A seashell?"

"Ooh." Isabel pressed close and caressed it with a careful finger. "A *chicoreus spectrum*. What a find."

Her fingers were long and slender, perfect for playing the

organ. Daniel froze. What a thing to think. He held the shell out to her. "It's all yours."

She backed up and put her hands behind her back, her eyes locking with his. "Don't you want it? Those are hard to find, and it's in perfect shape."

"You seem to appreciate it more than I can. Look what it did to me." Balancing on one leg, he displayed five red spots on the tender arch of his injured foot. At least the skin hadn't broken. "It looks like a conch shell covered with tiny swords and, I assure you, they're sharp."

A smile bloomed on her lips. He could hear Theresa saying, "Don't be such a baby."

Isabel made no such comment. Accepting the shell, she swished it through the waves and drained the seawater. "I collect shells. This will look beautiful in one of my montages." She tucked the two-inch seashell into a net bag that the little monster would doubtlessly saw its way out of. "I am sorry about your foot."

He noted the sparkle in her eyes. "Sure you are. Go ahead and laugh. My sisters would."

"You have sisters? All I have is my twin brother. I always wanted a sister."

"I have three. How many would you like? Actually, you can't have Theresa. She's married now, and her husband might object."

Isabel's laughter spilled over him.

"You don't mean that." She grabbed his arm. "Oh, look. Look at that shell."

A pinkish object the size of Daniel's fist tumbled in the surf. It teetered on the edge of a drop-off into deeper water.

"We have to get it." Isabel tried to follow the shell's progress, but the waves pushed her back.

Daniel timed the waves and managed to snag the shell on

his foot. With a soccer kick worthy of any team in Brazil, he directed the shell toward shore. A wave smacked him in the back. His wallet must be soaked.

Isabel reached down to snatch the shell, getting a face full of seawater. She danced around in the surf, joy shining from her eyes. "Look at this. Can you believe it? It's a *bullata lilacina*. Usually you have to dive twenty-five yards deep to find shells like this. And it's not even the right time of day for the tides to bring them in."

Daniel couldn't help but laugh at her exuberance. "Consider it an early birthday gift from the sea. Uh, when is your birthday?"

She spun around, holding the shell aloft. "Two months ago."

"Oh, well. Hmm. Please excuse its tardiness."

Her laughter tickled him.

She lowered the shell, cradling it in her hands. "Tardiness excused. This is so fabulous."

Several cigarette butts littered the beach in front of them. Since he saw no trash barrels, he dug a hole with his foot and pushed in the butts. They'd disintegrate, he hoped.

She watched him, her head tilted.

He offered a sheepish grin. "I can't abide litterbugs who think we appreciate their butts."

She nodded. "That, and broken glass. Although sea glass is a good find. Worn smooth by tumbling in the waves and in different shapes, they work well in my designs."

Beyond her, Daniel noticed a man watching them. Or, more likely, her.

"That sunbather is sure interested in us."

Isabel didn't turn around to look. She stepped closer to him and spoke in a low tone. "Don't call him a sunbather. People like to joke about that, but it's serious business. He's a coast watcher in the Brazilian army, watching for submarines trying to land spies or an invasion."

The man sat under what appeared to be a giant bird's nest propped up by four long, spindly branches. A moderate breeze could blow down the shelter. His low, wooden beach chair didn't look comfortable, and Daniel didn't see a picnic basket to sustain him. Even a fervent beachcomber would find the job monotonous.

Another man appeared over the dune.

"Looks like his relief has come. This guy's watching us with binoculars."

Isabel glanced around this time and stiffened. "I need to go. This way." She started off in the opposite direction. "Are you ready to go?" Her words drifted over her shoulder.

Before hurrying after her, Daniel studied the watcher. Now he noticed the man's clothing was too formal for beachwear. Blond hair, unusual in northern Brazil. A German? The man lowered his binoculars and stared back, not minding if he showed his face. His arrogant face.

Why did he frighten Isabel?

Chapter Five

As he walked beside Isabel, Daniel continually glanced back. Knowing he came along with her without questioning her was a balm to Isabel's shattering sense of security.

Uwe Schneider. Here, in Natal. Why? Because of her? The image of his cold, gray eyes haunted her. A wave of nausea swept over her, and she pressed a hand to her abdomen. Everything had been going so well, but now he would try to ruin her life. Again.

Of course, with this being a big American base, he might be spying or planning sabotage. And he might expect her to be his accomplice.

"Tell me about this guy."

Isabel dragged in a deep breath. "He's from Germany. My father and I believe he may be a saboteur and wants to recruit my brother. Marcos says he wants me." A shudder wracked her. "My life would be a nightmare in his hands. He believes women are only worth doing men's bidding. We need to tell the security officials on base."

"You're right." Daniel guided her through town with a hand at her back. He checked his watch and headed for the Mercado Publico. "The farmer's market will close soon. I want to see if pineapples are still available while we're here. I'll miss this back in the states."

Isabel huffed a little sigh. Pineapples? With Uwe Schneider nearby? Maybe Daniel wasn't taking this calamity seriously after all. True, they'd just met and hardly knew each other.

He approached a produce stand with a big grin. "*Boa tarde meu amigo.*"

She blinked. He knew Portuguese?

"Have you seen any suspicious-looking strangers who might be German spies?"

The seller chuckled. "Maybe. Two men walk by. One tells other, watch for blonde lady."

Daniel's smile faded. He described Uwe, surprising Isabel with all the details he had noted.

The seller nodded. "*Sim.* That was boss man."

"Keep watch for him. He likely is a bad man." Daniel paid for his pineapple and, scanning the area, led Isabel away. "I'll report your sighting on base today. You can sign a statement or whatever they want you to do when you come in tomorrow. Right now, let's get you home. If he did follow us, I think we've lost him. I don't want him knowing where you live."

The thought chilled her heart. She pictured him banging on the door. Or barging in and making demands. "I thought I'd be safe here."

"With a little precaution, there's no reason why you shouldn't be." At a main street, he looked both ways. "Where do we board the trolley?"

"The Bonde? It will turn at the corner here." They joined a few other pedestrians. "I didn't realize you speak Portuguese."

He laughed. "I could say good afternoon to my friend, but

not much else." The Bonde arrived, and they hopped aboard. "On base, officers are required to take language classes."

"Required? Even if they never leave the airbase?" The base had everything they needed. Shops, services, a chapel. Of course, it did lack the beach.

"All part of our effort to strengthen ties of friendship with Brazilians. We have a ten-week course and attend three times a week. Since I'm off flying so often, I miss a lot." He nudged her. "I'm glad you speak English, so we can still be friendly."

Heat spiraled through her, melting the chill. He liked her. What would Papai and Mamãe think of him? He and Papai were both pilots, so they'd find much to talk about. And Mamãe? She'd be pleased with his courtly manners. Mamãe could honestly say he was a sweet boy.

When they disembarked from the Bonde, she watched Daniel gaze around. "Is it like your hometown?"

"Nope. You don't find stucco houses or red tile roofs in Milwaukee." He removed his hat and ran his hand through his short hair. "And I have to admit, it's hard to imagine windows without glass."

She nodded. Attached shutters could be closed for privacy or protection from rain, and louvers provided ventilation. They failed, however, to keep out lizards and spiders and other creepy crawling things. "My mother insisted on glass in the windows when we moved to Recife. She finds it appalling how easy it is to listen to neighbors, or for bugs to fly in."

"My mom would totally agree." He burst out laughing. "Although even glass windows in a closed-up house didn't prevent the neighbors from hearing Mom scream when a grasshopper jumped on her in the living room."

Isabel shuddered. She didn't know what a grasshopper was, but it didn't take much imagination to picture a bug suddenly landing on her.

She indicated the house she lived in. "*Casa grande.*"

It wasn't grand. It was small for four women. The cramped bathroom had no counter space, and a perpetual scum line marred the tiny bathtub. The stovepipe had a nasty habit of filling the kitchen with smoke. But the house offered independence.

"How many live here? One of your housemates is the Used girl, right?"

"Two Used girls." Isabel turned aside to hide her smile at the term. "My roommate is Brazilian."

With one arm cradling his pineapple, Daniel shoved his other hand in his pocket and rocked back on his heels. "I think a lot of servicemen rent homes in this area."

"They do. It has caused prices to rise. We pay twenty dollars a month, but lots of houses are higher now." She tucked a lock of hair behind her ear. "Have you visited Cypress Gardens?"

He'd been watching a cat slink around the neighbor's house but jerked his attention to her sudden question. She gave him a wide-eyed look, waiting for his answer.

"Cypress Gardens. No, can't say I have."

Her jaw dropped. "Why not? They're so beautiful. You've been to Florida, have you not?"

"Florida, sure, Miami to be exact. Cypress Gardens isn't near Miami, though." He tilted his head. "It's not exactly a top-of-the-list tourist destination. How do you know about it?"

"It's at the top of my list. Huberto, my cousin, visited and sent us postcards. I still have them and hope to see it myself." She trailed off when a knowing light entered his eyes. "What?"

"I wonder if Huberto visited the gardens." He raised a hand when she opened her mouth. "I saw display racks of brochures advertising Florida's attractions. A couple buddies and I looked through them when we had a bit of free time in Miami. I remember the one from Cypress Gardens consisted of detachable postcards. We ended up visiting the beach."

Tears pressed against her eyes, a ridiculous reaction to discovering Huberto's possible perfidy. Okay, maybe not perfidy. He'd simply needed stationary.

Daniel touched her shoulder. "Just think. Now you can be the first in your family to visit Cypress Gardens. You can gloat to Huberto about what he missed."

How endearing of him to try to cheer her up. She smiled, then laughed. "You're right. And someday, I will see it."

"Well, hello."

Daniel stiffened at Sandra's greeting, which gave Isabel a measure of relief as she watched her housemate sashay toward them with a predatory gleam in her eyes. When they'd met on base, he hadn't seemed impressed by her, and Sandra knew he had roused Isabel's interest. Yet now, she tried to entice him?

"Hello, uh, Sandra?" He took a step back.

Her lips thinned before she smiled and touched his elbow. "Surely you couldn't forget my name already. We just met."

He moved away from her touch. "For a moment there, you sounded just like the nurse who accompanied the wounded on my flight yesterday."

"How interesting." Sandra snatched the pineapple from his grasp. "And how nice of you to come for lunch and bring this treat. Come on in. Graziela should have everything ready."

Irritation flared through Isabel, followed by the desire to giggle at Daniel's flummoxed expression. "Would you like to stay for lunch? You'll have to if you want any of your pineapple."

Sandra paused at the door. "Hurry up, Issy. Graz probably needs help."

Daniel frowned and spoke in a low voice. "Does she treat you and Graziela like servants?"

Isabel rubbed her chin. "Here at home, yes, I guess she does. We're the Brazilians and she's the guest."

"Hmm." Daniel reclaimed the pineapple as he crossed the threshold.

"Why don't you sit here while they get everything on the table?" Sandra seated herself on the sofa and patted the cushion next to her. Daniel didn't even pause. He headed straight for the kitchen opening to the right of the living room. There, he came to a stop, and his eyes widened.

Isabel grinned at his reaction. She'd never seen a kitchen so yellow before. The towels, the dishes, the pans, the walls, all yellow. Even the gauzy curtains sported lemon appliqués.

Graziela sliced a loaf of bread at the counter. She looked up in surprise at their sudden entrance.

Isabel slipped around him. "Graziela, meet Daniel."

"*Olá*, Graziela. What a sunny room." He turned on the charm. "Do you have another knife and board? I'll carve the dessert."

After a confirming glance at Isabel, Graziela transferred the bread to a plate and pushed the knife and board toward him. "Use these."

Isabel ladled the thick lentil soup full of carrots, tomatoes, and spinach leaves into soup bowls and carried them to the table. Then she found a bowl for Daniel's cubed pineapple.

Sandra appeared in the archway. "Daniel, you're our guest. You shouldn't be working. Let Isabel do that."

He ignored her again, and Isabel's heart took wing. Selecting a juicy piece of pineapple, he held it out to her. "Try this. I do believe I picked a winner."

Isabel opened her mouth and allowed him to deposit the cube, a strangely intimate act. "Mmm. Very tangy. Sandra, you might not want to eat these. You'll get that burning sensation like you did on base."

"I'll be the judge of that." She snapped and stepped close to Daniel. "Let me try one." Her voice transformed into a purr as she looked up at him through her lashes.

Daniel held out the bowl. Isabel turned so Sandra wouldn't see her smile. Graziela caught her eye and nodded. Sandra's antics were obvious to them all. Daniel, bless him, didn't succumb to her flirtations.

As they sat down, he watched Graziela. "I've seen you. Where do you work?"

"I'm a waitress at the officers' mess."

"Aha." Daniel's exclamation startled them all. "Another waitress held a tray while you served bowls of soup. One of the soldiers jumped up, smacked his head on the tray, and she dropped it. Soup rained down on him. Chicken noodle soup is supposed to be good for what ails you, but that day, it ailed him."

Graziela covered her face. "That was so embarrassing." She said to Isabel, "The whole room went quiet, and we just stood there. Milena turned as white as her uniform."

Daniel waved away the comment. "Everyone knew it was his fault. This soup is good. Just imagine tomatoes like these dropping down the back of his shirt instead of noodles."

He showed no reluctance to chat with Graziela but didn't address any comments to Sandra. He answered her questions, but only briefly. Isabel might have pitied her, but her high-handedness rankled. Sandra knew Isabel was interested in him from the moment she mentioned him yesterday, but now she wanted him for herself. And since Daniel had opened Isabel's eyes to Sandra's bossiness, she realized Sandra had believed herself better than them all along. She didn't treat her roommate like this.

"Too bad Flora is working today." Isabel's thought popped

out. "I think you'll like her. She's a refined lady, but she knows how to have fun."

Across the table, Sandra opened her mouth, but Graziela spoke before she could.

"She blows soap bubbles for the neighbor children and also for their cat. Now the cat comes and scratches at our door, wanting to play with her."

Daniel paused before taking a bite of bread. "What about the children?"

"No, they don't scratch the door. They watch for her to go outside."

Even Sandra laughed at Graziela's misunderstanding.

After their meal, Daniel asked to see Isabel's seashell art. She led him to her room and pulled out two boxes from under her bed. He lifted the top design from one box. Setting it on her bed, he picked up the next, and the next. Awe-filled eyes met hers. "These are incredible."

Warmth washed over her. "I love working with shells."

Sandra appeared in the doorway. "All the pretty seashells from the seashore."

Her tone grated like a yowling cat. Isabel's lips twitched. Maybe Sandra was priming for a cat fight.

Graziela slipped into the room. She pulled out a wreath made of mostly white shells with a few pale blue ones. "Isn't this gorgeous? Or this one." She raised a wreath made of coiled rope and decorated primarily with scallops. She nodded toward the wall hanging Daniel held. A sprig of shell flowers lay on burlap fabric, framed by scallops. "Of course, those are pretty too."

"Are these for sale?"

Graziela didn't give Isabel a chance to answer. She turned the wreaths around. "The prices are on the back."

Daniel relieved her of the rope wreath. "Sold."

Sandra slithered alongside Daniel and trailed her fingers along his shoulder. "The base is showing a movie tonight."

He brushed off her hand like a pesky fly and ignored her. "My mom's birthday is in two months." He winked at Isabel. "I'll have to come back here to shop."

Isabel bit her lip even as she smiled. She'd love to do business with him again.

When he prepared to leave, she followed him outside. He started to say something, but hesitated.

"Something wrong?"

He sighed. "Graziela has indigenous ancestry, doesn't she?"

She hadn't expected that. "Yes. A grandparent was Portuguese, or maybe a great-grandparent, but most people in northern Brazil are more Indian or African than white. The races are all mixed up."

"Is that why Sandra expects her to serve? Although she tries to order you around too. Does she help out? Dust? Mop? Prepare dinner?"

Across the street, a neighbor poured a dishpan of water on her flowers. Her black hair and tan skin proclaimed her ancestry. She exchanged waves with Isabel.

"Rarely. I think it is fair to say Sandra wants to be treated as a queen. Her roommate, Flora, isn't like that. She's fun."

"Hmm. Well." He glanced at his watch. "First thing, I'll stop at Security and tell them about our watcher."

His words doused Isabel like ice water. For a brief time, she'd forgotten about Uwe. "I'll call my brother and ask if Uwe is still in Recife."

His smile didn't reach his eyes. "Be careful. Don't let him catch you alone."

He believed Uwe was here. She glanced both ways before going back inside. Then she locked the door.

Chapter Six

Daniel was summoned to the security office early the next morning. Guesses as to the reason filtered through his mind. Maybe they'd arrested Uwe Schneider. Maybe the German had a cache of weapons, or a layout of the base. Perhaps they wanted to commend Isabel for her vigilance.

Major Herdman's line of questioning took him by surprise.

"What do you know about this Isabel Neumann? Where's her loyalty?"

Daniel resisted the urge to feel his jaw and make sure it hadn't swung open. Surely this man didn't suspect Isabel of being a spy. If she were, why would they have reported the watcher?

"We met a couple days ago when I literally ran into her in the hallway. Then yesterday morning, I saw her on the beach, and she invited me to have lunch at her house along with two of her roommates. She mentioned her father moved the family out of the German community down south to avoid entanglements."

The major's mouth turned down. "This just happened to come up in casual conversation?"

A chill swept through Daniel. He had to tread carefully here. How had that conversation started?

"We talked about a song that encouraged my grandmother when my grandfather in Wisconsin had been interned during the last war. Isabel wondered if her father knew how Germans were treated in the States, if that's why he came to Brazil."

"Hmm." The major studied him like he was a zoo exhibit. "She's a foreigner who holds a critical job for the US military. I'm leery of anyone with close ties to the Nazis who weasels her way into a position where she can sabotage our planes."

Daniel's spine stiffened. "She has no ties to the Nazis, sir. In fact, her cousin defected from the German navy because Hitler appalled him so strongly. He works for our intelligence now. Her parents gave her and her brother names that are common in Brazil, not Germany."

"And yet her brother went to Germany for school. Have you considered her father may be a sleeper agent?"

Daniel's fingers clenched, and he forced them to relax. "Do you know the Germans tried to draft her brother into their army? Apparently, the family had a hard time getting him out of there. That doesn't sound like a predicament a sleeper would have gotten into."

"Have you met the father?"

"No, sir. He's in Recife. I'd like to talk with him though. He has his own air freight company. That might be something I'd like to do after the war."

Major Herdman scowled. "I want you to stay friendly with this Isabel. Keep her under surveillance. Let me know if this Schneider fellow you reported approaches her. That will be all, Lieutenant."

"Yes, sir." Daniel saluted and left. He couldn't consider

spending time with her a hardship. But what would Isabel think if she learned he was keeping tabs on her?

Outside, a jeep idled. "Hop in, Lambert." Captain Russell served as a scheduling officer for the ATC. "You have a special assignment for your flight to Ascension. You'll be shepherding a flock of P-38s."

After the slightest hesitation, Daniel hopped in. Lots of combat planes were ferried across the Atlantic through Natal. The P-38 Lightning carried enough gasoline to reach Ascension, and was a single seater. One pilot, no navigator. In order for them to safely travel over fourteen hundred miles to a little dot in the ocean, a transport plane guided them. This marked Daniel's first time to lead a squadron. No big deal, really. Just fly his normal route.

Parked along the perimeter stood a dozen twin-engine, twin-boom fighters. The booms extended from the engines mounted in the wings back into twin rudders joined by a horizontal tail. With the wings in front, each resembled a flying square with the cockpit centered in the wings. German pilots called them fork-tailed devils. Daniel itched to give the Lightning a test flight.

A group of pilots clustered in the middle of the lineup. Captain Russell eased to a stop. "Gentlemen, this is Lieutenant Lambert. He will guide you to Ascension Island. He'll be taking off in fifty minutes. Be alert for when you are called to taxi behind his C-47 to the runway."

A lanky pilot with his fists on his hips sneered. "We're to trust a pilot who's allergic to combat?"

The day soured. Of course, Daniel had heard the ridicule before. The Air Transport Command's initials also lent themselves to Army of Terrified Civilians. The labels galled him. He had not picked his assignment to fly transports. He'd been ordered to.

"If you'd prefer to go it alone, that's your option." Captain Russell didn't mind dressing down the young whelp. "You haven't flown in combat yet. It wouldn't surprise me if you wet your pants the first time you go up against a seasoned, ace Luftwaffe pilot."

"Okay, okay. I'll follow the coward." The insulting pilot scowled, but belatedly remembered military decorum. "Sir."

The other Lightning pilots shuffled their feet and looked around, probably wishing they were elsewhere. Captain Russell's stare had their cocky friend twitching his shoulders.

"May I remind you that in the military, you go where you are ordered to go? All transport pilots are assigned to their posts whether they like it or not. And transport pilots are chosen because they are the best. They can be relied on to do their jobs." The captain spun on his heel and headed for the jeep. "By the way, Lambert, have you gotten any time on the Dauntless lately?

"Last week. We had a blast."

One of the P-38 pilots sidled closer. "You fly dive bombers too?"

"Every chance I get." Daniel grinned. The man had combat in mind, but Daniel saw no obligation to enlighten him otherwise. Before he could be questioned further, he added, "The C-47 has its benefits. I have a navigator, a lavatory, walking around room, and a crew chief who serves drinks." He bit his lip to avoid laughing when Captain Russell's eyes widened. No need to clarify that last point either.

Daniel tapped the dashboard. "We should head to the plane. I need to verify the crew has checked everything."

"Like drinks?" The captain said no more as he sped along the perimeter track.

Daniel grinned but stayed silent.

The cargo door was closed when they arrived. Kenny

Wright and Hal Busch loitered by the truck still parked beside the plane. Daniel immediately started his walk-around inspection. Captain Russell wandered over to Daniel's crewmen, but he didn't give it any thought. Kenny ducked into the truck's covered flatbed as he completed his tour.

"Hal, do you have all the dope on the P-38s flying with us?" Daniel asked his radio operator.

"Yes, sir. The captain says there shouldn't be chatter. They have our frequency if they do need to call us."

Captain Russell leaned against the truck with his ankles crossed. "I suspect the only thing you may hear from them is a whiny 'Are we there yet?'"

Daniel drew a deep breath. "Yeah. All right. Let's saddle up. Kenny?"

"Be right with you." A thump came from the truck.

"I thought we were all loaded."

Kenny vaulted off the truck and grabbed a sack. "We sure are." He headed for the plane, holding up the sack. "Just a little last-minute something I needed to fetch."

Reggie glanced up from the switches when Daniel entered the cramped cockpit. "Are the chicks ready to follow us?"

"I guess so." Daniel angled his left leg over the throttle quadrant and under the control column, avoiding the rudder pedals. Balancing with a hand on the back rest, he swung his right leg over and dropped onto the seat. It had been a while since he banged his shins on any of the flight apparatus. "The senior pilot in that squadron feels superior to us noncombatants."

He grinned when Reggie muttered something he probably wouldn't want his mother to hear. Reggie had dreamed of flying fighters. Being assigned to cargo planes, and as a copilot, irritated him, but he fulfilled his job with good grace.

Daniel chuckled. "I didn't catch his reaction, but some of

the others seemed impressed when Russell asked if I'd flown a Dauntless lately."

"Ha. That reminds me. I scheduled us to fly 'em next Wednesday." Reggie smirked. "Klein and Edson will fly too. We'll beat 'em up in a dogfight again."

The base kept five of the Navy dive bombers for the pilots to use for recreational flying. After long, tedious flights with nothing to look at but clouds and water, tearing up the sky in the combat planes proved a great way to alleviate pent-up energy. Daniel loved the freedom of soaring up or down and executing tight turns without worrying about damaging cargo or upsetting passengers. He chuckled to himself, imaging Billy Boy Nelson's comments if he flew the C-47 like the bombers.

"I need to see if I can tag along in a PBY one of these days," Daniel said. "If I wasn't flying C-47s, I'd want to fly PBYs."

His boyhood friend Stefan flew the seaplane, hunting U-boats in the North Atlantic. Daniel tried not to envy him. After all, Stefan was based in Iceland, which was as cold as its name implied. No, Daniel didn't have it bad being based in tropical Brazil, especially with the beach nearby. Even if it meant flying stodgy cargo planes.

"Landing on the water must be a thrill," Daniel mused.

"Not for me. No siree. I'm partial to land, myself." Reggie waved to the ground crewman who'd pulled out their wheel chocks. "Looks like we're good to go."

They taxied along the perimeter to the runway. Coming toward them were the dozen P-38s. Reggie whistled. "Funny looking flying machines. I wouldn't mind trying one out. I hear they do a lot of photo recon work. I doubt they accuse those boys of being allergic to combat."

The fighter planes rose quickly into formation, flying in four vees of three. The hostile pilot flew at the front of the closest vee off Daniel's wing. No surprise that he was their flight leader.

"That guy is crowding us." Daniel leaned forward to peer out Reggie's window but couldn't spot the other planes from his position. "How are the vees on your side?"

"Looking good." Reggie craned his neck to see the tail-end Charlie. "Kind of surprises me. When I think of fighters, I think of independent action."

"Don't forget they're fresh out of training camp. Give them time to relax." Daniel checked the formation on his side again. Had that guy crept closer?

The desire to climb another thousand feet filled him. No, they were at their prescribed altitude. He hated to deviate from orders, and that thought rankled. One reason he'd been assigned to cargo planes was his trustworthiness. He followed orders. Combat pilots risked themselves and their planes, and maybe they achieved heroic deeds, but the military didn't want their cargo risked.

They trusted him. That should please him. Daniel had a sneaking suspicion the combat boys would say that made him the military equivalent of a mama's boy. Fragments of Bible verses ran through his mind. *God set the members every one of them in the body, as it hath pleased him. ... Whatsoever ye do, do it heartily, as to the Lord, and not unto men. ... My grace is sufficient for thee.* He was where he was supposed to be.

Settling in, he studied the instruments. Chatting with Reggie would help to pass the time, but everyone would hear their conversation over the headphones. That might not be so bad with Kenny and Hal, but Billy Boy wouldn't hesitate to insert snide comments or twist their remarks to his own advantage. It hadn't taken Daniel long to learn to guard his words around the navigator.

Over three hours into their flight, Kenny came into the cockpit.

Daniel did a double take. "What do you have here, Kenny?"

"Captain Russell told me I'm supposed to be serving drinks to you guys." The crew chief shrugged. "Sorry. I didn't know that." He held out bottles of Coke to both pilots.

Accepting one of the bottles, Daniel chuckled as he held it out while Kenny used a bottle opener to pop off the top. He took a sip, then swiveled around to hold the bottle up to the window and tip it toward the nearest Lightning. "I told the arrogant combat pilot that among the benefits of a cargo plane is a crew chief who serves drinks. I surprised Captain Russell with that tidbit." He took another sip that tickled his throat. "Is this why you were scrounging around in the truck right before we left?"

"Yup. I don't know if these are compliments of Captain Russell or the Air Force, but it's a nice touch. I hear there's a new bottling plant in Natal to keep us supplied." Kenny pocketed the bottle opener. "Enjoy. I have to get back to my bottle before Hal guzzles it."

"Bless that misguided young man for his runaway tongue." Reggie clinked bottles with Daniel and swallowed a mouthful. "Ahh. A friend in England griped that Cokes are rarer than four-leaf clovers, and if they do find them, they're never refrigerated."

They were nearing Ascension when Hal called over the interphone. "The P-38 pilots are getting antsy. They're nearly out of fuel."

"We'll be landing in about twenty minutes," Bill Nelson said.

"Tell them, Hal, and let them know we'll start descending, so be watchful. And give them Ascension's frequency. Then alert Ascension to their arrival."

Soon Daniel spotted the isolated island in the middle of the Atlantic. Cloud cover hid all but the tip of the highest volcanic hill. He'd bet more sooty terns inhabited the island than men. The noisy birds gave the airbase its name of Wideawake Field because of their constant loud cawing, day and night.

He didn't envy the men based on Ascension. A silent chuckle rose in his mind. Being a transport pilot based in Brazil wasn't bad at all, especially when he was tasked with keeping an eye on a beautiful young lady. He looked forward to returning to that assignment.

Chapter Seven

A *month later*
"No, you cannot load the plane this way. The tail will drop, and it will crash." Isabel raked her hand through her hair. Why was this fool so bullheaded? He was a member of the plane's crew. His own safety was at stake.

What had Flora called men like this? Smart Alex? Because they were men, they thought they knew better than silly women. This man, a radio operator from his insignia, had no sense in his head at all.

"Look, doll, I'm the airman, not you. Now give me the manifest so we can get out of here."

Isabel hugged the clipboard to her chest and glanced around for the loadmaster. Extending both ways in the loading area, cargo planes angled into their parking spots in front of the long, low-slung operations building. Towers rose above them where controllers watched over the activity.

Five enlisted men stood around, some leaning against the cargo trolley, some with their arms crossed, all watching the show. She recognized some of them as loaders. Why didn't they say anything? They knew better than to load a plane like this.

Three officers strode up. Two pilots and a navigator. The rest of the crew. A pilot asked, "Are we ready to go, Johnson?"

Johnson swore. He called Isabel a name worse than doll. When he reached for the clipboard to grab it away, she spun away from him. "You cannot have clearance." She aimed her words at the pilots. "This airplane is poorly loaded. It will crash."

One of the officers stepped up to the cargo door and peered inside. "Johnson, are you out of your mind? Get that jeep out of there."

Isabel sighed, her shoulders slumping. A voice of reason.

The other officers crowded him at the door. The pilot, his face splotched with red, added his own venom directed at his radioman before turning to the loaders. "Get this load done properly."

The men jumped into action, only to snap to attention at a cry of "Ten-hut."

Isabel pivoted to see a general stalk into their midst, a major at his heels. "What's going on here?"

The general's bristly eyebrows hunched low over his eyes. His razor-sharp gaze fastened on her before focusing on the pilot. The plane commander.

The pilot's Adam's apple bounced up and down with his gulp. "We were expecting to take off, but discovered our plane is incorrectly loaded."

Isabel couldn't stop a gasp. He made the shoddy loading sound like her fault. She clenched the clipboard hard enough to make the pencil pop out of the clip.

The pilot glanced her way and his face paled. "This, uh,

woman wouldn't allow us to sign off on the manifest, and now we're waiting for the load to be fixed."

What had been his first choice of word for her?

Isabel pulled in a deep breath. At least he'd acknowledged the blame lay elsewhere, sort of. But why was that major staring at her like she was a laboratory specimen? Chills danced up and down her spine. He believed this was all her fault.

She stepped back as the general harangued the hapless loaders and the radioman. A quick search of the area revealed no friendly faces. Daniel flew farther away by the minute, on his way to Ascension. Captain Carter might be dashing hither and yon somewhere on the base, but not here. She hadn't seen Hank, the loadmaster who usually checked off on her loading charts, at all today. His absence explained the snafu.

She pressed her lips tight. Daniel had enlightened her on that word. Situation normal, all fouled up. Things didn't normally go this badly, though. The loading chart was clear. Why had it been ignored?

As though reading her thoughts, the general strode toward her with the ranking loader and asked to see the chart. The major joined them, still watching her rather than studying the chart.

The general glowered at her. "So why was the jeep placed in the rear?"

Why indeed? She turned to the loader.

He swallowed. "The ramps weren't here, so we were delayed, but we had to get the plane ready so it wouldn't miss its takeoff time slot ..."

Isabel's brows had shot upward at the beginning of his rambling excuse and the general raised one of his own bristly brows at her.

"The ramps are right there." She pointed at a small

stockpile sitting between this plane and the next one. Enough ramps waited to service three planes.

"Yes, yes, the ramps were here." The loader spoke breathlessly. He'd been caught in his effort to shift the blame. "The jeep was delayed. The sergeant told us to get everything else onboard in the meantime, so they wouldn't miss their window."

The pilots, huddled near the cargo door, glared at their radioman. He looked away. One of the loaders dropped a crate. It burst open and grenades bounced everywhere. The loader cringed and covered his ears. A lot of good that would do if the weapons exploded. Even Isabel knew grenades didn't explode if their pins weren't pulled, and none of the pins had fallen out.

The general closed his eyes. "And we're supposed to win this war with these clowns."

The major continued to watch Isabel. "Where were you when the jeep arrived?"

She refused to show how much his hostility hurt. "One of the other planes I watch had a mechanical failure with its load. I had to find a technician to repair it. When I returned here, the plane's cargo had been loaded mixed up as you see." Heat surged to her face. She was mixing up the English words. "So I would not advance it for clearance."

The general's gaze skewered the loaders. "It never occurred to you that a one-ton jeep outweighs all these crates? Did you learn nothing before being assigned here?"

Isabel glanced around again. Several other planes waited for clearance. And there was Julius, one of the loadmasters who could sign off on the loads. Probably looking for her. With the general busy scolding the men, she strode in Julius's direction. More trouble immediately popped up.

"Hey, baby doll, I've been looking for you. How 'bout clearing our bird to fly?" Clarence Berelli, a loader who fancied himself irresistible to women, hopped from a jeep and slung his arm around her shoulders. "Things are gettin' behind here."

His touch was akin to spiders crawling all over her. She ducked away from him and brushed off her shoulder. Realizing the major still stared at her, she kept any emotion off her face. The general seemed to be conducting the reload. She hurried toward the waiting C-47.

"Hey, wait for me, baby." Berelli yelled loud enough to call the hogs back home on his family's pig farm. "I got us a jeep right here."

She didn't break stride or look back. Ride with him? No, no, no. He'd take that to mean they were dating. She'd heard enough to know his idea of a good date consisted of drinks and a tumble in bed. He already acted far too familiar with her.

Flipping through the pages on her clipboard, she located his plane's chart. Everything appeared to be in its proper place, but she needed to board the plane to be sure. Only a crate sat below the door. "Would you please move the stairs up to the cargo door?"

Berelli snorted. "Just climb on in there, baby. We don't want to waste time."

The gleam in his wolfish eyes broadcast his anticipation of a show if she had to clamber into the plane wearing a straight skirt. Two young loaders barely out of high school also watched with silly grins. No help there.

"We haven't got all day, baby doll. Let me help you." Berelli latched his beefy hands to her waist.

A whiff of body odor engulfed her as he loomed over her. She tried to knock his hands away, but he snaked an arm around her.

"Feisty. I like that." He pulled her against him.

"Sergeant, release her."

The deep voice ripped through the air. Berelli groaned, but he stepped back. He jackknifed into a salute at spotting the general. His elbow hit Isabel's ear.

She stumbled away, holding one hand to her ear and one wrist over her nose.

"Miss?" The general left Berelli at attention. "Are you all right?"

It wasn't possible to give someone a bloody ear like a bloody nose, was it?

"Yes, sir, I think so." Her ear stopped ringing. Oh, he must wonder why her hand was practically covering her face. "I'm trying to smell my perfume instead of ..." Oh dear, how could she say this in a ladylike way?

The general didn't need an explanation. "Yes, there is quite a stench here, isn't there?"

He glanced beyond her, where the loaders were suddenly trying to look busy. "Privates, bring those stairs over."

They tripped over their own feet in their rush to comply.

Isabel scrambled into the plane and squeezed between pallets until she was out of sight of everyone. She leaned against a crate and dropped her head in her hands. Could the day get any worse?

Taking a deep breath, she straightened and adjusted her purple sweater. The lightweight cotton knit kept her comfortable and, while it was pretty, its plainness kept it from being provocative. She sighed. Maybe her attire didn't matter. She might as well wear sackcloth. The men around here either found fault with her because she was a woman or assumed they could take advantage of her because she was a woman.

Except for Captain Carter. And Daniel.

A quick glance at the stenciled identifications on various crates assured her this plane was balanced well and ready to fly. As she turned back to the door, her foot hit something that clanked. Crouching, she sighed again. Not ready to fly.

Berellli appeared at the door. "Is everything ready to go in here, ma'am?" His sickly sweet voice could curdle cream.

"No, it is not. This tie-down must be repaired first." She flipped the loose hook, and it clattered on the floor.

Berelli's mouth swung open. Then it snapped shut as he spun around. "Jenkins! Ah, never mind." He grabbed a toolbox and leaped aboard. Isabel eased around another stack of crates to stay out of his way as he fixed the problem himself.

She hurried down the steps and stopped short. Captain Carter awaited her. A glance around showed no sign of the general and that unnerving major. They must have summoned him. "Do ..." She had to clear her throat. "Do I still have a job?"

His eyes widened, but he grinned. "You better believe it, *ma belle* Isabel. I'm not giving up my human calculator."

She relaxed and even managed a wan smile. Captain Carter had no ear for languages and was immensely proud of his two-word French vocabulary. He had never confessed who had told him how to say "my lovely," but she found his appellation for her touching.

"General Peterson tells me you've had a lousy day with a bunch of jerks."

From the sudden silence inside the plane behind her, Isabel knew Berelli heard the captain.

"I want you to go see Corporal Kramer in the administration office. She'll help you get outfitted with a Red Cross or a WAC uniform. You won't have any insignia, but at first glance, you'll look official. Tell her you need the battle dress, which includes trousers. That'll be more appropriate for scrambling around in the aircraft."

Behind her, a loud bang meant Berelli had either slammed the misbehaving tie-down into position or he had thrown his wrench against the fuselage. He stomped off the plane without looking their way.

Isabel's thoughts raced. Appearing official might make the men take her more seriously. But slacks? Would she change into her uniform when she arrived on base? Imagine the looks she would get if she wandered around town in slacks. She'd seen Red Cross girls at the USO club, but they wore dresses. Why would they need battle dress trousers? How often did the ladies in the Women's Army Corp wear slacks? What would Mamãe say?

Captain Carter interrupted her inner musings. "Give this memo to Corporal Kramer." He turned to his driver. "Veillon, take Miss Neumann to the admin building and find the corporal. I'll sign off here."

He disappeared into the aircraft, and Isabel headed for the jeep in a daze. The first benefit of wearing slacks became apparent. Climbing into a jeep while wearing a skirt always posed a challenge.

By the end of the day, exhaustion consumed her. She trudged down the lane toward the gate, clutching the bundle containing her new WAC uniform. Laughter gurgled up. Could she be arrested for impersonating American military personnel? Had Captain Carter thought of that?

"Isabel. Yoo-hoo. Wait up."

She turned to see Flora teetering toward her at high speed in impossibly high heels. Her breath caught as Flora stumbled but recaptured her balance before toppling. She grasped Isabel's arm. "Whew. I spotted you from halfway across the base, it seems. Didn't think I would catch up."

"Someday you will break a leg wearing those shoes."

"Nonsense." Flora gasped for breath. "I have strong ankles and a determination to stay upright. Okay. You're in a hurry for home, I guess?"

"No hurry really. Well, yes, I guess so. The beach. That's what I need."

Flora peered at her. "Do I detect a note of discouragement?"

"Today was not worth waking up for." Isabel laughed at Flora's flummoxed expression. She offered a brief explanation of all that had gone wrong. "When I worked at the mess hall with Graziela, the men patted our bottoms and said things unacceptable in church, but there were several women and we supported each other. Now I am alone with all these men."

Some women thrived in this situation, but not her.

"And they're acting like fools. Men do that so well." Flora pursed her lips and studied the clouds. "Think about it. Men resent us for taking jobs that have always been considered their turf. They resent our presence, unless we cater to their baser desires. I've overheard the most amazing conversations they have when they think no women can hear them. Locker room drivel, I call it. They are the most contrary creatures."

Isabel chuckled. Flora often made insightful statements with a comic twist that left her wondering how serious her housemate was. "I believe men say that about us."

"Pshaw. They are all brawn and no brain. Most of them, anyway. How about your Daniel?"

Her Daniel. If only.

"I believe he knows how to use his brain. He was quick to learn about the man who watched me on the beach."

"Ah, yes. Be careful if you do go back there. Daniel's flying now, isn't he? Too bad. You need an escort. I'm sure you know Sandra's got her eye on him. Although, according to Graziela, he demonstrated his smarts by ignoring her. I must say, I'm eager to meet him."

Isabel preferred to introduce her to Captain Carter. The

way these two liked to talk, they'd either get along fabulously or drive each other crazy.

She and Flora caught the Bonde for the trolley ride to their neighborhood. Flora kept her laughing with a tale about office shenanigans. Isabel had a spring in her step when they arrived home. And tomorrow would be even better. Daniel would return.

Chapter Eight

A Week Later

Flying west late in the day had the disadvantage of the sun being continually in Daniel's eyes. Time for a break. He waved at Reggie's control column. "Take it."

With the plane in Reggie's capable hands, Daniel eased out of his seat. He nodded to Hal Busch and glanced at Bill Nelson, who ignored him. Making his way to the rear of the plane, he wished Kenny was along on this flight, but a crew chief wasn't always necessary. He squeezed into the lavatory and splashed water on his face, trying to hold it to his eyes. They didn't appear bloodshot in the tiny mirror's reflection, but they sure felt gritty. He dragged his sleeve across his face rather than use the none-too-clean looking towel.

On his way back to the cockpit, he paused at Hal's compartment. "How's it going?"

Normally a somber sort, Hal's eyes gleamed as he offered his headset. "I'm picking up some German, I think. And it's getting closer."

Daniel held the set to his ear. A strong Teutonic voice gave the coordinates of a ship riding low. A juicy target, no doubt. He handed back the headset. "Let me know when the signal is strongest."

A big grin crossed Hal's face and he nodded.

Daniel hurried back to his seat. "There's a U-boat in the vicinity. Probably two. Hal's listening to their transmissions. And one reported a nearby target."

"He's not going for it himself?" Reggie reached for his binoculars.

"Maybe he's out of torpedoes. Or maybe it's a supply sub. What do they call those?" Daniel scanned the ocean on his side of the plane.

"Milk cows. Is Hal radioing their position?"

"We don't know exactly where they are." Daniel accepted the binoculars when Reggie offered them.

A moderate wind kicked up high enough waves to make sighting a slim dark shape difficult. He'd nearly missed spotting a freighter chugging along to the south. Only the smoke billowing from the stacks announced its presence. A sub wouldn't offer any such hint.

Then Daniel's pulse jumped, and he rubbed his eyes. He had to be looking at an enemy submarine. "Look there. Ten o'clock."

"Whooee. Hal, get up here." The radio compartment sat behind the cockpit.

Their radioman skidded into the cockpit, bringing his own binoculars. "Wow. Where's the other one? Do you want me to radio its location to the navy?"

A decision came quickly. "No. They may be monitoring us and will dive. We'll act like we're unaware of them." Daniel continued to search the ocean. "We'll drop down and you can flash Morse code to warn the freighter. They can radio the navy."

"There, see it, kid? Nine thirty." Reggie pointed forward. "Grab a flashlight."

"The sub we saw must be the attack sub." Daniel put the C-47 into a descent. "He couldn't have observed from his position that the freighter is low in the water."

Hal returned with a twelve-inch diameter searchlight.

"Whoa." Daniel ducked to avoid being conked on the head. "Where did you get that?"

"It's part of our cargo. Must be defective or something that they're sending it back, but it works." At five hundred feet, he began signaling. "Danger approaching. U-boat off our port." He glanced at Daniel. "How far back is it?"

"A couple miles? No more than four. Too close for comfort." Daniel straightened his headset over his ears. "Nelson, what's our ETA?"

"If you come north five degrees to correct our course, we'll see land soon."

Daniel exchanged glances with Reggie. Maybe they hadn't included Nelson in ogling the U-boat, but he was well aware of the circumstances. His sarcasm irritated Daniel. Keeping them on course was his job, even when they deviated to warn an ally of danger.

With the message sent to the freighter and acknowledged, he gained altitude. Without using the intercom, he yelled at Hal, "Can you send a message to Kenny? He should be at the field."

Hal shrugged and nodded. *Maybe.*

"Tell him to be ready to join us on our dive bomber flight."

Hal's eyes bugged.

Reggie speared a glance at Daniel before he grinned and

nodded. "You can come, too, kid," he told Hal. "And we'll need some bombs. Tell Kenny to ask Calderson to load 'em."

An inkling of doubt tickled Daniel's heart. "Who's Calderson?"

"I met him at a card game, and he's in ordnance," Reggie said. "Bit of a maverick. He understands how to get things done."

"Should I be worried?" Daniel asked.

"Nah. He'll load the bombs and then fill out the paperwork. Otherwise, that sub will be back in Germany by the time everything's filed."

Why did Daniel get the feeling they were shaking hands with the devil?

REGGIE CAREENED the jeep around the corner and skidded to a halt near the Dauntless dive bombers. Kenny stood beside one of the planes, watching the bombs being shackled to its belly. He scurried over. "Do you usually carry bombs on your mock dogfights?"

"We're not dogfighting or mocking." Daniel grinned. "Saddle up. We're going after a milk cow."

Hal remained wide-eyed as he climbed out of the jeep. "A German supply sub. We saw the attack sub going after a freighter. Now we're taking a turn at some action." He raced over to Reggie's plane, which was already idling.

The five-hundred-pound bomb weighed down the dive bomber. In the pilot's seat, Daniel eased the plane right, then left, to get a feel for the difference. He smiled. Heavy, but not sluggish. Over the radio, he heard Reggie brief Klein and Edson on their plans. The four planes flew in a trailing line at twelve thousand feet, with Daniel in the lead.

Finding the sub didn't take long. Over the intercom, he spoke to Kenny. "I really didn't expect them to still be on the surface."

"Looks like they're just loafing. There's no wake."

Past conversations with dive bomber pilots rolled through Daniel's mind. *When the target disappears under the plane's nose, push the stick forward to dive. Right before pushover, increase the engine RPM to high.*

A moment of doubt struck him as he nosed the plane over. He'd never practiced a dive bombing, much less on a live target. Real bomber pilots trained incessantly before going to battle. What did Daniel think he was doing?

The plane hurtled downward, and the sub grew in his windshield. He resisted the urge to pull up.

Bomb release should occur around two thousand feet. "What's our altitude?" He did know the gunner called out their height during real dive-bombing flights.

"How would I know? The altimeter is spinning like a top. Hey, they're shooting at us." At least Kenny didn't sound panicked. "Not very good, are they? Must not have dive bomber experience."

Neither did Daniel. He wanted to laugh. Scurrying shapes on the sub became men. Lots of men. What were they doing, having a picnic on deck? This close to the Brazilian coast?

He yanked on the release lever to release his bomb and hauled back on the stick. The plane responded, grudgingly, but they were still dropping too low. Had he missed a step? Raise the dive flaps. He grabbed the orange knob. Those flaps acted as air brakes during a dive, but now they needed speed. They skimmed above the waves and wobbled up to five hundred feet. Sweat trickled down Daniel's arms. He didn't know the plane's parameters. This stunt could have torn the wings off.

"You got it." Hal's scream over the radio nearly burst his ear drums. "Like a pickle in the barrel. You dropped it right in the conning tower, sir."

Daniel pulled around in a wide circle. Men leaped off the sub as flames flickered around the conning tower. Ripples thirty feet away showed where Reggie's bomb scored a near miss. Gunners at the aft machine gun continued to fire as Edson began his dive. Instead of releasing his bomb, he fired his guns. The enemy gunners dove overboard.

"They're tame now. Can you go a little lower and slow down? I'm trying to take pictures."

Daniel laughed, more in relief than humor. Trust Kenny to strike a note of irrelevance. "You brought a camera?"

"You bet I did. I hope they turn out. This is great."

The Germans climbed back onto the sub, and more men emerged from a rear hatch.

Reggie's voice sounded in Daniel's ears. "Doesn't look like the sub's going to sink. The damage to the conning tower will prevent them from diving, though. Hal's calling the navy to send a destroyer to pick up the survivors."

The survivors. Men had died in the bomb blast. He, Daniel Lambert, had killed them. Nausea swirled in his gut.

"Maybe we can grab the sub." Klein's southern drawl identified him. "That would be a coup."

Daniel shook his head, unmindful that they couldn't see him. "I'm sure they'll scuttle it before letting us grab it."

Losing a supply sub would surely hurt the Germans. He had to concentrate on that aspect of the bombing.

A PBY flying boat came into view and joined the Dauntlesses in circling the sub. The pilot radioed them. "How'd it become disabled?"

"Lieutenant Lambert dropped a bomb down the conning tower." Kenny's voice sounded gleeful.

The PBY pilot sounded skeptical. "The normal method of hunting subs is dropping depth charges."

"From a dive bomber?"

"Hmm."

For the first time, Daniel considered that he might be in a heap of trouble for going after the sub. They should have reported the milk cow's position to the navy when they landed after their flight from Ascension, not gone after it themselves. They knew nothing about dive bombing protocol. True, none of them were wounded or killed, and the planes were undamaged. True, too, that supply subs were high-priority targets, but not for noncombatant spare-time warriors.

An icy fist replaced the heat in his gut. Might he be facing a court-martial? Ridiculous. And yet, this was the military, which seemed to thrive on contrariness. Desk jockeys jealous of fighting men went out of their way to make life miserable for the combatants. Except, he wasn't a combatant. That mattered, right?

A snatch from a childhood prayer drifted to the front of his chaotic thoughts. *Lord in heaven, hear my prayer. Keep me in thy loving care.*

What have I done?

Leaving the PBY to babysit the Germans, the dive bombers turned toward Parnamirim. Just before they made landfall, Edson jettisoned his bomb. It dropped into the ocean, followed seconds later by a geyser of dirty water. It must have hit bottom before exploding. Daniel laughed. Isabel needed to beachcomb after the next high tide. A lot of shells may have been dislodged and thrown toward shore. She could reap a bonanza.

He left the airfield immediately after checking in the

Dauntless. Reggie hurried after him. "Wait up. Where are you going in such an all-fired rush? It's time for chow. Soon as Klein finishes his report on the tire pressure of his bird, we'll head over."

Daniel glanced back at Kenny and Hal, busy regaling the ground crewmen with tales of their exploits. Kenny snapped photos to finish off his roll of film.

"I could be court-martialed for this."

Reggie hooted. "Are you nuts? You'll get a medal. You bagged an enemy submarine. A supply sub."

"That wasn't our responsibility. We should have reported it to the navy."

"And let them have all the fun?"

A laugh burst from Daniel. PBYs had to fly low when they lined up on the subs to drop depth charges. The U-boat gunners were no slouches with their anti-aircraft cannons. They knocked down plenty of planes. Stefan's last letter reported he'd returned to his base with more holes than a colander.

Reggie made a point. The navy did account for most U-boat losses. Maybe the air force would be so tickled over bagging a supply sub that it would overlook his transgression.

All talk in the mess hall centered on the submarine. The news had spread like wildfire. Daniel's mouth twisted. No surprise, really. Not the way Kenny and even recalcitrant Hal couldn't button their lips.

The diners greeted Daniel and his dive-bombing buddies with cheers. As soon as they sat down, the wait staff served them, even though others were already waiting. They weren't able to eat, though, as men crowded around, eager to question them.

"Why was a milk cow so close to shore? I thought they stayed out in the gap where planes can't catch them."

"Did you check your plane over to make sure you didn't pick up a few bullet holes?"

"How low did you dive?"

"You think those guys ever saw a dive bomber before? I bet they shook in their shoes watching you scream down on 'em."

"How many Krauts did you kill?"

A vice squeezed Daniel's chest, and his appetite waned. A gentle hand touched his shoulder. "Here's a treat for you, Daniel."

Graziela placed a dish of pineapple chunks in front of him.

The pressure eased. "Thanks, Graz."

She jerked suddenly and pressed closer to him. Glancing beyond her, Daniel spotted a leering face. He must have pinched her backside. "Shove off, McCormack. This is a lady."

Mocking hoots turned McCormack's leer to a scowl. Daniel sighed. Had he just made an enemy? Or would McCormack seek revenge on Graziela? He leaned back and caught her eye. "Don't be out after dark on base by yourself."

She nodded, patted his shoulder, and slipped away to the kitchen.

When he and Reggie left the mess hall, he caught the whiff of a cigarette before McCormack's voice came out of the gathering darkness. "Hey, Lambert, what's the little tart to you?"

Daniel's fists clenched. "She's a very nice lady. Not a plaything for your pleasure. Leave her alone."

"How do you know her?" McCormack tried to loom over him, but he lacked the height.

"I had lunch at her house. Her roommate is a ... friend." He couldn't really call Isabel his girlfriend, although he'd like to.

McCormack caught his hesitation. "Oho. So, you're having a dalliance with the locals."

"Shut up, McCormack." Reggie got in his face. "Not everyone has a sordid little mind like you."

McCormack took a step back. He frowned at Reggie like he thought he'd been insulted but didn't know the meaning of *sordid*. Turning away, he jerked a thumb toward the mess hall. "Come on, Lambert, introduce me to your little friend."

"Nothing doing. I told you, she's not a harlot."

"Come on, introduce us."

"You've already made a poor impression on her. And don't think you can sweet-talk or intimidate her into changing her mind."

"What's she doing on base anyway?"

"Working hard at a job made difficult by guys like you. Americans pay a far better wage than anything the civilians can get locally. Don't ruin it for her."

A fellow C-47 pilot sauntered out of the mess hall. "Your girl had a lousy time with a bunch of clowns today. She would have loved to have you there to go to bat for her."

Daniel tensed. "What happened, Cy?"

"First, an idiot radio operator ordered his plane to be misloaded, and then they tried to blame her. A general happened by and read them the riot act. Meanwhile, a sleazy loader asked her to check his plane and tried to manhandle her right there on the tarmac. Good thing the general was still around. I saw Carter send her off in a jeep. She smiled at him, so I guess all's well."

Daniel checked his watch and glanced up at the sky. Too late to head off base. Too bad she didn't have a telephone at the house. He wasn't flying tomorrow, so he'd haunt the base until he found her.

Cy swung around as he continued down the walkway. "Oh, by the way, word came that the Germans scuttled your sub.

The navy boys picked up forty-eight survivors." He continued on his way, whistling.

Forty-eight survivors. Those milk cows usually had around sixty crewmen. Dinner settled like rocks in his gut. He'd killed a dozen men.

Chapter Nine

A whole, beautiful day off. Isabel stretched in bed. The temptation to snuggle into her pillow beckoned, but she threw off the sheet and rolled to her feet. The beach's siren call cast a stronger hold upon her than extra sleep.

Uwe Schneider wouldn't be up before sunrise, would he? If he'd been following her, he might know she liked to go to the beach at dawn. What would he do? Yell at her? Order her to obey him? Grab her and ... and what?

She hesitated in the kitchen. She'd promised Daniel she wouldn't go out alone. Too bad they hadn't made plans. He should be back from Ascension now and have the day off as well. Pouring a glass of juice, she gazed out the window while sipping it, contemplating the day.

The coast watcher would be there. She'd stay within sight of him. She could do this.

Isabel opened the door and gasped. Daniel stood there, his hand raised to knock.

"Good morning, Sunshine."

She sagged against the doorframe and laughed. "I'm so glad it's you. And what sunshine? The sun isn't up yet."

"It's hiding its face because it knows it can't compete with your sunniness." Daniel offered his arm. "Were you expecting someone else?"

"I wondered if Uwe knows early morning is my favorite time at the beach. I decided I would be fine if I stay near the coast watcher. He'd watch me."

Daniel snorted. "I'm sure he would, but I'm not sure if I approve of his watchfulness."

His eyebrows bounced as his gaze dropped to her toes and back up.

Isabel's cheeks heated even as she grinned at his leer. "Will you do a better job of safeguarding me?"

"Indeed I will." He patted her hand, tucked in at his elbow. "We need to see if any seashells came ashore after being bombed."

"Bombed?" Her voice squeaked. "Was Natal bombed? Or the beach? I didn't hear anything."

"Just one bomb was dropped offshore. We went out in dive bombers yesterday. Edson released his bomb before making landfall, because landing with bombs isn't encouraged. We'll see if any loosened shells have washed ashore."

"You go out with bombs? I thought you flew bombers for recreation."

"Yeah, well, we found a U-boat lurking beyond the horizon and wanted to see if we could change their minds about torpedoing a freighter." A shadow flickered across Daniel's face and disappeared.

He wasn't telling her everything. "What happened to the U-boat?"

"They scuttled it. Word is that they had some mechanical problem and couldn't dive. When the navy charged in, the

German sailors opened the seacocks or maybe set off charges. They weren't going to let us grab the boat."

Isabel studied his face. He stared straight ahead, not meeting her gaze.

"You said Ed dropped his bomb. Did you and the others have bombs?"

A small smile appeared. "Edson. You can call him Eddie." His chest rose and fell. "Yeah, we had bombs. We dropped them at the sub."

She waited for him to elaborate. "Did you change their minds?"

"Yep."

"Daniel, what happened?"

He stopped. "My bomb hit the sub. At least twelve men didn't get off. I killed them, Isabel. I killed them."

She shivered at the bleakness in his eyes. Tugging on his arm, she continued to walk. "My dad says, if you want to know what hell is like, go to war."

"Yeah." The word sighed out of him.

They walked in silence for a long minute. "I think of the guys who fly the heavy bombers. The pilots fly the plane, the navigator directs their path, and the bombardier releases the bombs. Lots of bombs fall on houses. Lots of civilians die. Who's guilty? The pilots? The navigator? The bombardier because he dropped the bombs? Collective guilt? Mission after mission. How do they live with it?" Daniel rubbed his forehead. "The Germans started the war, killing thousands in Poland, followed by every other country in Europe. They have to be stopped."

"There weren't any civilians on that submarine."

"No, at least I hope not. It was a supply sub. Maybe the attack subs drop off the odd civilian." Tension radiated off him. "'Straight is the gate and narrow the way, which leads to life, and few find it.' That means, of those dozen men yesterday, maybe a few found themselves in heaven. Most of them have discovered that while war is hell, there are places even worse. They have no more chance for the salvation of their souls."

"They should have settled that before they headed off to war."

"Yeah." His tone indicated he still felt guilty. "I keep reminding myself that in the Bible, God called King David a man after his own heart. David was a warrior. God told the Israelites to wipe out the Philistines. There's a time for war and a time for peace." At the top of the dune, he stared across the waves. "Maybe it wouldn't matter as much if we weren't fighting Germany, my mother's homeland. There's a remote chance I had a distant cousin on that sub."

Continuing to the shore, they removed their shoes and let the waves lap their feet. They strolled through the surf in silence, but Daniel took her hand. His gaze lingered on the waves, the horizon, the gulls soaring above them, and all the while his thumb stroked her skin. His touch sent shivers through her. Maybe he needed that human contact while his conscience was troubled, but he wouldn't have held Sandra's hand. Or Flora's or Graziela's. He held *her* hand.

His grip relaxed as he glanced around. "This is in line with Eddie's bomb." He searched the beach. "Doesn't look like any shells were knocked loose."

Isabel spotted something tumbling in the surf and towed him deeper into the water, unwilling to let go of his hand. She scooped up a shell. "Hmm. Nothing special. Look. There's a little hole. Whatever creature this served as a home to moved out because of that."

Daniel tilted it in her grasp. "Definitely not bomb damage."

"Not bomb damage." Chuckling, she turned it around. "This side is nice. It's still usable."

He stopped short. "Uh-oh. There's a bit of bomb damage."

She followed his gaze. The waves deposited two dead fish on the beach. Farther along, a trio of gulls fought over something. Another fish, no doubt. They were a good size and would have delighted a fisherman. As she watched, another seagull landed by the nearest fish and pecked at the eye.

"Ew."

Daniel pivoted her around. "How about we go back this way?"

They finally sat on the sand and watched the waves.

"My grandmother always told us to concentrate on things that are pure and just and of good report. She would tell me to stop moping about the dead men. There's nothing I can do to change things. Think about positive things." He propped his arms on his knees.

Isabel missed the connection through their hands. "She sounds like a wise woman."

"She is. I miss her. So, positive thoughts." He winked. "I'm thinking of the men who survived. I wonder how they are liking captivity."

Isabel dropped her imperfect shell as she laughed. "I doubt they would consider that a positive thought." She traced a circle in the sand around the shell. "When my cousin Huberto was with us, he told us about the battle when the *Graf Spee* was damaged. Artillery shells slamming into the ship. Shipmates collapsing, their blood spurting. His eyes had a glassy look, like he was back on deck. The battle seemed to go on and on."

She shoved up a pile of sand, like a bulwark for the seashell. "Three bombs were dropped on their U-boat?"

"Only one hit."

"A quick attack. Over before they knew it." She cocked her

head. "They shouldn't have traumatic memories, should they? That's positive."

An hour passed as they shared stories of their families. He told her of Thanksgiving feasts at his grandparents' house with all his cousins. It sounded wonderful. Isabel's mother had only one brother with three sons. She had only her brother Marcos. Daniel's big family with sisters and girl cousins captured her imagination.

He suddenly vaulted to his feet. "Jumpin' Jupiter."

What? Isabel's thoughts stumbled. How had he done that, going from sitting to standing in one second? Had he spotted Uwe? Jupiter? The planet? She rose in conventional fashion. "What's the matter?"

"I have to be at a Portuguese class in"—he checked his watch—"forty-five minutes. The instructor looked right at me when he said, 'I will see you next time.' He doesn't appreciate us pilots being off on business trips so often."

Hopping on one foot, he jammed the other into his shoe. "Are you ready to go home?"

"No." She searched the beach. "Go on. I'll be fine."

Indecision warred with his need for haste. "Okay. Be careful. Maybe I can catch the Liberty Bus. How about meeting for lunch at the Mercado Publico? Noon? Then we can go sightseeing on the Bonde."

"I'll be there. Go." Her heart smiled that he wanted to see her again so soon.

He sped off, leaping a small dune and disappearing from view.

Picking up the shell, she dropped it in her net bag and continued down the beach, waving to the coast watcher. Without Daniel, the beach lost some of its allure. She turned inland. She could get some cleaning done before meeting him.

THE MILITARY'S Liberty Bus's main drop-off site was a small plaza on the edge of the downtown area. Isabel saw the bus leaving the area, but Daniel was nowhere in sight. The bus ran on a regular schedule. Maybe he'd be on the next run. Or maybe he'd catch a ride with a supply truck or other base vehicle. Maybe she should go straight to the farmer's market. Indecision paralyzed her.

A hand grabbed her arm hard enough to cut off the circulation. "Why are you spending so much time with the American enemy?" The German words spat into her ear.

Uwe had found her.

She tried to pull away, but he tightened his grip. "Let go of me. You are the enemy."

"You will come with me." He forced her to turn away from the plaza.

Another man loitered at Uwe's side. "Where we taking her?"

Even from three feet away, his foul breath gagged her.

Disbelief battled with terror inside her. Nearby stood three men, deep in discussion. She screamed. "Help! Help me."

Uwe slapped her across the face. When the men stepped toward them, he released her with a shove. She ran without looking back and plunged into the farmer's market.

The Mercado Publico was crowded, but a swift look around brought disappointment. Daniel was nowhere in sight.

Chapter Ten

Daniel rushed out of the classroom, eager to return to Natal and find Isabel. Speaking to the locals in their own language made sense, but wrapping his mind and tongue around the strange words and remembering their meaning while keeping a conversation going? Whew. Good thing he'd learned German while growing up, or he might balk at learning Mom's native language.

"Daniel, wait up." Reggie nearly stumbled over a chair, so intently did he peruse the class handout. *"Vamos jogar beisebol depois do lanche."*

"Play baseball after a snack? Sorry. No can do. I'm going into town to have lunch with Isabel."

"A snack?" Reggie stopped to study his sheet, blocking the rest of the men from leaving. Daniel tugged his arm to get him moving. "Are you sure about that?"

"Lunch is *almoço.*"

"Well, anyway, wanna play some ball?"

"No, I'm meeting Isabel ..."

"Lieutenants Lambert, Klein, Wendt, Edson. Report to Colonel Sanborn's office immediately."

The hairs on Daniel's arms stood at attention as the corporal bawled his announcements from the doorway. It had been too much to hope their little tangle with the submarine had gone unnoticed by the brass.

Reggie's face blanched. "Now we find out if we get a pat on the back or a kick in the pants."

Daniel considered possible repercussions. Instead of the kick in the pants, he'd be kicked down to second lieutenant. He'd be grounded for a month and assigned to hard labor. A disciplinary letter would be attached to his service record and a copy sent to his parents. They'd take away the dive bombers. He'd be transferred to a combat unit, although not flying the Dauntless, since that was a navy airplane.

Positive outcomes? He'd get a pat on the back and a letter of commendation.

The four pilots filed into the colonel's office and stood at attention. Sanborn eyed them from beneath bushy brows. He leaned back in his chair, arms crossed. "I understand you boys are trying to prove you're not allergic to combat."

Daniel's breath whooshed out of him. Either that was just the colonel's opening salvo or he wasn't too upset.

"Why didn't you inform the navy of the U-boat's presence?"

Reggie answered with his question from yesterday. "And let them have all the fun? Sir?"

"Psh." The colonel probably didn't mean to verbalize his scoff. He studied a report on his desk. "Yesterday at approximately 1600 hours, four combat-retired Dauntless dive bombers intended for recreational flying dove on an enemy supply sub, releasing five-hundred-pound bombs. One bomb exploded in the conning tower. As a U.S. destroyer approached the sub, the crew scuttled it. Forty-eight survivors were picked up."

He drummed his fingers on the report. "Anything you'd like to add? For instance, where you found bombs?"

Daniel waited for Reggie to say something, but his copilot had clammed up.

"There's a man in ordnance who, if plopped down in the middle of the Arctic, could outfit a platoon, sir. He gave us bombs with no questions asked." Daniel hoped Calderson would never demand something in return.

"Uh-huh." The captain maintained an excellent poker face. "Anything else?"

"No, sir." Daniel hesitated. "Do you know how many men were on the U-boat, sir?"

"Sixty-four."

Sixteen dead, and he'd pulled the bomb release lever. He swallowed. As Isabel said, they should have seen to their eternal destination before they left home.

The colonel's steely gaze remained fixed on him. Daniel raised his chin.

"Supply subs are priority targets," Sanborn said. "The navy is miffed that you went after it with only four bombs. Sinking subs usually requires several depth charges. With no diving practice, you took a big chance on bagging it and avoiding being shot down yourselves."

"Not really, sir. Gunners have a hard time scoring hits on a plane coming straight down on them. They have to elevate their guns at such a high angle. And high angle dives boost diving accuracy."

"You know this how, Lambert?"

"I had dinner once with a dive bomber pilot."

The colonel barked out a laugh. "And that makes you an expert." He laughed some more. "I'll tell you what's going to happen, Lambert. The First Lady, Eleanor Roosevelt, is coming to Natal in March. She's going to pin a Distinguished Flying Cross on you."

Daniel kept his jaw from dropping. A transport pilot with a DFC. And Mrs. Roosevelt wrote a daily newspaper column about what she did. Would she mention him? People in Milwaukee would read that and maybe stop heckling his family about his noncom status.

He couldn't wait to tell Isabel about this. His whirling thoughts screeched to a halt. Isabel. She was waiting for him.

"Thank you, sir. One question, if I may. The milk cow sent an attack sub after a freighter. We warned the ship, and we know they called for help. Did they get away?"

"They did, with their thanks. Dismissed, gentlemen."

Daniel caught a ride into town. Reggie and the others probably thought him rude to rush off. Couldn't be helped. He hopped off the jeep at Mercado Publico and dashed inside the sprawling building. The clamor of dozens of voices filled his ears. He dodged a little girl scurrying to a *caldo de cana* stall. He knew that peeled sugar cane was passed through a pressing machine to create the sugar juice. The one time he'd tasted it, he had puckered up from the sweetness like he'd drunk sour lemonade. Nooo, thank you.

Isabel knew he liked pineapple. He veered toward a produce stand. There she stood, still wearing that pretty blue dress decorated with white birds. Or were they seagulls? Of course. He smiled. To remind her of the sea. She watched two children squabbling over melons. Stepping up beside her, he touched her arm.

She gasped and jerked away. "Oh, Daniel. It's you."

He found himself wrapped in a bear hug. His arms came around her, and she quivered. He murmured in her ear, "What happened, *querida*?"

90

She relaxed and leaned back in his arms. "Sweetheart? Is that what you learned in class today?"

He shrugged. "No. I found it in my English-Portuguese dictionary." He didn't like the way her eyes seemed overly bright. "What happened? Did Uwe put in an appearance?"

A shudder wracked her. "I waited at the plaza to see if you came back on a Liberty Bus. He grabbed my arm." She pushed up her left sleeve and huffed. "He's making bruising me a habit."

Daniel gritted his teeth. That hoodlum. How dare he hurt Isabel? If Daniel hadn't been called to the colonel's office ... No, don't go there. What's done was done. He unclenched his fist. "What did he say?"

"He asked why I spend so much time with the American enemy. And I was to go with him." She paused to catch her breath. "Some men stood nearby. I called for help, Uwe let go, and I ran. That's all. Oh, and he had someone with him. A thug with very bad breath. Like a pelican must have from keeping fish in its beak."

She stepped away and looked around. "Are you ready for lunch? I saw *pão de queijo*. Have you had that? Balls of cheese bread. Or *bolinhos de bacalhau*. Cod cakes you'll find everywhere, from restaurants to street vendors. *Acarajé* is another street food, an African falafel. And we need to get some *brigadeiros,* chocolate balls that are real popular now."

Her rapid speech told him she was still jumpy. She wanted to change the subject. Fine, for now. He played with her hand. "Did you see any of those fried cheese pastry things stuffed with chicken?"

"Oh, yes. *Pastel de queijo.* Although they might be stuffed with ground beef. Or pineapple. Over here." She gripped his hand and tugged him into another aisle.

They purchased a selection and headed to the plaza where

they found a bench. Daniel devoured a cheese ball before biting into a falafel. "What's in here?"

"Mashed black-eyed peas and ..." Her voice faltered when his cheeks puffed out.

He gulped down his mouthful. "Peas?" He grabbed his bottle of *Suco de Uva*, the grape juice he preferred over any other local drinks, and drank deeply. "And what else? Onion?" At her nod, he tapped his chest with a fist. "I'll be belching for the rest of the day. Good thing I won't be flying soon."

Taking his falafel, she offered a melon slice. "Soothe your taste buds with this." Then she pushed forward the little bag of *brigadeiros*. "And chocolate is always good for what ails you. That's what Flora says."

The melon juice did wash away the heat in his mouth. He reached for a chicken-filled pastry. "I'm sorry I was late. Reggie, Edson, Klein, and I were called on the carpet."

Across the way, four young men strode down the sidewalk. All wore white suits that were the preferred fashion for Brazilian businessmen. Sailors in dress whites blended in well. Daniel nodded toward the men. "If they showed up in Milwaukee dressed like that, they'd be laughed out of town. Do the men wear white to reflect the sun and stay cool?"

Isabel barely spared the men a glance. "Probably. White suits are not the fashion in the south. Of course, the men there are mostly German."

He studied her. "What do you consider yourself to be? Brazilian or German?"

"Both. Neither." She shrugged. "I don't know. I don't want to return to Florianópolis. The war is changing it. But I'm not comfortable here. I don't fit in. Have you noticed, among the waitresses at the mess hall there are no blondes? When I first worked there, the other girls were friendly, but they looked at me like they wondered why I was there. Many people have mixed blood. Portuguese and Indian, or Indian and African, African and white. There is not the segregation here that Huberto says is in the United States for Africans, although most scholarly jobs belong to white people here."

As she spoke, her busy fingers shredded a pastry. "I feel more comfortable on the airbase, except for when the men treat women like we're stupid or"—her voice dropped to a whisper— "like we are all prostitutes."

"I heard you had a lousy time with a bunch of clowns."

She shuddered. "Clowns? There was nothing funny about them." Selecting a cheese ball, she began pulling it apart. "What was wrong with the carpet?"

Daniel savored a chocolate ball. "What carpet?"

"You said you were called about the carpet."

"Oh." He wiped his fingers on his handkerchief. "Being called on the carpet means being rebuked for wrongdoing. Which in our case, means explaining about sinking the submarine, why we didn't summon the navy, diving in the Dauntlesses without any training, so on and so forth. But we're not in trouble." He made an exaggerated show of wiping sweat off his forehead. "In fact, I'm to receive a medal when Mrs. Roosevelt comes to Natal in March."

Isabel's eyes bloomed. "Mrs. Roosevelt? Your president's wife? Oh, Daniel, how wonderful. What an honor for you."

He spread his hands. "Yeah, I guess. I don't agree with her on everything, but she does a lot of good. She's more in touch with the common man than her husband is."

"He was here in January. Did you see him?"

"Nope. Flew out to Ascension on the day he flew in. We learned later he was on his way back from meeting with Churchill in Casablanca."

"And President Vargas came up to meet with him." She bundled their leftover food and hopped up, her unhappy demeanor gone. They needed to talk about Uwe, but he hated to spoil her mood now.

"You mentioned sightseeing." She swung her shoulder bag behind her and clasped her hands. "Have you seen the cashew tree?"

"Cashew tree? Do we get to eat some nuts?"

"Yes." She grasped his hand and pulled him up from the bench. "We'll have to take a taxi because it's twenty minutes south, and the Bonde doesn't go there. It's an amazing tree."

It *was* amazing. Daniel had a hard time believing one single tree could cover an area the size of two football fields. "This is like walking in a forest. Hansel and Gretel's forest, the way the branches have grown all over the place."

Isabel nodded. "The branches grew sideways instead of upwards. Then, instead of just touching the ground, they sent down roots, enabling it to spread over two acres."

Elevated wooden pathways enabled them to walk above the branches along the ground instead of stumbling over them. Daniel paused and looked back. "I think this qualifies as a metaphor for life." He reached for Isabel's hand as they continued on. "All the things that can trip us up and steal our joy, like my navigator or Uwe or the snarky combat pilots who don't respect us transport pilots. My Uncle Peter says to watch for heaven's little bridges that help us rise above the irritants."

He stopped to examine a cashew fruit hanging close to the path. "Actually, my grandmother prompted that illustration. One of her favorite Bible verses goes something like this. 'Looking unto Jesus, who for the joy set before him endured the cross.' And Uncle Peter said if you keep your eyes on Jesus, you're not going to see the obstacles in your way, so heaven bridges them for you."

"Heaven's little bridges. Hmm." Isabel's gaze wandered around the tree. Her hand tightened on his. "I like that."

They wandered around under the leafy canopy for over an hour. He'd brought Kenny's camera and took several photos. Before leaving, they bought some cashew fruits and nuts. On the way back to Natal, they stopped at Pirangi Beach and wandered some more.

When they returned to her house in the late afternoon, he chatted with Graziela in the kitchen while Isabel took her things to her room.

"Daniel. Come here." Alarm filled Isabel's voice.

He ran to the bedroom with Graziela on his heels. Isabel pointed under her bed. A box of gadgets rested there. "That wasn't here before. It's not mine."

He tugged it forward. "It looks like radio tubes."

"It's against the law for civilians to have them." She glanced at the window. The glassless window. "Uwe must have been in here. Or his stooge, Pelican. He'll probably make an anonymous phone call to the police and report me as a spy."

She was shaking, a hand over her mouth. Tears spilled over. Her voice cracked as she asked, "Why is he so fixated on me?"

Daniel thought fast. His first inclination was to comfort Isabel, but they needed to act. At the very least, Uwe was letting her know he knew where to find her. She needed a safer place to live, where enemies couldn't climb in through open windows. And they needed the police on their side.

"Graziela, would you bring the camera I left in the kitchen?"

She returned quickly, along with Flora.

He photographed the box still partially under the bed. Then he pulled it out completely and took more photos from various angles. "Do you have a large sack or a sheet I can wrap this in? I suppose the local police should be notified, but base security already knows about Uwe. I'll turn this in to them and let them contact the police."

Flora brought a tablecloth and helped him bundle up the contents.

Daniel turned to Isabel. "Try not to worry, sweetheart. If the police come, they won't find anything incriminating. Tell them base security knows you're being harassed by a probable German saboteur. Come to work a little early and meet me at Captain Carter's office. I hope I'll have some good news for you."

His gaze settled on each of the three women. They all looked a little shell shocked. If only they had a telephone.

"I'd better leave now, while it's still light out. If Uwe's watching, he might try to waylay me."

Isabel stifled a gasp and more tears spilled over.

"Wait right here." Flora held up her hand like a traffic cop. "I'll run next door and ask the neighbor to take you to the Liberty Bus stop. This is serious business."

"Thank you, Flora."

He hated to leave Isabel like this. This was a nice neighborhood, but if he had his way, she wouldn't be living here much longer. He gave her a quick, one-sided hug and followed Flora out the door.

Chapter Eleven

Isabel arrived on base early, determined to find one of heaven's little bridges to carry her over the trauma of Uwe's obsession with her. Last night's scene still chilled her to the bone.

A policeman had come to the house and insisted on searching it. He'd been vague, saying something about a report of suspicious activity. Sandra came home and staged what Flora called a hissy fit. She'd had the gall to turn on Isabel and accuse her of using her job to spy.

Flora had been a bridge from heaven, telling Sandra to be quiet and stay out of the policeman's way.

Graziela was another bridge. She stood beside her and told Sandra if she didn't like the present company, she could find herself a new place to live.

Sandra had puffed up, declaring with head held high, "I am a loyal American."

Graz had mimicked her pose, slipping her hand around Isabel's arm. "This is Brazil, and we are loyal Brazilians."

Isabel smiled at the memory.

Her smile faded. If Sandra moved out, would Flora too? They were colleagues and roommates but didn't appear to be close friends. Isabel and Graziela couldn't afford the house by themselves. How easy would finding two new compatible housemates be?

She took a deep breath. She was borrowing trouble. For now, she was meeting Daniel, and he was the best and strongest bridge of all. Thank God for him.

He waited for her in Captain Carter's office. The captain grinned at her. "This young whippersnapper has really put up his dukes for you."

"I don't understand a word you said."

Daniel raised clenched fists in a boxing stance, whirling his right fist in fast, tight circles. "Actually, I'd prefer saying I went to bat for you." He nodded to Captain Carter. "I prefer baseball over boxing."

The captain laughed, but then sobered and checked the time. "We'll be meeting with Major Herdman in fifteen minutes."

"Herdman? He was so suspicious of me when the loaders tried to blame me for the jeep being placed in the tail."

Daniel led her to a chair. "He's in security. He's suspicious of everyone. Those radio parts really grabbed his attention. He took them to the local police." He raised a brow. "I hear you did have a visitor last night."

"Indeed." She slumped in the chair before her mother's words rang in her mind. *A lady never slumps.* She straightened. "I don't understand why Uwe Schneider is so determined about me."

"He'll have a harder time getting to you now," Captain Carter said. "We're moving you into the women's barracks."

The rest of his words went over her head.

"The barracks? To live? I'm not American." She tried to rise, but Daniel kept a hand on her shoulder.

"Doesn't matter," the captain said. "You work for us. Important work. Your security is our concern. The brass is making an exception for you."

"What about Graziela?"

Daniel winced. "Sorry, no exceptions for her. But consider this. Being your roommate at the house puts her in danger. Theoretically, Uwe may try to use her to get at you. With you gone, she's safer. You could ask Flora to join you."

Graz, her best friend in Natal. Only friend, until she met Daniel.

"You'll still see her all the time, since she works at the mess. And living on base will be a whole lot more convenient." His eyes gleamed.

Convenient for her or convenient for him? A hot shiver swept through her. Spending time together would be so much easier.

"Time to see the major." Captain Carter grabbed a file and marched out the door. "Step lively now. We're going to conquer the beast in his lair."

"Conquer? So, this isn't decided?"

"It is." Daniel touched her shoulder briefly. "This is a formality. He'll issue you a new security pass and you'll return the one you have. He'll probably lecture you on proper procedures. Nothing you haven't already heard, but remember, he needs to feel important."

"Ahem, Lieutenant. That's a superior officer you're bashing." The captain tried to look stern, but his eyes twinkled.

Major Herdman breezed in. He didn't waste words. "This Schneider fellow may want to use you to gain access to the base to sabotage airplanes or steal supplies. The Third Reich has observers reporting on ships and their cargoes sailing out of South American ports. Schneider may try to extend surveillance over the U.S. military bases. Fortunately, the Germans have many agents with some training rather than a few well-trained agents, and they are easier to catch. We know this man's Achilles heel. You."

A funny feeling spiraled through Isabel's abdomen. The major better not suggest using her as bait. At least, he hadn't suggested she leave her job. Not to her, anyway. Maybe Captain Carter had already had words with him. All because she excelled at arithmetic. Funny how life turned out. Fraulein Richter, her grade three teacher, had thought she was hopeless when she didn't immediately understand how to multiply double-digit numbers.

By the time Isabel reported to the loading office, her head spun. The Americans were taking Uwe very seriously. He had been obsessed with her, believing her to be his, when she left Recife. Had moving to Natal and working for the Americans changed his plans?

She ran a finger down the list of the first plane's cargo. Several tons of radio equipment. Nothing like the stash under her bed. Enough for one person to contact a U-boat, Herdman suggested. Even secret inks and microdots for coding. Private ownership of radio transmitters was illegal in Brazil. Direction-finding equipment would be used to locate rogue sets.

Did they think Uwe had another radio? Maybe he wanted her to use the one he'd left in her room to contact him and share manifests from the base. Could he really believe she would do that?

Isabel closed her eyes and breathed deeply. Right now, concentrating on her job took priority. The figures for this plane weren't adding up. She calculated again. Still wrong.

This plane was four hundred pounds overweight. Grabbing her new military jacket, she headed out to the plane.

Isabel located Graziela in the mess kitchen before lunch. She hadn't been back here since she'd been on the wait staff. At Isabel's news, Graziela's eyes widened. "You're leaving?"

"Not my job. Just the house. I should be safer on base. And you will be too. Uwe shouldn't break in anymore if I'm not there."

Graziela sighed and turned back to the table. She set out small plates for dessert. "At least they're not terminating you. I worried they might."

Finding a knife, Isabel cut slices of a white sheet cake with chocolate icing and centered them on the plates.

"You shouldn't be doing that." Graz pulled the spatula from her grasp. "Remember Sofia and Luiza? They've asked me to join them in their apartment. I think I will. It's not as nice as the house, but" —she gave Isabel a sidelong look—"the company is better."

"Oh, good." Isabel clasped her hands together. "I felt bad about leaving you with Sandra."

Their laughter released some of the tension that had built up yesterday with her Uwe problems. Next on Isabel's to-do list was notifying her parents of her altered circumstances. Did Uwe still spend time with Marcos? Whether he did or not, her parents probably couldn't do anything about his behavior.

"Go on out and have lunch." Graziela prodded her toward the door. "I'll bring you a slice of cake."

Isabel peered out when one of the girls came in with an empty tray. Of course, mostly men sat at the tables. Daniel didn't seem to be among them. They hadn't made plans, and she couldn't expect him to spend all his time with her. She didn't need a bodyguard.

She glanced around the kitchen. No place here for her to eat without getting in the way.

"Go on." Graziela pushed her out the door with a smirk. "Be brave."

An older woman sat alone at the side of the dining room. She caught Isabel's eye and waved her over. "Please, join me. I feel like I must have a contagious disease the way everyone is avoiding me."

"Maybe they fear you'll tell their mothers if they are naughty."

"Hmm. I hadn't thought of that." The woman's eyes sparkled. "Not their mothers, but my husband. He's General Becker, and they won't want to get on his wrong side."

"The commanding officer of the base." Isabel nodded. "He would order them tarred and feathered for infractions. Or stripped and staked out among fire ant hills." She nodded again. "Best to avoid any situation where they will reveal their immaturity."

Goodness, Isabel's mouth was running away from her. She should keep it shut, except she had to open it to eat. Mrs. Becker's look of shock faded and her shoulders shook, like she was laughing.

"My dear, I think if George tried punishments like those, he'd be recalled and sent to Leavenworth, and not in a position of authority. Oh, but I would like to see the ants feast on a certain insolent young man." Mrs. Becker's eyes narrowed. "His poor mother must despair of his soul. Anyway," she brightened and leaned forward in a conspiratorial fashion, "tell me about yourself. Your attire has a military look which I suspect is to disguise the fact you are not."

Isabel touched the empty collar. "It's a WAC uniform without the emblems."

The story of the poorly loaded plane, Clarence Berelli, Uwe

Schneider, and her move to the barracks spilled out. Her face warmed at the realization of how pathetic she sounded, but Mrs. Becker had such a sympathetic demeanor, and talking to her was like talking with Mamãe.

"Hmm. Sounds as though things are working out." Mrs. Becker laid her knife across the top of her plate. "Tell me about your young man. Daniel. How does he make you feel?"

After the recitation of the last couple days, she uttered the first word to come to mind. "Safe. And happy. Comfortable."

"Your eyes sparkle just thinking about him." The general's wife smiled. "That's good. Also good that you're at ease in his presence. So many girls seem more concerned about moon dust and rainbows and butterflies." She shook her head. "Take some advice from an old lady who's been around the block, or in my case, the world. Butterflies are beautiful creatures, but fragile. They blow away in a stiff breeze and take away all the joy in life."

She reached across the table to pat Isabel's hand. "Rather than making your heart skip a beat, he should calm your heart when you're anxious. He should look at you with steady eyes rather than looking everywhere except at you. His smile should brighten when he catches sight of you. His hands should reach out to you day or night, blue skies or storms, ready to carry your burdens. If this describes your Daniel, your parents need to meet him, sooner rather than later."

A flock of butterflies erupted in flight within Isabel. They may be fragile, but these insects had lead-tipped wings.

She wanted to protest. She and Daniel had no understanding. They were barely dating. But the thought of something more with him ... The butterflies fluttered harder.

"He's American. I'm Brazilian."

"Didn't your father leave his home to follow a dream?"

His dream of flying had persisted after the conquering

Allies stripped Germany bare and forbade the country from manufacturing airplanes. Permits had to be obtained to fly what planes they had, and those were not easy to obtain, even for civilian use. Germany had too many pilots for the few flying jobs available, so of course Papai had to leave home.

He left for a job. Could she leave for love? Her fascination with America was what led her here to Parnamirim. The next step was going to the United States, like Huberto did. With Daniel?

If Daniel was the man for her. Her heart warmed and whispered, "He's the one."

Chapter Twelve

Daniel swung the bat. *Thwack.* The ball sailed beyond the outfielder. He dropped the bat and raced to first base. Second. Third. He could make it home. Probably. Maybe not. Mike Cobb had a wicked arm, and he'd finally snagged the ball. Better play it safe and hold up.

Lloyd Carter taunted him from the opposing bench. "What's the matter, Daniel? Allergic to home runs?"

"You wait, *el Capitan*. Me thinks you're going to strike out next time you're at bat."

Carter stuck his thumbs in his ears and wiggled his fingers like he was five years old.

Daniel made it home with the next batter and was met by a messenger.

"Colonel Sanborn wants to see you."

"You know why?"

"Guess you've been assigned a flight."

"To Ascension?" That would be odd. The flight schedule was made up a month in advance.

The messenger shrugged his left shoulder. "I don't know.

He didn't tell me. Just that you're supposed to get your ... *self* over there. Sir."

"You don't want to keep the colonel waiting, Daniel." Carter's grin stretched across his face. "Besides, your team doesn't need you."

"You're afraid I'll bat in more runs that your team can't counter."

Carter's reason for him to leave immediately had been in jest, but it held a lot of truth. Daniel didn't want to keep Colonel Sanborn waiting. And he was curious. This new flight must be out of the ordinary. At the end of the fifth inning, he jogged across the airbase.

At the administration building, he poked his head in the colonel's office. "You wanted to see me, sir?"

"Come on in, Lambert." Sanborn leaned back in his chair. "How would you like a quick visit to Miami?"

Miami? A quick visit. There wouldn't be time to include a quick side trip to Milwaukee.

"Sounds interesting. What's the cargo?"

The colonel's grin stretched as wide as Carter's. "Prisoners."

Prisoners? Did they have to clear out the brig? Did they have that many? Or did he mean ... "Germans?"

"U-boatmen, to be exact, from a recently demised sub."

Daniel pulled in a deep breath. "Do they know I bombed them?"

"Nope." Sanborn chuckled. "Think they might try to storm the cockpit if they knew? You'll have two armed guards with you. And there will be two planes. Klein will fly the other one. You'll leave tomorrow."

When Daniel arrived at the flight line the next day, the German sailors were already there. Each plane would carry two dozen. He spotted a white cap in the group over by Klein's

2

plane. Good. The white cap designated the sub's skipper, and he'd gladly allow Klein the privilege of flying him.

A forlorn-looking officer slumped against a jeep. Daniel tried to imagine how it would feel to be captured and sent to the enemy's country. He ought to offer a little hospitality.

"Wie geht es Ihnen?"

The man straightened, fully alert. *"Sie sprechen Deutsch. Wie ein Einheimischer."*

Daniel smiled. Nice to know he spoke German like a local. Wait. Each area in Germany had its own accent. "Where are you from?"

"Schwerin."

"My mother grew up there," Daniel said. "The Strieders emigrated in 1908. I grew up learning English and German."

"Strieder? My mother's best friend was a Strieder."

"Do you know her first name?"

The German tapped his chin. "Elisabeth."

"She's my mother. So your mother is Clara? Is she still living?"

"She is." Excitement animated the officer, but then his face darkened. "Last I heard."

Daniel nodded. More and more bombs fell on Germany these days. "They lost touch after the Great War."

"Ja, my grandfather died in the last year of the war. Starvation from the blockade. He insisted his family eat most of what they could find." The prisoner studied his shoes. "When he became ill in the bitter cold winter, he didn't have enough strength to survive. The family moved in with my grandmother's family in Stralendorf. Not far from their old home, but Germany was chaotic after the war."

"I'm Daniel Lambert, by the way." He stuck out his hand. "I'm the pilot of this plane."

"Konrad Buege." He shook Daniel's hand.

"May I ask why you were so close to Brazil's coast? I thought you stayed toward the middle of the ocean in the gap that planes don't cover."

Konrad glanced sidelong at the captain with the white cap. "Carelessness. We had a mechanical problem and had to stay on the surface. The captain didn't pay attention. We told him we were drifting too far west. He kept saying almost finished, almost finished. We should have started the engines to reposition, but no."

The captain stood off by himself. He must not be too popular with his crew.

Daniel wanted to ask if they'd been having a picnic on the deck, but that would reveal he'd seen the sub.

Konrad shoved his hands in his pockets. "I had never seen airplanes like the ones that bombed us."

"Dauntless dive bombers. They're used mostly in the Pacific by the navy, but we have a few here."

The fuel truck finished fueling the planes.

"Where are we going?" Apprehension filled Konrad's voice.

"We're taking you as far as Miami. It'll take a couple days. From there, I don't know where you'll end up. There are camps all over. Several are in Wisconsin. If you end up there, my mom will visit you. She'd love to hear about Clara."

"Visiting is allowed?"

"I guess so. My folks spotted some prisoners working on a farm. They were eating lunch under a tree." Daniel shrugged. "My parents stopped to talk to them. At least, Mom talked to them. Dad has Dutch heritage, but he's been around the Strieder clan long enough to know some German."

Kenny waved to Daniel from the plane's open door.

"Time to start the preflight checks. I'll see you later."

Bill Nelson stood at the top of the stairs in position at the door, a sneer marring his face. "You're awfully chummy with the enemy."

Daniel brushed past him. "Know your enemy."

He ducked into the cockpit and slid into his seat.

Reggie gave him a questioning look. "You did get a bit animated. Did you tell him you dropped the bomb?"

"No way." The wonder welled up within him again. "I greeted him in German, and he recognized my accent. He's from the same area where my mom grew up. And get this. My mom and his mom were best friends. He knew Mom's name. First name and maiden name. I knew his mother's given name, but not her surname." He snapped his fingers. "Dietrich. Clara Dietrich. They lost contact in the last war."

"Gonna tell her about him?"

"You bet. She'll want to know what happened to her friend. I'll call her from Miami."

"That'll cost big bucks."

"Really, Reggie? Ten dollars tops for a short call. That's worth it to talk to my mom. She'll be thrilled to hear her firstborn's voice."

Daniel pictured her reaction. She wasn't the screaming type, unless bugs were involved. She might laugh with joy or weep with thankfulness. After the call, she would dig out the few photographs from Germany and reminisce about Clara. Would the intervening years prevent their friendship from reviving? The Germans had suffered from the vengeful reparations inflicted on them. Frau Buege's father had died. Would she blame Mom for being an American?

"So, his mother's still alive?" Kenny lounged on the doorframe.

"Yes. Her father died of starvation during a cold winter, but he made sure his family had something to eat."

"They call it the winter of turnips, or something like that."

109

Hal Busch stood behind Kenny. "Turnips were meant for livestock, but it was all the people had to eat."

"Yuck." Kenny turned back to the cargo hold as the prisoners were led aboard.

"Did you ask him for her address?" Reggie ran his finger down the pre-start checklist.

"I will. I suppose the Red Cross might get a letter through, but that might bring his mother unwanted attention from the Nazis. If he ends up in Wisconsin, Mom can give him a note to pass along."

"Consorting with the enemy."

Daniel glanced back to see Nelson shake his head and grimace as though disappointed in him. Daniel clenched his teeth. He needed to request a new navigator.

The flight from Natal to Miami took more time in the air than flying from Natal to Ascension Island. Rumination filled his time. Why couldn't Marcos have met someone like Konrad Buege while he was in Germany? The man seemed like a polar opposite to Uwe Schneider. Of course, if Konrad had come visiting, maybe Isabel would have fallen for him.

An overnight stop in Trinidad broke up the time spent in the cramped cockpit, but Daniel still felt stiff and achy upon arrival in Miami. Rest would have to wait a moment though. The crew was scheduled for a two-night stay here. Tomorrow belonged to him, and he had plans. After a brief word with the officer who took charge of the Germans, he headed for the training office.

Early in the morning, he headed for the flight line. Kenny caught up with him. "Aren't you going to the beach, sir?"

"Naw. I can do that in Brazil. Today I'm heading to Winter Haven."

"Where's that?"

"Two hundred miles north of here."

Kenny trotted along. "You gonna fly one of those trainers?"

"Yep."

"You need a radio man?"

Daniel stopped. "You want to go with me, not knowing where I'm going?"

Kenny shrugged. "If I hang around here, they're likely to put me to work loading whatever we're hauling back tomorrow. Seems to me, the day will be more interesting with you."

The crew chief's camera hung around his neck. That would be good. So would the company.

"Saddle up."

When they arrived at Daniel's destination, Kenny's jaw dangled. "A garden? We're visiting a garden?"

"This place fascinates Isabel."

Fascination also stirred in Daniel now. Why were there so many young ladies dressed in colorful hoop skirts?

Kenny spotted them too. "Whooee. This is some garden." His eyes nearly fell out of their sockets. He handed Daniel the camera and took off toward a young miss clad in a crimson dress. "Outstanding."

Chapter Thirteen

Isabel and Graziela hopped off the Bonde near the dry goods store. Isabel glanced around. Guilt plagued her for going into town without Daniel's protection, but Graz needed fabric and Isabel wanted to get off base for just a little while.

Giving up her freedom didn't sit well with her, and that made her feel shallow. Men were fighting and dying to preserve freedom, giving up their lives for it, and she was complaining about being restricted to base?

A distant day from Florianópolis stirred her memory. Teenagers had been rampaging during Mardi Gras, and Mamãe wouldn't let her go to a friend's house. She had to stay inside for her own safety.

This was no different. A temporary situation until Uwe was no longer a threat. No big deal. And Graziela was with her. She wasn't alone. He wouldn't come after two of them, right?

Isabel looked around. He didn't appear to be anywhere nearby. Her shoulders relaxed, and she smiled at the sight of all the Brasilero men on the street.

"Have you noticed how the men all wear white suits? Daniel pointed that out to me. In the United States, the only white suits you see are the Navy's white dress uniforms."

Graziela shrugged. "White reflects the sun."

Isabel stepped off the brick-paved street and followed her into the store. Bolts of colorful fabric slowed her step. She touched one, then another. Too bad she and Mamãe's sewing machine had never become friends. She fingered a sapphire cotton sprinkled with crimson daisies. This would look fantastic sewn up like the dress a Hollywood actress wore in one of Flora's women's magazines. Maybe Isabel should buy it and ask Mamãe to create the dress.

Leaving the store with their purchases, Isabel gasped. She turned left and walked at a quick pace.

Graziela scurried to catch up. "We're going the wrong way." She hesitated. "Where are we going?"

Isabel's heart pounded in a frantic rhythm. "That big man in the ratty green shirt. That's Pelican, Uwe's lackey. Is he following us?"

Graz swept her hair behind her ear as she glanced back and gulped. "He is. He looks mean."

Isabel grew more frantic. They needed to hop on a Liberty bus. Pelican wouldn't be allowed to board too. But they were heading the wrong way. What to do?

"Let's go into the church." Graziela pointed to a large beige building with five front doors and two steeples. "He won't follow us into a church, will he?"

"I wouldn't put it past him." She dashed across the tree-lined walkway and yanked open a door, Graziela on her heels.

The interior was cool and dim. A long narrow nave ended with a crucifix at the apse.

"Come on." Graziela grabbed her hand and ran down the aisle.

Running in church seemed disrespectful, but God would understand. They'd come to His house for protection. Large archways on either side led to the transepts of the cross. They paused, looking around. Ahead lay more archways. Graz inched forward to peer through an archway. Behind them, a door creaked.

No, no, no.

Isabel rushed to join Graziela, and they ducked into the small area. Now they were trapped. Hunkering down behind a bench seat, she stared up at the crucified Christ. Blood dripped from His crown of thorns, His face battered, His mouth slightly open as though gasping for breath.

Father in Heaven, save us.

Beside her, Graziela whispered to the Virgin Mary.

Were they overreacting? Maybe Pelican was only supposed to follow them. Surely he didn't plan on grabbing Isabel in broad daylight. Maybe he hoped to slip something incriminating in her purse or steal it. He might want her base identity card.

Noise came from the sanctuary. What was he doing? Trashing the place? If he found them ...

She and Graziela exchanged glances. Graz's eyes must reflect her own trepidation.

"You there. What are you doing?" A deep voice came from the opposite transept.

The big man possessed a surprisingly high voice. He answered in bad Portuguese. "We are rounding up loose women. Two ran in here."

"Is that right?"

Isabel glimpsed the priest, tall and imperious in his cassock.

"You are not Brazilian." The priest's eyes widened. "You are German. Your mischief is not welcome here."

Stomping footsteps retreated down the aisle.

Isabel blew out her breath and slumped over. Too soon. Graziela's fingernails dug into her wrist. She looked up, up, up into the face of the frowning priest.

"I surmise you are the two loose women."

"No." Graziela's denial echoed off the high ceiling. She leaped to her feet and pointed toward the narthex where Pelican had disappeared. "That man is a saboteur, and his boss wants to possess my friend."

The priest offered Isabel a hand to pull her up.

"You were right when you said he was up to mischief." Her voice quavered and she cringed.

"He's probably waiting outside for us to leave," Graziela said.

The priest rubbed his chin with a thumb and index finger as he studied them. "Where are you headed?"

"The Liberty bus, to take us back to Parnamirim Field." Isabel's voice steadied. "We work there."

"Hmm." He turned around. "Come with me."

With a shrug, Graziela followed him. Isabel hurried after. The priest had sent Pelican on his way. He was unlikely to lead them to harm.

He led them to a kitchen in the back of the building, where two nuns inventoried the contents of a closet. "Sisters, these two young ladies are being followed by a ne'er-do-well. Dress them in habits and deliver them to the bus stop."

He disappeared out the door and the sisters blinked at them. One brushed off her hands. "Well, all right. I'm Sister Vitória and this is Sister Beatriz. Let's sneak you out of here."

In short order, Isabel and Graziela were garbed in black habits, including stiff crown bands under long black veils and wimples. At least they didn't need to wear the form fitting coifs around their faces. Maybe they were supposed to be novices. Isabel fought back a giggle. "It's hot under here."

Sister Beatriz offered a smile that seemed more like a grimace. "It won't be for long."

Sister Vitória lifted a sleeping cat curled up on a stool and set it on the floor. "Too old to jump, and we don't want to leave him stranded. We'll take the old Ford. This way."

Isabel and Graz were given several empty boxes to carry as part of their disguise. As they walked to the garage, Sister Vitória said, "We need to find more mouse traps. The one alongside the oven has vanished. Again. We must have very clever mice to figure out how to lug the traps away."

"The cat doesn't catch mice?" Graziela asked.

"That old cat is too blind to know a mouse if it smacked him in the nose." Sister Beatriz's disgruntlement rang through.

Sister Vitória caught Isabel's eye in the mirror. She raised her eyebrows and smiled. Her companion must be her cross to bear. Arriving at the plaza that was the main pickup point for the bus, she parked in the shade of a large tree. "You can wiggle out of the habits so you're able to run for the bus when it arrives."

They bumped elbows a few times, but both Isabel and Graziela divested themselves of the nuns' attire and smoothed their hair back into place. Just in time. A bus rumbled past the car. Isabel hopped out and headed to the bus stop.

Behind her, Graz said, "Oh, my fabric." Isabel glanced back to see her duck into the car to retrieve her bundle.

No sooner had Isabel turned back to the bus when she heard, "Nooo!"

Pelican held Graziela in his beefy grasp.

Sister Beatriz hopped out of the car and struck his shoulder with a kitchen ladle. He turned toward her, and Graziela escaped. She was gagging as she joined Isabel in outracing Pelican to the bus. "He smelled putrid." She held her arm out. "Oh, I feel contaminated."

Isabel collapsed onto a seat near the front of the bus. "Why is he so determined? By grabbing you, what did he hope to accomplish? That I would trade places?"

The bus seemed to tilt as a cold tight fist squeezed her heart. Uwe's obsession would give her nightmares for years.

The next morning, Isabel awoke with a start. Lying still, she listened to silence. She exhaled. No one had sneaked into the room. Easing out of bed, she raised the window shutter. High overhead, stars sparkled in a clear, inky sky. There, that might be the constellation Centaurus.

"Is it time to rise and shine already?" Flora's words ended in a yawn.

"I kept dreaming of Pelican or Uwe jumping out and grabbing me." Isabel sat on her bed. "It's hard to believe someone is so obsessed with me."

In the dim light, she saw Flora stretch out her arms before rolling onto her side and propping up her head.

"He's attracted to a pretty face and also your inner goodness, which he lacks. Although he may want to destroy that goodness. Maybe he sees you as a challenge to bring down to his level, which is in the gutter. You'd better not leave the base again without a whole squadron of men. Don't go out with just Daniel. I'll bet they have no scruples against knocking him over the head and leaving him for dead."

Isabel shuddered. She wanted to deny Flora's words. Would Uwe really kill Daniel?

Why not? He was German. Daniel was American. They were enemies. In war, people killed the enemy.

Uwe didn't belong in Brazil. He was up to no good, and not

only regarding her. He needed to be arrested. Only then would she feel safe.

She pulled on her new uniform. She hoped Daniel would return today.

★∘∘∗∘∘∗∘∘∗∘

"I TELL YA, that guy annoys the tar out of me."

Isabel peered around Captain Carter at the loader heaving bundles onto the conveyor. He wore a filthy T-shirt, more black than its original white. His arms were also streaked with black junk.

She pointed at his arms. "That's tar?"

The man looked at her in surprise. "Huh?" He held out an arm. "That's grease."

"You said tar is annoyed out of you."

Captain Carter laughed.

One of the guy's buddies howled. "We'll have to call you Tar Baby."

Did the guy redden? He scowled at his friend. "Tar baby nothing. I'm a North Carolina *tar heel.* Or, at least I would be if I'd gone to the university."

"Tar heels?" Isabel formed a mental picture. "Your mother must despair."

He blinked at her again. "Huh?"

"She'll never have clean floors if you keep scraping tar off your heels."

Captain Carter slung his arm around her in a neck hold. "Come along, Iz. Let's let these men get their dirty work done."

She was checking off the supplies waiting beside a C-47 when a voice said, "Finally."

119

She spun around to find Daniel standing two feet away, his hands behind his back. Her heart soared.

"You're here." She flung her arms around him and hugged him as though her life depended on it.

"Wow. You missed me." He returned her hug with one arm.

She stepped back, her face heating as whistles and cat calls from the loaders filled the air and Captain Carter said, "Ahem."

"I brought you something." Daniel held it behind his back. "Do you want to see what it is?"

She aimed for a touch of hauteur. "Why, yes. I believe I do."

With a flourish, he held out a brochure.

"Ooh." She accepted it as though it was fragile glass. "Cypress Gardens." Opening the cover, her eyes devoured the page. "Did you go?"

"Yes, I played tourist."

She gazed at him for a moment before flipping through the pages. "Ooh." Colorized photographs showcased beautiful flowers and young women dressed like Southern belles.

"If you get to Florida, you can apply for a job as a belle. All they do is stand around looking pretty. I wanted to ask if they had stools under all that skirt so they could get off their feet now and then, but I could just see my mother roll her eyes."

Isabel pressed her lips tight to keep from laughing. "That's all they do? Add color to the park?" What would it be like to wear a hoop skirt?

"As I understand it, a hard freeze damaged some of the flora, and the girls' wide skirts hide the bare spots. They also sell a lot of film at the park."

Captain Carter sighed dramatically. "You'll be useless now. Why don't you take an early lunch. Go on. Scram. And don't forget to eat while you're drooling over the flowers."

The mess hall was nearly empty. Isabel and Daniel claimed

a table in a corner where they were unlikely to be interrupted. A waitress served them with a smile and disappeared.

Isabel ignored the food and opened the brochure. "Was there a special reason you flew to Florida? Besides going to Cypress Gardens?"

"Since I sank the U-boat, Colonel Sanborn assigned Klein and me to fly the prisoners to the States. He likes to vary our trips so we don't get too bored with the familiarity of the same route and become careless." He leaned back, apparently no hungrier than she. "We only went as far as Miami. Since we had a free day, I visited Cypress Gardens. I wish you could have gone with me."

"I do too. Was it as beautiful as these pictures?"

"Better." He huffed a laugh. "Kenny went with me so he wouldn't be assigned to load our plane. All those girls drove him a little crazy. He had his camera, and I think I took a photo of him with each and every one of them."

Daniel picked up his spoon. "Anything interesting happen for you while I was gone?"

"Pelican." She set aside the brochure. "He chased us into a church, and then he grabbed Graz when we were running for the Liberty bus."

Daniel made her tell the whole story. Shivers swept over her as she relived the previous day. "I don't understand why Uwe is so obsessed with me. That question keeps going through my mind over and over." She twisted her hands in her lap. "I try to pray about it, but I don't think God is listening."

"Sure He is." Daniel placed his hand over hers. "You don't deserve this, but consider all the people who hurled insults at Christ during His crucifixion. He didn't deserve that. He understands your pain. Think of this as being worthy to suffer as He did."

"Because I'm a Christian?"

121

"Satan will get to you however he can. This is just a blip, less than that, in light of eternity."

Isabel smiled. "Your grandmother's wisdom?"

"Granddad's. His internment during the last war was unjust."

"Hey, Lambert." Klein stalked across the mess hall. "Colonel Sanborn wants to see you and he's not happy."

Chapter Fourteen

Daniel poked his head into the colonel's office. "You want to see me, sir?"

"Get in here, Lambert, and close the door."

Klein was right. Sanborn wasn't happy. He glowered across his desk. "What's this I hear about you getting too chummy with the enemy?"

Daniel's first inclination was to laugh. "Did Nelson file a complaint?"

The colonel's right brow rose. "Your navigator. Sit down and talk to me."

Sitting gingerly on the hard-backed chair, Daniel attempted to gather his scattered thoughts. The little boy within screamed at him to tar and feather his nemesis. Billy Boy had it coming. Whining, however commonplace it may be, wasn't professional.

"I initiated a conversation with one of the German prisoners before we took off. Nelson made comments about consorting with the enemy."

The colonel started clicking his pen. "How do you two get along?"

"We don't."

Sanborn barked a laugh. "Why not?"

"Near as I can figure, he feels like he should be aircraft commander because he's older than me. He tries to order all of us around. When that doesn't work with my copilot and me, he just harasses our two enlisted men until I tell them, in his hearing, that they take orders from me."

Daniel took a deep breath. "He's always been cantankerous. He never misses an opportunity to criticize me. Like when we took the prisoners to Miami, I presented him with a perfect chance to taunt me about talking to one of them."

"And this is the basis for a complaint? A casual conversation?"

This could get tricky.

"It wasn't casual, sir. It was amazing. The German's name is Konrad Buege. He looked sad, I said *hello*. I noticed we have the same accent from the Mecklenburg-Schwerin area. Turns out, his mother and my mother were best friends growing up in Schwerin. Mom's family emigrated and they lost touch in the last war." He had to stop and swallow.

Sanborn arched his eyebrows and waited.

"I telephoned Mom from Miami," Daniel went on. "She was so excited to hear her friend may still be alive. I asked the officer who took charge of the prisoners if Konrad can go to a camp in Wisconsin. If he does, Mom will be burning up the miles to visit him, in spite of gas rationing."

"So, you were consorting with the enemy?" The colonel's words didn't sound good, but the glint in his eyes seemed amused.

"Hands across the waters, sir. This war can't last forever,

and then it will be time to restore what's broken, including relationships."

"Have you tried to replace Nelson on your crew?"

"I've thought about it often, but I figure he's my cross to bear."

"Hmm. We'll see about that. What about your girlfriend?"

Daniel nearly choked on his saliva. "Isabel's a Brazilian citizen who's never been to Germany and has no wish to go there. She's being harassed by someone we assume is a German saboteur. Major Herdman at times seems to suspect her, but I suspect he'll report his own wife if she names their baby Ursula or Franz."

The colonel dropped his pen. "His wife is having a baby? How would you know that? She's tucked away at their home in New York."

"I, uh, assumed she's here. That is, I saw the major with a pregnant woman."

"Hmm. Very well. Dismissed."

Daniel wandered outside into bright sunshine and reached in his shirt pocket for his sunglasses. His conversation with the colonel left him discombobulated. "We'll see about that," he'd said, regarding Nelson. What did that mean? Would Sanborn transfer him off his crew? Daniel could only hope.

But the major. He'd been awfully cozy with the woman. If she wasn't his wife ... Good grief. Daniel may have opened another can of worms.

He needed to see Isabel. She'd probably be back at her loading station. He flagged down a jeep for a ride to the airfield.

A long trailer had been delivered to the staging area, and Isabel was directing the unloading. Crates were being divided among three airplanes. He noted cargoes of tank shells and radio equipment. Hauling the shells was almost, but not quite, as bad as hauling fuses, which exploded easily.

Isabel joined him, several pages fluttering on her clipboard. Not only did her brain work like an adding machine, but she managed to coordinate several tasks at once.

She glanced up at him. "Everything okay?"

"Best case scenario, I'll get a new navigator. I'd call Billy Boy a birdbrain, but that would be an insult to birds. They fly thousands of miles without maps or devices. If he's transferred, I'll be relieved."

"No more snarky comments?"

"Snarky?" He chuckled. "Where'd you hear that?"

"One of the loaders." She grinned, pleased with her growing English vocabulary.

"I worry about you with all these roughnecks. Some of them use pretty raw language. Even some of their less obnoxious slang might raise a few eyebrows, like saying you have a housewife in your pocket, or you need some happy cabbage."

Her head tilted. "Do I want to know what that means?"

"*Housewives* are sewing kits, and *cabbage* means dollar bills." He grinned as she gazed at him through narrowed eyes. "Are you up for a movie tonight? I hear *Down Argentine Way* is being shown. Have you seen it?"

"No. It's an interesting choice. Do you know Argentina and Brazil aren't too friendly?"

"Carmen Miranda is in it. Isn't she Brazilian?"

"Yes, but I heard she filmed all of her scenes in New York. Let's go. It could be interesting."

THE NEXT DAY, Daniel reported to the airfield for an evening takeoff. As he performed the visual outside inspection of the plane, Reggie joined him, sipping a cup of coffee. "Did I see you and Isabel at the movie last night?"

"That would be yes." Daniel checked the tire inflation.

"I get the feeling you weren't impressed."

Daniel grimaced. "I knew it was a musical, and there are some good ones. But do people really take over a dance floor to do their own dance like Betty Grable did?" He shrugged and moved on to the left propeller, running his hand across it to feel for nicks. "It was colorful, certainly, with lots of energy. I think that was the first time I heard Carmen Miranda sing. I thought she'd have a sultry voice, but ..."

"Kind of squeaky?"

"Higher than I expected." Daniel removed the pitot head covers.

"The story was kind of lame." Reggie ticked off the plot on his fingers. "Guy meets girl to sell her a horse. Guy's father hates her family, so the sale's off. She follows him back to Argentina and meets Dad under an assumed name. Dad agrees horse can race, but someone tries to fix the race. Horse wins anyway."

"Here. Make yourself useful." Daniel handed him the pitot covers. "That actor who played Dad was miscast, in my humble opinion."

"Did Isabel enjoy it?"

"She was impressed that Betty Grable danced so well in high heels." He peered into the wheel wells for leaks in fuel or hydraulic lines.

Daniel checked off the last of the outside inspection list as a jeep pulled up. Colonel Sanborn hopped out. "Lambert, meet your new navigator. This is Flight Officer Mike Green." He pushed a slight kid forward. "Have a good trip."

Daniel and Reggie stared at Green, who held out his hand. Daniel finally stuck out his own hand to shake. "Welcome aboard."

Reggie was blunter. "How old are you?"

Mike tried to stretch higher. "I'm twenty-three and a graduate of the University of Georgia."

Daniel blinked. He'd never heard such a strong southern accent. "So you're right out of navigation school?"

"No, sir. I flew on a northern route for two months before I was transferred. A couple of doctors figured I'd do better in a warmer climate. The cold weather kept causing respiratory ailments."

Daniel got the gist of his explanation. Visions of going off course because he didn't understand his new navigator's directions filtered through his mind, but he pushed them aside. "Have you been south of the equator before?"

"No, sir, but I know about navigation rules being different here. Such things as changing plus signs to minus in my equations. Determining drift from whitecaps on the ocean is the same in both hemispheres. I shouldn't have any trouble finding our way. My wife says I have a built-in compass."

Reggie spewed out a mouthful of coffee all over the pitot covers. "Your wife?" he wheezed. "You're married?"

"Everyone seemed to think getting married before I left for training was a good idea, in case I don't make it home to Savannah. Then, when I was assigned to transport, some of them thought we could have waited, but it's already done."

Daniel tucked his clipboard under an arm. He wanted to ask if Mike thought he should have waited, but that seemed too personal on first acquaintance. He opted for, "Does she mind that you're not in combat?"

"No, sir, I think Vivian's relieved. Her brother's scornful. He's a marine."

"Right. Can he navigate across a thousand miles of empty ocean and hit a tiny island?" Daniel exchanged a glance with Reggie. "By the way, I'm Daniel Lambert and this is our copilot, Reggie Wendt. No need to *sir* us." He turned to the plane and emitted a sharp whistle. Kenny and Hal popped into the doorway, and he waved them down. "This is radioman Hal Busch and crew chief Kenny Wright. Boys, meet our new navigator, Mike Green."

They both looked down on him.

"You're not going to try to order us around, are you?" Kenny asked.

"I don't figure that's my job," Green said.

"Then we'll get along fine. Come on, I'll show you to your office."

As they disappeared into the plane, Hal's voice floated back. "Can't say I'll miss Billy Boy."

"Him and me and all of us." Daniel sighed. "I think we just received a get-out-of-jail-free card."

He boarded the plane and checked over everything on his way up to the cockpit. The state of the radio compartment brought him up short. "What's going on, Hal? Is there a problem with the radio?"

"No, sir." Hal didn't look up from whatever he was rummaging around in on the floor.

"So, why has the radio been disassembled?"

"It's not." Hal's head popped up and he gazed around, looking bewildered by the mess. "Oh, uh, I'll get everything put back in order right away." He slumped in his seat and began what had to be a tedious task.

"If nothing's wrong with it, why's it in pieces?" Reggie picked up a part, but Hal grabbed it back.

"I'm trying to find my immunization card."

"Oh boy." Daniel patted Hal's shoulder and continued to the cockpit. He turned back. "Will reassembly delay us?"

"No, sir. It's not as bad as it looks." Already Hal was snapping and twisting things together at an impressive rate.

Reggie stayed behind. "How could you lose your immunization card?"

"It was in my wallet, and then it wasn't."

"He's already torn apart the barracks." Kenny tugged on a cargo strap and cinched it tighter. "Now he's hoping it slid down somewhere in the radio gear."

"If you can't find it, you'll have to have all those shots again." Reggie wasn't being helpful.

"I know, sir, I know. A dozen of 'em."

"At least they're spread out. You don't have to have them all at once," Kenny said.

"Yeah, three rounds, two weeks apart. All that means to me is, I'll be puking up my guts three times for one of 'em, and my arm swelling so much with another that my shirts don't fit."

Kenny stepped up to the cockpit. "Glad it's not me." He grabbed for his wallet and flipped it open. His posture relaxed as he held up his card. "Whee."

Daniel quietly checked for his own card. It was tucked in where it belonged. He chuckled. And why shouldn't it be there? He never removed it.

Reggie finally dropped into his seat, and they began their preflight checklist. A floral scent hit Daniel's nostrils as a slender hand reached in front of him, dangling his watch. He looked up into Isabel's smiling face.

"In case you suspect you're overdue to find the little island."

"I never missed it." He slid it onto his wrist and motioned for her to lean down. "We have a new navigator, and his southern accent is hard to understand. We may end up off course."

A frown puckered her brow. She turned to Reggie. "How's your Southern?"

"Don't you worry. I'll keep him on his toes."

"Is your radioman concerned about him? He looks so upset."

Daniel glanced back toward Hal. The radio was back together. The poor guy sat slumped at his desk, head in hands and fingers raked in his hair. "He lost his immunization card."

"Can't he replace it?"

Reggie smirked. "Not without getting all the vaccinations again. Ten or twelve of the stinging beasts."

"Do you have your cards?"

Daniel patted his pocket. "Safe and secure."

Reggie's smirk disappeared when he slipped his hand in his jacket pocket. He jerked up from the seat and felt his pants pocket. "Aw, rats. I left my wallet in the drawer. Smithers interrupted me, and I shut the drawer without retrieving it."

"Well, fortunately for you, you won't need any money on Ascension. And if there's an immunization card spot check, you can hide with Hal." Daniel swallowed a laugh. He rather enjoyed seeing Reggie on the edge of panic after he'd been unsympathetic with Hal.

Isabel poked his shoulder. "Are any women based on Ascension?"

"I've seen nary a one, except for pin-ups. Of course, nurses do pass through." Daniel squeezed her hand. "Care to stow away and see it for yourself?"

"That sounds like a good way to lose my job." She interlaced her fingers with his. "Interrupting you while you are preparing to fly is another way." She included Reggie in her admonition. "Don't forget a step on your checklist here."

Daniel gave her a two-finger salute. "See you tomorrow."

She left, to be replaced almost immediately by a routing officer. "New orders. We're mixing things up to keep crews from getting bored. Did you all bring your kits? From Ascension, you'll fly a North Africa route. Have fun."

Daniel stared out the windshield. He wouldn't see Isabel tomorrow. Botheration.

Chapter Fifteen

Isabel laid out her seashells on her bed. She hadn't had much opportunity to design new creations. Now, with Daniel gone indefinitely, she had lots of time to fill.

That man who'd jumped into Daniel's plane quickly hopped off and told her the *good* news. Daniel was off to Egypt, Morocco, and Oran. He'd be gone for at least a week.

A week.

She heaved a sigh. If not for the war, what were the chances he'd go there? He might enjoy seeing all those places. What did she know about them? The pyramids in Egypt, camels, strange smells. Daniel didn't appreciate strong odors. That might be a problem.

She divided her shells into three groups. Lots of scallops, some pretty spirals, bright orange cones. What she needed was background material. Feathery ferns and coral branches. She needed to go to the beach.

How likely was Uwe keeping constant watch on her? Did Pelican hang around the base entrance, hoping to see her leave? Every day? Surely not.

The airmen often went to the beach for recreation. There was even a Red Cross USO club at the beach. Isabel didn't know any of the men well enough to ask to tag along. They might get the wrong idea. She didn't know any of the women who staffed the club, but someone in the barracks must know. Traveling with a group ought to be safe enough.

Flora burst into the room. "Such a dreadful day. Just look at this. My last good pair of silk stockings. Ruined. And even nylon stockings are rationed to make parachutes."

A large bandage covered her shin. All around it, the stocking was torn away.

"Goodness, that looks painful. What happened?"

Limping to her bed, Flora collapsed upon it. "I'm walking with Ann—have you met her?—to the jeep. We're supposed to attend a meeting. A couple guys are digging around a scrawny bush, or maybe it was a tree, I don't remember. Anyway, things aren't going the way they like and one guy yells, 'Ah, forget it,' and tosses aside his trowel without checking for passersby." She groaned. "I thought my leg was broken."

"I'm guessing you didn't make it to the meeting."

"Bingo. After seeing me to the infirmary, Ann went. There was supposed to be a really cute guy there." Flora rubbed her arm as though chilled.

"Was your arm injured too?"

"Yes. That doc insisted on giving me a tetanus shot. Even though I'm sure I've had one not so many years ago."

"Wasn't it listed on your vaccination card?"

Flora turned her head to look at her. "I don't have one. I'm not in the military."

"Oh." Isabel told her about Hal losing his card. "If he doesn't find it, he'll have to have all his vaccines again."

Flora groaned again. "He has my complete and utter sympathy. Just this one shot is killing me."

"Would I need all those vaccines if I go to the United States?"

"Going that way, I don't know what you might need. Not cholera or yellow fever, like if you went to Asia or Africa."

Daniel must have had them, since he was on his way to Africa. Good thing she hadn't stowed away.

✦·❖·✦·❖·✦·❖·✦·❖·✦

"Hurrah for me. Lucky thing I pinched this loser's card. He's had the works."

Isabel barely heard the enlisted man's words of triumph as a Liberator bomber lumbered by on a parallel taxiway. The fellow waved a small piece of manila paper that blew out of his hand in the bomber's prop wash. It fluttered onto the muddy lane near her, where a truck promptly ran over it.

She stepped around several puddles and picked up the paper, which could be folded twice to be the size of an index card. Through the mud, she read IMMUNIZATION REGISTER. The name typed in could scarcely be read. She caught her breath and rubbed her thumb across it. Yes, it said Busch, Harold N.

The man who had lost it charged over to her. "Thanks for saving my card. I'd hate to lose it."

She recalled his triumphant words. *I pinched this loser's card. He's had the works.* She remembered Hal's devastation.

"So, Hal, what's your serial number?"

"Huh? How should I know? I didn't memorize it."

"Come on, lady. Just give it to him," one of his pals said.

She stepped back. "You can find it on your dog tag."

The man pinned her with a menacing look.

An officer pulled up in a jeep. Captain Carter. Isabel nearly wilted. With him sat a man whose armband read MP. Military police. "What's going on here?"

The three buddies backed away.

Isabel held up the muddy card. "I know Hal Busch. This is not him. He pinched Hal's immunization card."

The officer held out his hand. "Let me see your dog tag."

Isabel could see that the name and serial number didn't match the card. "Where did you get this?" Carter asked.

"I found it."

One of his friends decided to be helpful. "The guy left it lying on his bed."

The thief growled.

Captain Carter's brows rose. "Lying out in the open, waiting for anyone to help himself?"

"No, it was in his wallet ..." The friend clamped his mouth shut as the thief turned red.

All three men ended up getting a ride to the MP headquarters.

Captain Carter handed Isabel a stack of manifests. "Fortunately for you, I'm guessing they'll be transferred to a hot, humid Pacific island. Somewhere where they won't be able to take revenge on you. Aren't you lucky?" He winked and gunned his jeep to continue on his way.

Lucky her. As if Uwe and Pelican weren't enough.

And Clarence Berelli. She'd caught the loader eyeballing her a couple of times since the general had scolded him for manhandling her. Why hadn't he received a transfer to Timbuktu or those steamy jungles? She wouldn't want him to catch her out alone after dark.

Maybe working on the airbase wasn't the best idea. The captain appreciated her work though, and she enjoyed it. As long as the men didn't harass her.

Thousands of men lived here. They lacked female

companionship. That might explain why they acted so poorly in her presence. Or was that the way they were raised in the United States? The boys in Florianópolis hadn't acted like them. Leering, making snide innuendos, grabbing. Was that how the American boys had treated girls in school?

Not all of them, certainly. Not Daniel. He treated her like a lady. And his crewmen were always polite. Of course, they didn't want to get on Daniel's wrong side.

Later in the day, she pedaled to the shed. Now that she wore pants for work, Isabel used a bicycle instead of depending on jeep rides between the office, the cargo planes, and the airfield shed that constituted an on-site workroom. She found Julius, one of the loadmasters, frowning over a chart. "Do you have a problem with a load?"

He glanced up and, spotting her papers, held out his hand. After a quick flip through them, he tossed them on a makeshift table consisting of a sheet of plywood nailed to four unequal boards. "Some numbskull, I'm assuming, put together these loads."

He offered her the chart, but before she could take it, he pulled it back. "I dunno. This needs ta be verified." He pointed at the two planes on the tarmac. "They have identical split loads. Makes sense. Put half on one plane, half on the other. If one don't make it, the guys in Africa still get half their order. But mixing medicine with toxics? That don't sound right. Hold off on those birds."

Isabel watched him stalk off before pulling out another chart. This load made sense, including refrigerated whole blood. A glance around revealed no little Frigidaires. She grabbed a pencil and sketched the layout.

A headache throbbed. Lowering the pencil, she massaged her temples. Her workday was ending, just in time.

Returning to the barracks, she slipped into her room. No

sign of Flora. She must have hobbled to work. As Isabel clicked the door shut, a flash of white registered in her peripheral vision.

Had a piece of paper fluttered from ... where? It didn't lie on the floor. Had it floated under the bed? She bent to look, but her head whirled. Later. She'd look for it later. She collapsed on her bed. If only she had an ice bag.

A slight noise sounded like it came from nearby. Opening her eyes, she glanced around without moving her head. Nothing. It must have come from the room next door.

Something suddenly landed on her pillow and hit her head. She shrieked. Uwe? Had he gotten on the base? Into her room?

The door flew open. A brunette from down the hall stood in the doorframe. "What happened? Did you see Ghost?"

"No." How could she be expected to see a ghost? "I was hit on the head." By something that wasn't there. Her head throbbed, either from the headache or the hit.

The brunette stepped inside, another shorter woman replacing her in the doorway. A frown puckered her brow. "Who hit you?"

A strange sound came from under the bed.

The second woman pushed into the room and fell to her knees. "It *is* Ghost."

Seconds later came a loud "Yow."

The woman re-emerged in triumph, holding high a small cat by the scruff of its neck. A small *white* cat. The cat waved its paws, claws extended. "Mrrrawr."

The woman grabbed its flailing claws and tucked it into the crook of her arm. "Stop that, naughty boy." She bopped him on the nose. "No more hissing and snarling."

The cat relaxed and began a loud purr.

"I've been kicked in the head by a cat." Isabel sat up and

propped her head on her hands. "Better than a horse, I guess."

"Let's start over, shall we?" The first woman smiled. "Hi, I'm Eloise, she's Cynthia, and the runt, as you've no doubt surmised, is Ghost. He probably slipped inside when you opened the door."

The flying piece of paper she'd thought she'd seen.

"I'm Isabel. Are you with the USED girls like Flora?" She waved toward her roommate's bed.

"No, we're with the Red Cross." Cynthia rocked the cat like a baby. "We work at the USO club in downtown Natal and, when we're lucky, at the club on the beach."

The beach.

"When will you next go to the beach club?"

"Hmm." Eloise tapped her chin. "Today's Tuesday. In three days? Yes, I'm going to the beach on Friday. Want to come along?"

Isabel scrambled to find her weekly work schedule. Friday was beautifully empty. "I'd love to come. I always spend as much time hunting for seashells as possible so I can make my designs." She pointed to her work bench.

"Oooh." Cynthia shoved Ghost into her cardigan pocket, ignoring his yowl. "These are gorgeous. What do you do with these?"

"I sell them."

"Really? How much for this one? May I buy it?"

"Of course, when it's finished." Isabel named her price in US currency.

"You should bring them to the club." Eloise gingerly picked up a painted sand dollar. "I'll bet the men here will snap them up to send to their wives or mothers or girls back home."

Isabel's headache had vanished. She had new friends, access to the beach, and an outlet for her art. All she needed now was Daniel.

Chapter Sixteen

Finding Ascension Island in the middle of an ocean was akin to finding a needle in a haystack, Daniel had been told. Nothing but water all around, and each wave looked pretty much like the next. No matter. Their new navigator nailed it, locating the seven-by-ten-mile island in the standard nine hours of flight. They'd gassed up and headed farther east than they'd ever been before.

Their first stop was Kano, an ancient, walled city in Nigeria on the southern edge of the Sahara Desert. The lack of sanitation kept them from exploring.

Then they had to fly north over the desert and the Atlas Mountains to Oran on Algeria's Mediterranean coast. Like the ocean, the desert had no landmarks. Mike Green showed no concern, and they took off.

Halfway to Oran, the port engine's oil pressure dropped. Moments later, the starboard engine also experienced a spike.

"What in the world?" Reggie tapped the gauges, a useless gesture. "Let me play with the mixture."

"Sand in the engines?" Daniel studied the instruments. "I

wouldn't have called it a sandstorm in Kano, but there was a lot of stuff in the air." He reduced their altitude while watching the engine temperatures rise. "The engines will seize at this rate. Mike, where are we?"

"Smack dab in the middle of the Sahara. Nothing around for five hundred miles."

Daniel's gut wrenched. "We have to land. Now."

Questions rose in his mind. How firm was the sand? Would they sink in? Would the landing gear snap off? They wouldn't be able to take off in that case, but neither could they fly again if he did a belly landing.

He reduced their speed, hoping the slowest possible speed would lessen the likelihood of damage.

The sand loomed ever closer. It appeared wavy, like ocean waves. At least they provided him with a wind direction. He nudged the right rudder, causing the tail to turn to the left and the nose to the right, into the wind.

"Kill the engines?" Reggie sounded like he was gritting his teeth.

"No, we need to flare our landing. A flat approach is less likely to dig in."

They touched down. The left wheel must have touched first, because the plane wanted to skew around. Daniel's arms ached from gripping the control column. His legs trembled from pressing on the toe-operated brake pedals. The plane lurched to a halt. He shut down the engines.

"Why would both go bad at the same time?" Mike stood behind them. "We put the engine covers on. I know they're for cold weather, but shouldn't they work against sand?"

"Apparently there's a flaw in the system." Daniel leaned back, breathing heavily. They'd done it. Landed in one piece. Whether they could take off again remained to be seen.

"Now what?" Kenny's shoulders slumped, his hands shoved into his pockets.

Daniel blew out his breath. He'd received a three-minute briefing on flying over the desert. "Here's the situation. We keep a lookout for Arabs. If they come, only one man is to leave the plane. The rest man the machine guns."

"Ah, what machine guns?" Hal's face drained of color.

"The captain wasn't too clear on that." Daniel reached into a case attached to the bulkhead and withdrew a pistol, which he handed to Reggie. Next, he pulled out a sack. "We have a small supply of gold coins. Also, documents in French and Arabic which will supposedly ensure our safety. And, of course, that universal sign of friendship, a stash of chocolate bars."

He heaved himself out of his seat. "Okay. Time for a lesson in engine tune-ups."

"Who's the teacher?" Kenny cracked his knuckles.

The sound sent a shiver down Daniel's spine. He opened the cargo door. "Come on, guys. Haven't any of you ever worked on engines? Remove the cowling, look for sand where it doesn't belong. Kenny, grab your tools. We'll need some sort of scaffolding to reach the engines. Let's empty some of these crates."

A large part of their cargo consisted of radio equipment. One beautifully-sized crate contained classified instruments. It had something to do with radar, Daniel had been told, and wasn't to fall into enemy hands. He'd been given a small grenade to destroy it, if necessary, but would rather not do so inside the plane. He slapped the crate. "Let's start with this one."

Two men had to hold the wobbly platform steady while Daniel and Kenny checked out the engine. "Look at this." Kenny ran a finger along an opening. "There's a gap just behind the engine cowling."

"And the sneaky sand spotted that and rushed in." The platform teetered when Reggie twisted around to yell at Hal. "Take a look at the other engine. Does it have the same gap?"

"Yeah. It's crusted with sand."

With a lot of grunting and heaving, they wrestled the cowling off the port engine. Daniel's heart sank at the grit coating the cylinders. Air blasting or hosing might work, but they had neither option.

Kenny snapped his fingers. "I've got an idea." He leaped off the crate and hustled into the plane, returning shortly with a box and a grin. "I wondered why someone needed us to haul paint brushes, but maybe they're for us." He pulled out an inch-wide brush. "We can give 'em a try."

Two long hours later, Daniel took a cautious step back. He mopped his face with a sodden handkerchief. "I wish we could flush it out."

"Ouch." Kenny pulled his hand out of the engine. Blood oozed from a scrape across his knuckles. "All we've got is our drinking water, and now I need some for first aid."

"It must be a hundred and ten in the shade." Mike still wore his shirt, even though the others had all discarded theirs.

"Yeah, well, we're not in the shade." Reggie's tone bordered on surly, and he hadn't had his arms buried in the engine.

Daniel sighed. As plane commander, it was his job to keep their spirits up, but discouragement flooded him.

"Hey, look at this." Hal rushed over from the rear door. "I was reading our manifest. Look at this one. It's abbreviated, but that's an air compressor, isn't it?"

"Now you tell us." Reggie reached for the clipboard, causing the crate to wobble. Daniel and Kenny jumped down before it tipped. "Oops. Sorry."

Daniel took the clipboard. AC. He flipped to the layout sheet and pointed to a spot. "It should be right there. Find it."

"It won't have any gas in its tank." That concern didn't stop Hal from jogging back to the plane.

"No problem. Siphon some out of the fuel tanks."

"High octane? Is that okay?"

"Of course it is." Reggie boosted Hal through the door with enough strength to send the poor guy sprawling. "Wars aren't won by being inflexible. Grab the initiative and work the problem."

"Are you saying that's why he's an officer and I'm not?"

Had Hal just cracked a joke? Daniel chuckled. His crew seemed to be in high spirits now.

Reggie had the compressor fired up before Mike managed to clear away the crate. Things were looking up.

Another hour passed and they were nearly back in business. Mike and Kenny finished screwing the starboard engine's cowling back into place while Reggie dragged the crate back to the door and raised it high enough for Daniel and Hal to pull it into the hold.

"Are all the tools accounted for? I'd like to get back in the air as soon as possible." A bath would be nice, but that wasn't possible. Daniel hadn't even seen a mirage of water.

"Uh-oh. Too late." Hal nodded to the east. "Company's coming. Looks like they're riding horses, or ... Are those camels?"

Arabs. A prickly sensation had Daniel shifting his shoulders and rubbing his neck. Good or bad. This could go either way. He hopped out of the plane. "Hal, stay inside. Reggie, stay with him. You're appointed to guard the plane and the cargo. As soon as we have a feel of the situation, Hal, raise someone on the radio and keep them apprised of what's happening."

Per instructions, only one man was to leave the plane if Arabs turned up, but Mike and Kenny stood frozen by the engine. Frozen? In this heat? Daniel wanted to laugh.

No, he wanted someone else to deal with this encounter. All he knew about Arabs was from *Arabian Nights,* and that was a book of tortures. Would they hang them by their thumbs? He took a deep breath. He'd been on the debate team one year. Somehow, he doubted that qualified him for international negotiations.

The fast-approaching party consisted of eight men dressed in robes and head scarves. Despite being sticky with sweat, Daniel put on his shirt and asked Hal to fetch his cap. He would present as a dignified officer.

Their visitors arrived in a cloud of dust. One of the men uttered what sounded like a demand. Nothing that sounded like *shalom*. This must not be a peaceful greeting.

Another man spoke what seemed to be another language. Not German. What Daniel wouldn't give for Isabel's talent with languages.

Mike stepped up beside him and replied, apparently in the same language. Daniel forced himself not to gape at his navigator. He looked like a kid, had a wife, and now appeared to be saving their necks.

The conversation went back and forth while Daniel imagined his hair turning gray. He quietly cleared his throat.

Mike rocked back on his heels. "This is Philippe Yergeau. He's French, but he enjoys the nomadic life, I guess. They want to know why we are on their land."

Daniel kept his jaw from dropping. "Their land?" In the middle of nowhere? Asking to see a title of ownership was probably not a good idea. "You told them we had to repair our plane, right? We didn't take anything from the sand. I mean the land."

Mike shrugged. "We disturbed it. Philippe says they expect payment."

They probably wanted to paw through the cargo, but that

wasn't going to happen. Most of it would be useless in the desert anyway. This is why they had the gold coins. "Think he'd like to read our French documents?" Daniel held up his hand before Mike could ask. "Tell him we were about to have a snack before leaving. Would they like to join us? We've got candy bars."

He turned to Kenny. "Get the goods."

Mike added, "And your shirt."

One of the men turned out to be a sheik with a sweet tooth. He loved the chocolate, even though it had softened to a mess. He also helped himself to the gold. And he made a show of studying the Arabic documents, although Philippe revealed he couldn't read.

Daniel watched the supply of candy disappear with a twinge of alarm. What would happen when it was gone?

Mike sidled close. "Philippe says they have a two-way radio and have summoned more of their tribe. They'll be arriving shortly."

"Yeah. Here comes a sandstorm."

Daniel followed Kenny's gaze. From the size of the sand cloud, a large group approached. "We don't have any more chocolate bars."

Mike shook his head. "I doubt the sheik wants any for them. It's supposed to be women who will prepare a feast for us. The sheik wants to reciprocate."

Prepare a feast? They could be here all night. Daniel's hope of reaching Oran before dark disappeared. He sighed. As Reggie said, wars were won by being flexible.

The new arrivals immediately set to work building fires, raising a goat's-hair tent, unrolling carpets soon covered with unrecognizable food stuffs, and slaughtering a goat. Daniel hoped no one noticed that he flinched when they slit its throat. The Arab ladies would impress his mother with their speed in setting it to roast, but he had to wonder about the sanitation.

Mike voiced another cause for concern. "The sheik has never flown."

"We are *not* taking him for a ride."

"I think Philippe knows that. They're testing us. Seeing how far they can push."

Daniel surreptitiously studied the Frenchman. No older than mid-thirties, probably. Had he come to the desert to avoid conscription? The German occupation? "Can you find out if he's had military service? If he understands military protocol?"

Mike had to repeat most of his words. That bothered Daniel. Mike's southern accent made his English hard to understand. What did it do to his French? He leaned close to Kenny. "Do you speak any French?"

"Only a few words, but I don't know what they mean."

"Huh?"

Kenny cleared his throat and sang, *"Frère Jacques, frère Jacques, dormez-vous? Dormez-vous? Sonnez les matines. Sonnez les matines. Din, din, don. Din, din, don."*

Behind Mike, Philippe exploded in laughter. He gasped out a comment before laughing some more.

Mike enlightened them. "He says Kenny sings a lullaby. Or tries to, anyway. Sorry, Kenny, but you'll never be an opera star."

Kenny drew himself up in a huff and crossed his arms. "Well, bully for him. Who'd want to be in an opera?"

Daniel patted his shoulder. "He doesn't or he wouldn't be here." He glanced back to Philippe. "We never spotted anything that looked like an oasis. Are there really watering holes with palm trees around here?"

The translation came back. "Just over that rise the tribe

came over. A large lake and many trees. Underground springs of cold water replenish it. Other tribes are camped there too."

Daniel mulled that over. They'd been on the ground for four or five hours before the sheik and his men arrived. "How far exactly? Easy walking distance? Or maybe don't ask. Even if it's close by, we can't all go and clean up."

It was bad enough that Reggie and Hal had to stay in the plane instead of joining them for the meal. These people were friendly enough, but what did Daniel know about Middle Eastern customs? If they left the plane, they'd likely return to find it stripped of all cargo.

Philippe asked about them.

"Tell him they have to monitor the radio. The base knows we had engine trouble and we are waiting to hear their instructions." Daniel took another bite from his bowl of roasted vegetables flavored with spices he couldn't identify. He speared a thick round slice. "What is this? I feel I should know it."

Philippe asked the girl serving them. "Onion, zucchini, eggplant, sweet potato, tomatoes, peppers."

That didn't exactly answer his question, but he smiled at the girl and nodded.

Late in the evening, the tribe finally prepared to leave. The sheik approached Daniel with the girl. He pushed her forward with many words.

Philippe coughed and said, "The sheik presents you with his daughter to be your wife."

Chapter Seventeen

What a narrow escape.

Daniel leaned back in his seat and closed his eyes. They'd made it to Algeria. Let the rest of the crew handle the usual arrival procedures. He felt as limp as a worm.

"You okay, buddy?" Reggie jiggled his shoulder. "You've hardly said a word since leaving the desert. You're not regretting leaving the little wifey-poo behind, are you?"

Sometimes Reggie was a pain in the neck.

"I've been imagining my mother's reaction to that child."

That's what the girl was. A child. Fifteen years old, max. What was the sheik thinking? That'd be like a foreigner coming through Milwaukee while he was growing up and his dad offering him Theresa or Gretchen. *Here, mister, take my daughter.*

One side of Daniel's mouth kicked up. Sure, there'd been days he would have been thrilled if Dad had given Theresa away. But, come on. Seriously?

The girl didn't speak English. He didn't speak Arabic. Their lifestyles were a world apart. The sheik must view her as nothing more than a cook and bed warmer.

"I've been imagining Isabel's reaction." Reggie chortled. "Maybe she'd start making puppy-dog eyes at me."

Daniel pushed himself out of his seat and brushed passed his copilot. Correction, sometimes he was a sheik-sized pain in the neck.

A sergeant appeared in the doorway. "Sir? You're to report to headquarters. I have a jeep ready."

A colonel waved Daniel into his office and pointed to a chair. "So, Lieutenant, you didn't want a bride."

"I should have brought her along and taken her to some protective agency. Her father's likely to hand her off to the next guy who passes through. He could be a brute, for all the sheik knows."

"Lives are cheap here. Women's lives especially." The colonel leaned back and hefted a pair of filthy boots onto the corner of his desk. "How'd you weasel out of the nuptials?"

"The Frenchman with them told the sheik that the military won't allow marriages during the war or civilians on the airplane. The sheik didn't seem too surprised." Daniel shrugged. "And my navigator, who speaks French, said I have a girl who expects to be my number one wife."

The colonel chuckled. "That may have done it. Now, you boys are free to explore Oran. You can get a feel for what you're missing by declining the marriage." He winked, and his feet thumped to the floor. "Mechanics are tearing apart your engines to be sure they're ready for a trans-Atlantic flight. Then you'll fly to Casablanca and pick up a bunch of wounded to start homeward. Dismissed."

A little shuteye would have been great, but Daniel didn't expect to pass this way again. The crew didn't waste time in heading into Oran. The city bore evidence of French colonial influence with oriental touches. Arched portals led through walls daubed with clay. Dry thatch covered roofs. Women cooked in clay pots redolent with the scent of spices Daniel failed to recognize.

Men wore robes and headdresses in varying colors. The way they grouped together made him think the colors denoted their status or origin. Arab women were covered from head to toe, while other women wore western clothes. Outside a mosque, a communal trough allowed worshippers to wash their hands and faces before entering. A donkey attempted to drink and was shoved aside.

A nearby market beckoned. He should find something for Isabel. Plenty of stalls offered woolen goods. Pretty scarves and stuff, but not too practical for tropical Natal. Carpets and copper items. Mountains of spices that would last a lifetime in Mom's kitchen.

He turned to his crewmen. "Are any of you buying souvenirs?"

Mike eyed something hanging in a wool stall. "I don't have any francs. Do you think they take dollars or Allied military currency?"

"They'll be glad to take your money of any kind." Kenny moseyed over to a booth with wooden carvings. He held up a monkey with a toothy grin. "These are kind of cute."

Hal spotted a carving of a kitten curled up. "My mom loves cats." His brow puckered when he opened his wallet. "I was sure I had a five spot."

"Maybe it's with your immunization card." Kenny pulled out his own wallet. "Here. I'll loan you a buck."

As he tucked the wallet back into his hip pocket, he whirled around. "Hey."

Daniel glimpsed a young boy run into the crowd, bare feet

flashing beneath his dirty robe. "Pickpockets. Better keep your valuables in your shirt pocket."

He was about to give up on finding something meaningful for Isabel when his gaze fell on a stall that seemed to be full of junk. There, in the back, could that be seashells? He took a step into the booth and the two attendants began yelling about their wares. They must think the louder their voices, the more likely he'd understand their language. He squeezed past them. Nearly hidden by some feather contraption sat a shell sculpture. Three large painted scallops created a backdrop for a fourth which held tiny shells and a small bottle. Ink? How about that. A decorative inkwell.

Isabel could create something much nicer, but this might give her ideas. As he was about to pick it up, he noticed a tray on the floor. Small shells overflowed. She would love these.

Pulling out a dollar, he indicated the inkwell and the tray of shells. The woman grabbed it, bobbing her head. He scooped up his treasures.

Reggie shook his head as they strolled on. "You could have gotten a lot more stuff with that buck. You're giving us a reputation of being gullible Americans. You're supposed to bargain."

"This is a bargain." Haggling didn't appeal to him. "Nothing else there held any appeal, and she sure couldn't give me change for a dollar."

"Hey, we don't leave real early tomorrow, and there's a beach nearby," Kenny said. "You can find more shells on your own."

Daniel grinned. "Excellent idea. Sometimes, Kenny, you're a genius."

Mike wandered back to a wool stall. The two staff women shouted and pushed garments in his face. He fingered a thin, cheery yellow bolero. "What do you guys think? Would this be fashionable in the states?"

"Sure. My sisters would wear that with dresses that only have straps over the shoulders." Daniel found a multi-hued blue one. Elise's birthday came in a few weeks. "How much do we offer for these?"

Mike pulled out a bill and one of the women snatched it out of his hand, smiling at both of them.

"Two for the price of one." Mike inclined his head. "Not bad."

"Just hope they fit. They're non-returnable." Kenny pointed to a row of food stalls. "Let's find something to eat."

Early the next morning, Daniel, Reggie, and Mike found their way to the beach before the sun peeked over the horizon. Few people ventured out at this hour. After the noise of the market, the silence refreshed Daniel. He removed his shoes and socks and allowed gentle waves to wash sand over his feet.

A plump conch-like shell in variegated maroon and gold tumbled in the surf. He rescued it and smiled at his prize. Just the kind of shell Isabel loved.

A starfish that looked more like an octopus languished on the beach. He'd never seen anything like that in her collection. A tiny olive-green sea urchin shell with a small hole in the side would delight her. He even found quarter-sized pieces of sea glass in shades of orange, yellow, and green, sanded smooth by wave action.

"You've got more here than you bought at that shop yesterday." Mike had picked up a few shells for his wife.

In the distance, a horn wailed.

"What's that?" Reggie sniffed the air. "A fire alarm or a call to pray?"

"Pray for safe flights back to Ascension and Natal." Daniel secured the mouth of his sack of shells. "I'm ready to return."

Back at the base, Hal met them with a worried look. "Bad news. Kenny's sick. Food poisoning."

"Huh. All that rot gut he ate at the market really was rot gut." Reggie twirled his cap on his finger. "Now what?"

Daniel pursed his lips and exhaled. "We'll have to leave him behind."

Chapter Eighteen

I sabel managed to arrive at the tarmac within seconds of the Skytrain turning off the perimeter track. The plane appeared tired, plodding forward at a slow pace, hydraulics squealing as it lurched to a stop. Sunlight glared off the cockpit windshield but didn't prevent her from seeing Daniel. Finally, he was home.

Home.

No, she meant back in Brazil. This wasn't his home. And maybe not hers for much longer. She could hope.

The propellers stopped spinning, ground crew chocked the wheels, and ambulances lined up at the cargo door. So, they'd been hauling wounded.

Four men emerged from the tiny front door, which was little more than an escape hatch. They deplaned without disrupting the medical staff. No sign of Kenny. He must still be busy inside, helping remove the injured soldiers.

Daniel handed something to Reggie and headed toward her. The rest of the crew followed in his wake.

"You're a sight for weary eyes." Although he smiled, his

eyes looked ready to close. He dropped his bags, held out his arms and she stepped into his embrace. His chest heaved in a sigh.

"A grueling, whistle-stop tour of Africa, was it?"

He groaned. "Fine by me if we aren't sent back. It wasn't all bad, but …"

"Engine trouble put us down in the Sahara Desert," Reggie said.

"Right smack dab in the middle of the desert," Mike said. The new navigator was obviously comfortable with the crew.

"Then a sheik arrived. He was concerned that we'd disturbed the sand." Daniel's mouth twisted with a grimace. "Our supply of chocolate placated him."

"So much so, he summoned their womenfolk to come roast a goat, and he wined and dined us." Mike tapped his fist to his chest like he had heartburn.

Isabel grinned. "Tasted like chicken, didn't it?"

"No." Daniel kept one arm around her shoulders. "It tasted like spice."

"And then the sheik decided Daniel would marry his young daughter." Reggie shook his head as though still in disbelief.

"Marry his daughter?" Isabel wanted to laugh, but the men before her were serious. "How young was she?"

"No more than fifteen, I'm sure," Daniel said. "He pushed her forward, expecting us to take her with us. If not for the French guy with them who translated for us, I don't know if he would have finally accepted that I belong to the military now, and the military would not allow the marriage." Daniel's hand tightened on her arm. "I was ready to sweat bullets."

Reggie chuckled. "We should have brought her along. She could keep our room clean, shoes polished, all the nitty gritty stuff. She'd never know the difference."

Hal Busch scoffed. "Lieutenant Lambert would never marry a foreign woman."

Heat flushed through Isabel. He wouldn't marry a foreign woman? Spots danced before her eyes and she felt faint. Weren't they courting? She'd been imagining a wedding. Wasn't she special to him?

Daniel pulled her closer to him. Before he could ask what was wrong, she blurted out, "Where's Kenny? Did you leave him with the sheik to pacify him?"

Reggie snapped his fingers. "We should have thought of that."

Daniel gave a laugh that didn't sound amused. "We left him in Oran. Algeria. He indulged in the local cuisine and ended up with food poisoning. His stomach kept erupting, so he's still in the infirmary there. He'll follow in a day or two."

"He begged to stay with us," Mike said. "We didn't want to chance the plane ending up smelling like vomit, so we said *no*. Wouldn't have mattered. One of the wounded guys kept barfing. The plane ended up stinking anyway." He waved his thumb to Hal and back to himself. "We could have brought Kenny and laid him out between our stations."

"Oh, Hal, I have something for you." Isabel fished in her pocket and pulled out his immunization card.

He didn't immediately recognize the mud-stained card. Then his face lit up. "Yahoo." He grabbed her in a hug, nearly jerking her off her feet.

Daniel rescued her. "How'd you find it?"

After she explained, Reggie planted his fists on his hips. "That was kind of careless of you, Harold."

Hal shook his head. "It wasn't out in the open. I hid it under a stack of laundry. All I had was six dollars, and he stole the five-dollar bill."

"Don't worry, Reg. He'll be more careful in the future,

won't you, Hal?" Daniel twisted Isabel's arm to read her wristwatch. "What's the local time? I need some shuteye. Meet me for supper? Five o'clock?"

She nodded.

He gave her a big smile. "I brought you something. You'll like it." He turned to a waiting jeep. "Come on, guys. Come on, Hal. We'll drop you off."

Isabel watched them drive away. She pivoted and stared at their plane, now taken over by the ground crew.

Lieutenant Lambert would never marry a foreign woman.

Her dreams shattered like glass.

Somehow, she managed to get through the next few hours. Concentration proved difficult. Where had she misread him? If he wasn't serious, why did he pursue her? Round and around, questions swarmed, demanding answers she didn't have.

As soon as her shift ended, she escaped to her room and collapsed on her bed.

He brought her something. Something she'd like. Surely it wasn't one of those voluminous robes Arab women had to wear. She wouldn't like that. He acted like he cared for her. He just didn't want to marry her? Did he simply want a girlfriend in Brazil while he was so far from home? He couldn't be toying with her. Not the man she'd come to know.

A glance at the clock had her up and dressing for dinner. She didn't want to be snarky, but she hoped Reggie and Mike didn't join them. Or did she? Did she need a buffer?

Daniel met her at the entrance to the mess hall and kissed her hand. "You look exceptionally lovely this evening."

"Hmm." She smoothed a hand down the skirt of her magenta dress. "This isn't one of my nicest dresses. Are your eyes still tired?"

He led her to the end of a table in the farthest corner. "How have you been?"

"Fine. Busy. Missed you."

He covered her hand, his thumb brushing back and forth. "Any trouble with Uwe?"

"Not a peep out of him. Nor any sign of Pelican. I even went to the beach with the Red Cross girls. Maybe he's given up."

"You can hope, but I doubt it."

She looked down. "Me too."

"What's wrong?"

His quiet words brought her gaze back up. "Nothing's wrong. You're back. That's good."

His eyes narrowed. The way he studied her made her squirm.

"Something's not right. Be honest. A lack of communication can kill a relationship."

She stopped breathing. What kind of relationship did he consider them to have? Could she ask him straight out if he thought of marrying her?

She took a deep breath. "You remember that I'm a foreigner to you, yes?"

His brows shot up and his thumb stilled.

A minute passed. Maybe two. Or maybe ten seconds.

Understanding relaxed his face. "Hal said I wouldn't marry a foreign woman."

She bit her lip and toyed with the napkin on her lap.

"Isabel." His thumb rubbed her hand with urgency.

She raised her eyes.

"Hal doesn't include you in foreign women. None of us do. He meant foreign culture. A Middle Eastern Arab woman and a Christian American man? That's like mixing gas and water. Won't work. You, yes, you're Brazilian. But you're part of the Judeo-Christian culture of western countries."

Her heart pounded. He wasn't proposing, of course, but it sounded an awful lot like he'd been envisioning marriage too.

161

"During training, one of the guys met a great gal. They hit it off, crazy about each other. But he was from stuffy, uptight Boston and she was from laidback California, and it was like they were from different cultures. Their friendship crashed and burned. You, though, I think you'd fit in just fine in Milwaukee. My mother did, and she was a foreigner from Germany."

She tingled all over as hope soared.

A waitress brought their meal. She was a friendly girl Isabel remembered from her days working in the mess, but for the life of her, she couldn't recall her name.

The hall filled up, and they shelved their talk for later. Some of the fliers spotted Daniel and ragged him. "Hey, Lambert, where's the little Arab bride I heard about?"

"Her father was most insistent, but I had to tell him my girl is adamant about being my number one wife."

Isabel's glass thudded down on the table, and she clapped a hand over her mouth to avoid spitting out her pineapple juice. "Number one wife? How about only wife?"

"No, it's a great idea," a freckle-faced pilot told her. "You could insist she do all the housework."

"Lambert, your navigator has an accent as thick as thieves," another man said. "Do you think your Frenchman recognized what he was saying in French?"

"Doesn't matter. We got out of there with our cargo intact and the girl left behind." Daniel looked grim. The incident must have really shaken him.

"Maybe you can go back and say you changed your mind."

Daniel shook his head. "I have no intention of returning to the Sahara. I prefer my sand on a beach."

As the teasing continued, Daniel's responses became shorter and he ate faster. Isabel didn't enjoy the banter either. The men considered the incident a joke as long as it happened to someone else.

She eyed a dark-haired man who always leered at women and made lewd remarks. Flora knew about him and called him a bandy rooster. He probably would have taken the girl and made her life miserable, not caring that she was a human being with feelings.

She studied Daniel. So well-mannered, so thoughtful, so much fun. "You said you brought me something."

His sudden smile lit up his face. "Are you curious?" He surveyed the food on the table. "Had enough? Let's blow this place."

An image of the mess hall exploding flitted through her mind before she scooped up the last bite of beans and drained her juice.

They stopped at his barracks and he came back out with a box large enough to contain a pair of boots. When she tried to peer inside, he turned away.

"Uh-uh-uh. Not yet." He glanced around. "Nothing should be going on in the chapel. Let's go there. I'm tired of listening to planes roar overhead."

Hundreds of planes took off or landed every day. At peak times, a plane landed in Natal every three minutes. A four-engine plane rumbled above their heads, one engine spitting and sparking. Isabel tensed, waiting to hear a crash on the runway, but the sounds of the evening didn't change. "Instead of hearing singing birds on the wing, we hear mechanical beasts. I hear gulls at the beach, but I do miss birdsong."

The chapel was a beautiful white stucco building with a red tile roof and steeple. It bore no resemblance to the churches in Natal or Recife. More like the churches in Florianópolis, but without the half-timbered styling.

They settled into a pew near the back of the sanctuary, and Daniel placed the box between them. Something bundled in a cloth lay on top. She lifted it out, and the cloth dropped away.

She gasped. "Shell art." Three large scallops provided a backdrop for a small display centered around a short bottle. "What is this?"

"An inkwell." Daniel shrugged. "It's not a thing of beauty, but I thought it would give you ideas. You can make something so much better. And it doesn't need an inkwell. Just the scenery you're so good at."

He seemed embarrassed by his gift. Then his words soaked in. It did give her ideas. Yes, she could create something beautiful. "I wouldn't paint the scallops like this. Maybe I can use something other than ink."

She turned it this way and that as possibilities flitted through her mind. A mental inventory of her shell supply brought a twinge of concern. "I'll need to go to the beach. I need more seashells."

Daniel pushed the box closer to her and she heard a jangle that sounded an awful lot like ...

"Shells." She scooped up a handful, and beautiful, colorful seashells of all sorts slipped through her fingers. "Oh, oh. Oh, Daniel, look at all these shells. Oh, look at this one." She held up a fat, round spiral. "And this one. Oh Daniel." She plopped the shells back in the box and lunged forward to hug him.

A chuckle escaped him as his arms came around her. "I think I nailed this."

"I love them."

She leaned back as a voice said, "I say, am I interrupting?"

They jerked apart to find a minister approaching down the center aisle. Isabel wanted to crawl under the pew. He must think they'd come in here to ... What had Flora called it? Neck? Make out?

She straightened her back. "Come see what Daniel brought me from Africa."

The minister, a sandy-haired man about forty years old,

leaned forward for a look. "Seashells by the seashore. Quite an assortment, it appears."

"Isabel's a seashell artist." Daniel touched her shoulder. "In no time, these will all find a place in one of her masterpieces."

His boasting warmed her heart.

"Is that right?" The minister picked up the fat spiral. "I've never seen one like this before. Such a wonderful variety in God's creation." He set it back. "I saw a seashell arrangement at the Engineering Department. Delicate little thing. Was that your work?"

Delicate little thing? Was that a compliment or an insult?

"My roommate Flora works at USED, and she bought one of my arrangements. That may have been it."

He nodded. "You have a good imagination to create something like that. My artistic ability, I'm sad to say, is limited to drawing stick figures."

The sun was setting by the time they bid farewell to the minister and strolled around the base. Daniel carried the shell box and draped his other arm around her shoulders. "Have I told you about my friends?"

"No. I know you have sisters you're willing to share."

He chuckled. "Ah, yes. Well, John, Stefan, and I have been buddies from the time we were in kindergarten. We did everything together, including dodging my dear sister Theresa and our cousin Gloria. They always wanted to tag along. Pests, they were. Gloria's a great gal now. She's a naval nurse on a hospital ship in the Pacific. Aunt Maren and Uncle Peter are proud, but concerned."

"And Theresa's married, right?"

"Yep. She's her husband's problem now."

Isabel elbowed him. "You love her."

"Most of the time." He sighed. "Actually, her husband, Lawrence, is home from Africa now, minus his lower leg."

"He was in the army?"

"Graves Registration. The Germans booby-trapped a corpse, which exploded when the men tried to retrieve it. Lawrence's shrapnel wounds developed gangrene."

"Where are your friends?"

Daniel took a deep breath. "In harm's way."

He gazed across the base to where planes landed, but Isabel didn't think he actually saw them.

"One of my earliest memories of the three of us took place in second grade. Our teacher, Mrs. Lester, called us the unholy trio."

"What a terrible thing to say."

"Yeah, I thought so. We all have Bible names. I guess she thought we should behave better. All we did that day was feed one of her fish to a starving stray kitten."

"You didn't."

"Oh, yes, we did." His hand fluttered on her shoulder. "The fish was a bully, always snapping at the other fish in the aquarium. She tried to suspend us for stealing. Our parents were summoned to school. My folks were away, so Uncle Peter, who's a reporter, and his lawyer friend showed up. They made her worry about her job security for being cruel to eight-year-olds on a mercy mission. Turns out, in the end she adopted that poor kitten. She may have had some good qualities, but they're all overshadowed by that incident."

"Your uncle, of course, knew you couldn't be guilty."

"Of course. I was always a little angel." He cleared his throat to prevent a laugh. "He's my godfather and I'm his namesake. Daniel *Peter* Lambert. Anyway, why am I telling you this?"

A small dog trotted up and she stooped to pet it. Several of the servicemen had acquired dogs. Or cats, like Eloise and Cynthia.

"You started by saying your friends are in harm's way."

"Right. We're all pilots. John started lessons in high school and, of course, Stefan and I joined him. His college prospects weren't good, so he joined the navy right after high school. He flies fighters off an aircraft carrier. His letters are vague, but he seems to be dating an Australian nurse. He was upset about the Japanese torpedoing an Australian hospital ship."

"And Stefan?"

"He flies amphibians in Iceland."

"Iceland. Brr."

"Big time. No lazy days on the beach for him. He hunts U-boats going after the convoys. They have to fly low, which makes them susceptible to the U-boat deck guns. Anyway, he has a girlfriend."

"An Icelandic woman?"

"No, a Canadian gal who went to school in the U.S. and joined the Red Cross. She's French Canadian from Quebec." He stopped and turned to face her. "You see, we like foreign women."

With one arm grappling the box of seashells, he leaned closer. Her breath caught. He was going to kiss her.

His lips brushed hers with a feathery touch. Then they settled more firmly. Isabel tasted pineapple. She loved pineapple. Her arms entwined around him of their own accord and tugged him closer. When he leaned back, she breathed again. Then he kissed her once more. She could get used to this. Her heart tap-danced in delight.

They continued walking around the base holding hands. Words weren't necessary.

Back in her barracks room, she spread out her new cache of shells. She twisted the inkwell arrangement this way and that. The piece didn't need a gimmick like the ink bottle, but it could have charm if she could figure out what to add.

Flora came in with Eloise. "Did you go to the beach?"

"Daniel brought these from Africa."

Eloise plucked the inkwell from her grasp. "Hmm. Kind of a weird thing to put with shells. What if it drips?"

"I'm trying to think of something else. All I've come up with is a key holder."

"Or coins or earrings." Flora trailed a finger through the shells.

"Excuse me, Flora." Eloise tapped her arm. "I need a flashlight."

"Right." Flora rummaged in her drawer and pulled out the light.

It lit up in Isabel's mind. "Candles. I can put short, stubby candles in these."

"Oooh. Make one for me." Eloise handed back the inkwell. "With a bayberry candle if you can find one."

Isabel's shell order list kept growing. Between her job and time with Daniel, she didn't have much time for crafts.

A sigh escaped her. Day after tomorrow, Daniel would fly back to Ascension. She'd fill the time with her shell designs. Maybe she wouldn't even notice his absence.

Yeah, right.

Chapter Nineteen

Two weeks had passed since Daniel brought Isabel seashells, and she'd used them all up in her creations. Her talent amazed him. When he looked at a bunch of shells, he saw shells. She saw them as flowers and angels and sea horses and candle holders.

"We need to go to the beach early one morning," he told Reggie and Mike as they barreled toward the runway in late afternoon. "Isabel needs more seashells."

Reggie took his eyes off the road as he careened around a curve. "Is she still having problems with that Kraut saboteur?"

"Not lately, but she's been careful. The moment she drops her vigilance though ..." Daniel's words trailed off as he imagined what might happen if Schneider got his hands on her.

"What does she do with the shell stuff she makes?" Mike clapped a hand on his cap to keep it from flying off.

"Sells them. People see her designs and ask her to make them one. Did you see the framed beach scene I have? Her creation. I need to box it up and send it to my mom."

Mike whistled. "That's beautiful. I thought it was all stuff like that inkwell. Think she'll make one for me? Vivian would like that."

"Come see her when we return. She may have a waiting list, depending on how many orders she has." Daniel smiled. Everyone was impressed with her talent.

They arrived at the plane to find a group of men standing around. "These must be our passengers. Some special group that needs to get over there pronto." Daniel consulted his clipboard. "I think they're paratroopers to be dropped behind enemy lines."

"They'll be squeezed in tight." Mike glanced skyward. "The weather's supposed to be rough. Maybe they won't bounce around too much if they're tight."

"I asked Kenny to rig stretchers along the upper rack. A few will be able to stretch out and get some rest, but they'd better tie themselves down or they may be pitched off."

"I'm glad we're guaranteed seats, uncomfortable as they are." Reggie wheeled into a parking spot by the ground crew's shed.

No sooner had they climbed from the jeep then a loud voice said, "Oh, no. We're depending on a coward to get us to Africa?"

Silence descended. Daniel's good mood evaporated. He recognized the malcontent. Phil Colton had been in his high school class, a braggart and a bully. Just how did he expect the plane to get them to Europe without a pilot?

The group's commanding officer studied Daniel and his crewmates before asking, "You have a problem, Colton?"

"They're sissies, flying in the backwaters instead of in combat."

The CO rocked on his toes. "May I remind you, Colton, that

you go where the military sends you and do what you're told to do?"

Colton shrugged one shoulder.

Kenny jumped into the fray. "Lieutenant Lambert flies combat in his spare time. And next week, Mrs. Roosevelt, the *First Lady*, is gonna pin a Distinguished Flying Cross on him for dive bombing and sinking a German supply sub. Single-handedly."

Daniel headed for the plane. "Come on, Kenny. You know the Krauts scuttled their boat as soon as the navy showed up."

Colton's smirk slid off his face.

One of his comrades asked, "Did you really sink a U-boat?"

Daniel waved off the question. "I don't like to toot my own horn."

Kenny skedaddled into the airplane on his heels. "Toot your horn?"

"Colton's brother bragged about how becoming his company's bugler would keep him out of the front lines. I'm sure Phil, here, caught the reference."

In the cockpit, Hal hovered close. "Reports coming back from outbound crews say the storm is bad about four hundred miles out. Some planes reported icing. Kenny found a supply of bags for puking. Not enough, though, if these guys have full stomachs."

"Ah, the joys of flying. Okay, tell Kenny to start loading them."

Reggie came in from his exterior inspection. "Shipshape. Are we ready to go?"

"Give those guys the dope, will you, about how bad it may get?"

Daniel probably should have done the briefing himself, but he didn't want to face Colton and his pals. Maybe he *was* a sissy, but rank had its privileges. He started the first engine.

Their flight proceeded smoothly for the first three hours. Then the clouds built up.

He mused aloud, "They're too high to fly over. Too low to fly under without the risk of ending up in the drink."

Reggie agreed. "And we don't know how far they extend to the right or the left. Trying to go around could take us too many miles out of the way, and we might run out of fuel."

They had to fly straight through. The air became rougher. Daniel struggled to hold a steady course.

They'd been bouncing around for an hour when a sudden, eerie blue light flickered and streaked across the window. He leaned to the side window and gasped. The propellers glowed blue, set in a blue circle around the engine.

"St. Elmo's fire. We're in an electrical storm." He glanced at Reggie, who stared wide-eyed out the front window. "Take a look at the engine."

Reggie took a quick glance before his gaze swept the controls. "A whirling dervish. Everything seems to be working."

"It's harmless." At least, that's what Daniel had heard.

No sooner did the words leave Daniel's mouth when icing struck. The controls stiffened and required all his strength. The engines coughed. Bits of ice flew off the propellers and clattered against the fuselage.

"Sit back down." Kenny's yell startled him. "Don't touch that door. Where do you think you're going? We're over the middle of the angry Atlantic."

Daniel had trouble cuing his intercom mike. "What's going on back there?"

"One of these clowns panicked and wants to get off. His pals are sitting on him now, but they all look ready to wet their pants."

If Colton had been the panicky passenger, Kenny would have said so.

He came back on the intercom. "The, uh, special passenger has coated himself with barf."

Daniel allowed a smile as he wrestled with the controls. "How is it for the rest of them?"

"Stinks to high heaven. They've been barfing like babies. I wish I could open a window."

"I didn't know babies barfed so much." Sweat glistened on Reggie's brow.

A lightning strike hurled the plane onto its side. The luminous dials of the controls went haywire. The artificial horizon indicated they were upside down. Daniel grabbed a pen from his pocket, held it out, and dropped it. It fell forward, down and to his left. They weren't inverted, but they weren't flying level. And they were plunging downward. He strained against the rudders and control column.

They needed a miracle to avoid crashing into the sea.

A voice with a Texas twang reverberated in his memory. 'Sonny, in the old days, we didn't have all these fancy instruments. Just the needle, ball, and airspeed. Pay attention to them."

Just like that, Daniel was back in flight school, flying with a crusty old pilot instructor who'd flown biplanes in the last war.

His thoughts settled. He concentrated on the turn and bank indicator and the climb and descent needle. They'd dropped low enough for warmer air to revive the airspeed indicator. He hauled back on the control column and the plane leveled off.

Before he had a chance to catch his breath, a massive updraft shoved them hundreds of feet higher. His heart hammered in his chest as though trying to get out.

"Going up to kitchen wares. Next stop, children's clothes."

Kenny's voice in the intercom sounded somewhere between laughter and concern.

Just as suddenly, the draft dissipated and they dropped.

"Oof." Any laughter disappeared from Kenny's voice. "Bargain basement coming up, where you'll find lots of good deals you won't want to miss."

"Like a watery grave?" Reggie slumped in his seat, still gripping the controls.

Daniel must look the same. He flexed his fingers, then his toes. Everything ached. He wasn't prone to airsickness, but these aerobatics were pushing him to his limit.

The compass still wallowed like it was drunk when the buffeting eased. He dared to hope they were coming out of the storm. A faint light appeared ahead. The plane flew out of the murkiness. Stars twinkled overhead.

"Hallelujah." Daniel's relief came out in a whisper.

He stared at the beautiful pinpoints of light before rousing. "Mike? Where's the southern pole star? We need to find it to fix our compass. Do you see it? And get a fix on our position."

"Got my sextant ready to go." Mike must already be in the astrodome. "Ah, there it is ahead of us. Polaris Australis, also known as Sigma Octanis. It's not very bright. We're north of our route. Come south three degrees. I'll get more fixes to finesse our heading."

Daniel used the time to set the directional gyro to zero on the pole star. According to his watch, they had two more hours of flying time. Two hours? They'd been four hours out when the storm got really bad. Could they really have been in it for three hours? No wonder he felt like a basket of laundry, ready to be hung out to dry.

"Kenny? Any chance of getting to the lav?"

"None whatsoever. Even if there was a clear path, you'd

end up puking if you tried to slog through this stuff. Their lunch is all over the place."

"That's just great." Reggie shifted around in his seat as he muttered. "I don't trust those relief tubes."

Daniel nodded. "Hal? Do we still have a supply of cans under your desk?"

"Yep. It's all yours while I stretch my legs."

As Daniel pressed past Mike, the navigator leaned down from the astrodome and yelled, "Good thing it's night and I can take some star fixes. I don't think we're too far off course."

The paratrooper leader shuffled forward like an old man. "How much longer?"

Daniel hid a grin. "Under two hours. How'd your boys like the electrical storm?"

"If I'd known that was coming, I would have forbidden them to eat first."

"I'll open my side window and let some air blast through. It won't be able to go out the rear, but hopefully it'll change the atmosphere in here."

Daniel glanced around the dim cargo hold. Hard to tell which arms and legs belonged to which bodies. The troopers were a picture of abject misery. Phil Colton huddled near the front. As Kenny had reported, Colton, like the others, was coated in barf. Kind of glassy eyed. Green around the gills.

Daniel grinned, returned to the cockpit, and opened the window. An arctic gale rushed through.

By the time they landed, everyone had revived at least a little. Kenny opened the front hatch, leaned out, and took a deep breath. "Smells like a lovely day on Ascension. Thank you, folks, for flying with us on Goonie Bird Airlines. You may now disembark through the rear door. Please be sure to gather all your belongings and all of your barf. We hope we don't see you again real soon."

Daniel smiled. What would they do without Kenny?

He should get up and do something. Exactly what, he couldn't remember. Now that they were safely on the ground, his brain seemed to be taking time off. He unclenched his hands from the controls. His muscles quivered.

"Like a bowl of jelly."

"Yeah." Reggie appeared to be in the same shape. "For a while there, I didn't think we were gonna make it."

"Oh ye of little faith." Daniel leaned his head back. All those hours, and days, of repetitive training made sense. When the chips were down, the instruction came back to him. Even in the twangy voice of a curmudgeon who liked to chomp on stinky cigars. Thank the Lord for that old scoundrel.

Time to get cleaned up. He heaved himself out of his seat and grabbed his duffel bag.

The CO of their passengers loitered beside the aircraft. "I don't know much about flying, but I'd say you pulled off a miracle to get us here."

Daniel shrugged. "It was one of our worst flights." He bobbed his head. "Okay, it was *the* worst."

The CO chuckled. "My life flashed through my mind. I thought we were goners."

"There's a steady stream of planes going back and forth between here and Natal. We're waiting to hear if any of them didn't make it." Daniel gazed across the busy airfield, then shook off the depressing thought. He raised his duffel. "Now, though, it's time for a dip in the ocean to wash away the tension."

The CO frowned. "We were told we can't take showers."

"Because there aren't any. This rock has limited fresh water. You can get a basin for washing and shaving." He eyed the filthy clothes of the paratroopers. "Wade into the water fully dressed. Wash yourselves and your clothes, then stand up on a rock in the wind and let it blow you dry. Once you're dry, take off the salty clothes, use a dampened cloth to brush the sea salt off yourself so you won't itch all the way to your next destination, and dress in clean clothes."

He wanted to laugh at their befuddled expressions. But, hey, they were headed to battlefields where they'd find conditions a whole lot worse. Mama wasn't around to do their laundry anymore.

"Just follow that trail. Keep heading west and you'll come to a cozy little bay."

"You're not going there?"

Daniel grinned. "I'm going further afield to a beach that will be," he eyed them up and down, "a little less polluted."

The CO chuckled and offered his hand. As he led his men to the trail, Phil Colton hesitated then nodded. No smile, but Daniel recognized the emotion that lurked in Colton's eyes.

Respect.

Chapter Twenty

An airplane roared overhead.

Isabel awoke with a start. Planes flew over at all hours. Why should this one be different?

She jerked up, staring around the dark room. Daniel. She had planned to surprise him and see him off at the airfield.

Groping for her flashlight, she shone it at her clock and groaned. Three fifteen. Too late. Maybe that was him flying over.

It was a stupid idea anyway. How would she have gotten to the field? Walking in the dark was dangerous. Just the other day, a bicyclist had been struck by a jeep. According to Kenny, the man's shoulder had been scraped clean like a snake sheds its skin.

She stifled a giggle. Kenny had such a way with words. Daniel's mimicry played again in her mind. *Kitchen wares. Next floor, children's clothes.* While the plane was out of control in a fierce storm, Kenny joked. Maybe it was his way of coping.

Daniel coped by wrestling the plane into submission, saving all their lives. Even the nasty schoolmate acknowledged his feat. And when Daniel returned from this trip, Mrs. Roosevelt would award him a medal for sinking the sub.

Isabel hugged her knees. Of all the women on base, admittedly not nearly as many as men, Daniel liked her. Maybe even loved her. He'd practically said he thought of marriage. Daydreams of being his wife fired her imagination. What would it be like to live in Milwaukee and share a home with him? If he continued flying, he'd be away for days at a time, like Papai. Mamãe worked on projects to fill the time. Isabel could work with her seashells. But where would she get them? Milwaukee bordered a huge lake, but Daniel had said it didn't have shells like the ocean.

A yawn escaped, and she snuggled back down in bed. She'd start work late today, after lunch. Time for more sleep.

⁂

"WAKE UP, LAZYBONES."

Someone wiggled Isabel's shoulder. She pried open an eye. Flora. "Hmm?"

"I have to go into town this morning, and I want to stop at that fabric store you mentioned. This zipper's broken and I need to replace it. I hate sewing, but I need this skirt. Will you come with me?"

Isabel yawned and, through bleary eyes, stared at the clock. Nine? "Daniel's already gone."

Flora shrugged. "That's okay. I doubt he'd want to visit a fabric store." She huffed at her reflection in the mirror. "You are so lucky to have thick, wavy hair. I can't do anything with this thin, stringy stuff."

Feet thumping to the floor, Isabel shuffled over. Grabbing most of Flora's hair above the ears, she twisted it around and pinned it up. The hair below her ears, she twisted and pinned to the back of Flora's head. "There. The Neumann double twist. Guaranteed until you step outside."

Flora turned this way and that. "Iz, you're amazing. Are you ready? You're not even dressed yet."

An hour later, they stepped inside the dry goods store. While Flora looked for zippers, Isabel found an eclectic collection of possible craft items. An appliqué anchor, a child's colorful beaded bracelet, even a tiny glass kitten curled up for a snooze. She balanced it on the pad of her finger. Oh, the possibilities.

"When is Mrs. Rosenfelt arriving?" The words hissed in her ear.

She nearly dropped the kitten before she clenched it in her fist. Uwe. She spun around. "Get away from me."

He grabbed her wrist. "Tell me when that woman is coming."

"I don't know. And it's none of your business."

She tried to pull free, but he wrenched her arm. Pain streaked up to her shoulder. "Let go of me."

"You will do as I tell you."

"Isabel?" Flora marched toward them.

Uwe shoved Isabel into the display rack. She ended up on the floor with merchandise raining down on her. Something stabbed her back.

"Isabel, are you okay?"

No, she wasn't okay. What did Flora think?

The proprietor hustled up. "What happened here?"

Isabel's vision spun, making her dizzy. She tried to focus on the owner. "Did you see that man? He's a German saboteur." Her gaze sought Flora. "I think he intends to harm Mrs. Roosevelt."

She rocked back and forth, clutching her arm close to her

body. Tears stung her eyes. Good thing Flora had rushed her through breakfast or it would be all over the floor now, like the mess on Daniel's plane.

Isabel held something in her fist. Opening her fingers, she found the little kitten, still snoozing. Tears spilled over. "Isn't this cute? I found several things, but I don't know what happened to them."

The appliqué anchor lay near her knee. She tried to reach for it.

Flora put it in her hand. "Your arm is bleeding where you must have hit a shelf." She turned to the proprietor. "I think she's in shock. Is there someplace she can lie down?"

A clerk joined them, saying the police had been summoned. They raised Isabel to her feet and propelled her to a back room. She longed to sleep, but Flora wouldn't let her. A man squatted down to her eye level. A club hung from his belt. Imagine the damage Uwe could do with that.

Someone else came. He pulled on her arm. That cleared her muddled thinking. She heard snippets. "Bad bruising ... not dislocated." At a fiery sting on her arm, she attempted to pull away. "Hold still ... disinfectant ... mild sedative." He pressed a glass of cold water to her lips. It tasted delicious. She hadn't realized her mouth was so dry.

A pair of sailors took them back to the base. As their jeep barreled down the road, Isabel realized she still gripped the kitten and anchor. "I didn't pay for these."

"Not to worry." Flora patted her hand. "The owner regrets that you were hurt in his store. They're on the house."

On the house? Had Isabel heard right? They were in her hand. Had she been injected with something that was making her so befuddled?

Everyone must consider her pathetic. She did. How could

she have fallen apart like that? At least Daniel hadn't seen her whimpering.

Back in the barracks, Flora wanted her to go to bed. "You need to rest."

"I need to do something." Her thoughts crystallized. Mrs. Roosevelt. "I need to talk to security. Mrs. Roosevelt may be in danger."

She tried not to squirm under Flora's gaze. Finally, her roommate nodded. "I'm off on a business trip of my own. My boss wants me to accompany him on a quick visit to Recife."

That sparked her interest. "My parents live in Recife."

Flora smiled. "I'll tell them *hi* for you."

When Isabel changed into her work clothes, she found a half dozen bruises decorating her arms, back, and legs. A chill shivered through her at the evidence of Uwe's animosity. He liked to say she was his, but he treated her so cruelly. Certainly he didn't love her. If Papai had agreed to a match, assuming Uwe had marriage in mind, life would have been unbearable.

As Isabel was about to leave the room, she noticed her letter from home on the bureau. Odd. It was no longer in its envelope. She peered under the beds and the bureau, finding Flora's missing bracelet, but no Neumann Air Freight envelope. Very odd.

Pondering the mystery, she bicycled to Major Herdman's office and gave a report before heading to the airfield. The loading of planes proceeded smoothly. Daniel's friends, Klein and Edson, had the first plane in her lineup. Their cheerful banter raised her spirits, and the morning's trauma receded.

"Hey, Issy, how about flying with me on Friday?" Edson sprawled across the plywood table. "I've got a dive bomber scheduled."

"Hmm, I don't know." She tapped her chin. "You haven't won any medals like Daniel with your flying."

He sputtered. "What, all of a sudden you're too good for us?"

She patted his hand. "Let's just say I have the option of flying with the best pilot."

"Boy, does he have you fooled."

Klein signed his manifest. "I think a loader over there has eyes only for you."

She managed a casual glance around. Clarence Berelli. "He's no friend to me."

Edson straightened up. "He giving you trouble?"

"He was disrespectful in the hearing of a general."

Klein whistled. "Better watch out around him." He put on his sunglasses and headed toward his plane.

"Don't eat all the cookies."

"Cookies?" He came back and snatched up the manifest. "I don't see anything about cookies."

She pointed to the seven sacks of mail. "Lots of those sacks include packages. What can they contain other than cookies or socks?"

"Man, we need a sniffer dog to find us a tasty package."

Isabel laughed as she filed their paperwork. She scanned the tarmac for the next plane to check. Berelli continued to watch her. A sigh slipped away from her. Why did she attract the attention of so many losers?

The next morning, Flora groaned and rolled out of bed. She pulled back the curtains. "Right. I'm back in Natal." She sang to the tune of "the White Cliffs of Dover. "It's going to be a beautiful day. Just you wait and see."

Isabel laughed. "It is. Daniel returns today."

"Oh, right. That too." Flora twirled around to select a dress. "You never mentioned how much bigger Recife is than Natal."

"No? Natal is about one fifth the size of Recife, which has about one quarter million people. Now you know."

"It's probably easier to disappear in Recife."

She wandered down the hall before Isabel could ask about her cryptic comment.

By the time her shift concluded in late afternoon, Isabel was ready for supper and hoped Daniel returned in time. A voice hailed her. "Isabel."

Not Daniel.

She turned around and gasped. "Papai?"

In the next instant, she was in his arms. Over his shoulder, Marcos grinned at her.

"What are you doing in Natal? Did you have a cargo to bring here?"

Papai stepped back and took her hand, examining the bruising around her wrist, shaking his head. He pulled her back for another hug. "We did. A last-minute shipment for USED. What does that stand for, Marcos?"

Isabel answered. "United States Engineering Department. Flora found you, didn't she? That explains the missing envelope. She needed it for your address."

After giving her a hug, Marcos shoved his hands in his pockets. He and Papai exchanged a look. "She said Uwe attacked you."

"His obsession with me is scary. I don't understand why he's so fixated on me." Isabel wrapped her arms around herself as shivers swept through her. "Flora and I had gone out early in the day. He must have someone watching the base all the time. I moved onto the base to be safe." She took a deep breath and let it out slowly. "What else can I do? It's hard being confined here. I can't even go to the beach when I want."

Marcos nodded to Papai. "Avoiding the beach is the big tragedy."

Her brother's teasing earned him a poke in the ribs.

"Is Daniel here?" Papai raised his brows. "I'd like to meet him."

"Flora had a lot to say, did she? He flew to Ascension Island yesterday and should be back today." What all had her chatty roommate said? She rose on her toes and squinted over Papai's shoulder. Tingles filled her midsection, like a flock of butterflies playing tag. "Here he is now."

Looping her arm with Papai's, she towed him toward the airplane that had just parked on the tarmac, its engines whining down. The malaria patrol boarded immediately, while an ambulance pulled up to the door. Most of Daniel's return flights featured wounded soldiers on their way home. After the plane had been fumigated, a motionless man on a stretcher was brought off. How heartbreaking to believe he was going home only to take a turn for the worse and be left behind at another foreign hospital. Another man waited to replace him on the homebound flight.

A ladder was placed under the front hatch, and the crew emerged. Another crew waited to take their places, and the two groups got together for a briefing. Daniel stood tall, confidently speaking and joking with the men. Isabel's heart swelled. How could Papai not be impressed? Up close, he would see that Daniel's clear sapphire eyes shone with integrity, kindness, and steadfastness. He couldn't find a better man for her.

She bit her lip. She mustn't get carried away. He hadn't proposed, despite his talk of pairing up with foreign women.

Daniel broke away from the airmen and strode toward them. He held out his hand to Papai and spoke in German. "You must be Isabel's father. She has your eyes."

"And her mother's nose." Papai shook his hand with a firm grip while touching his long nose. "I am pleased to meet you."

Isabel relaxed. Papai approved.

Daniel studied her. He took her hand, examining her wrist,

so reminiscent of Papai just minutes earlier. "What happened? Uwe?"

"The man is a menace." Papai growled. "And elusive."

Daniel's brows lowered. "Were you off base alone?"

"No." She curled her toes. "I was with Flora. We were in public, but he followed us into the dry goods store."

"Hmm."

Isabel sighed. She'd hear more from him later. He could be worse than Papai with his smothering concern. She pursed her lips to avoid the smile that begged for release.

They dined together at the officers' mess. Graziela brought dishes of chicken with rice. Marcos flirted with her, turning her cheeks pink but also putting a sparkle in her eyes. Isabel raised her eyebrows. Interesting. Daniel nudged her. He'd noticed too.

"Your mother didn't come?"

"No." She looked to Papai. "Why didn't she?"

"She is in Florianópolis for a few days for Opa's birthday. Had she known we would be coming here, she would have been hard pressed to decide where to go. She will be very disappointed to learn she missed this trip."

Isabel's thoughts kept straying to Mamãe as conversation swirled around her. As expected, Papai and Daniel couldn't not talk about flying.

Marcos fiddled with his fork. "Maybe I should look for Uwe."

"Would he obey if you tell him to stay away from Isabel?" Papai asked with raised brows.

Marcos shrugged and ate a bite before saying, "So, Isabel, what do you do in your job?"

Her mind wandering, Isabel struggled to follow the men's conversation. Finally, she gave up. If she and Daniel married, they would live in Milwaukee, Wisconsin. Papai and Mamãe knew about her fascination with America, but did they consider that she would actually move to the U.S.? Had she considered all the implications? How often would she see her parents? Milwaukee and Recife lay nearly five thousand miles apart.

Mamãe usually made a yearly visit to Florianópolis to see her family and friends. Sixteen hundred miles seemed like a long way off, but since Papai had his own air freight business, the distance wasn't a problem.

Love filled Papai's eyes whenever he looked her way. Could Isabel leave her family? In spite of the heat, she shivered.

Chapter Twenty-One

Eleanor Roosevelt arrived safely in Brazil. Natal was an early stop in her worldwide tour that would take her to Africa, the Middle East, and the Pacific. And she would devote a minute or two to award Daniel the Distinguished Flying Cross.

He blew out his breath. Whoops. A newsreel cameraman panned his camera in Daniel's direction. He stiffened his spine and straightened his shoulders.

Since the ceremony was taking place at the Navy's Fleet Air Wing base, a commodore made the welcoming introduction. As if anyone didn't know the First Lady's significance.

His sisters and mother would want to know how she looked. She stood taller than he expected. Nearly six feet, he'd say. Her print dress featured a paisley pattern, maybe. Flowers trimmed her hat. Elise once said she wore Pilgrim shoes. His gaze dropped to her feet. Yep. Shoes with a decorative buckle instead of shoelaces. How had his sister known about that?

The president's wife approached the four medal recipients lined up like truants at the school principal's office. He shot a glance to his right. Isabel and his crewmembers had claimed front row seats. Hands clasped under her chin, Isabel beamed at him.

Mrs. Roosevelt paused in front of him. The commodore handed her the DFC. "Sinking a U-boat is quite an accomplishment, Lieutenant Lambert."

He blinked. She knew his name? The commodore hadn't said anything. Oh, of course. His name appeared on his uniform.

"Yes, ma'am." Was that the right thing to say or should he have said thank you?

The softness of her voice surprised him. This was a woman who traveled the world on behalf of her husband, the President of the United States of America. She spoke with world leaders, championed the less fortunate, and influenced voters. Shouldn't she have a commanding voice?

She worked at pinning the medal to his uniform. Her forehead scrunched and her nose wrinkled as she concentrated on her task. Should he offer to help?

"This is certainly tough material. It should be used for children's play clothes." She sighed. "There we go. I didn't want to end up stabbing you."

He grinned. "No, that wouldn't have appealed to me."

"Congratulations, Lieutenant."

"Thank you, ma'am."

She moved on to the next man, and he exhaled. He glanced at Isabel. Palms together, her fingers clapped. Kenny must be using a whole roll of film. Daniel would send a photo to his family.

Ceremony concluded, Mrs. Roosevelt was whisked away to her next appointment surrounded by a bevy of marines. He joined Isabel and the guys.

Isabel rose on tiptoe to kiss his cheek. "That was wonderful. You and the First Lady of the United States."

"My sister will be pea green with envy. I'm just glad I didn't step on her toes in her Pilgrim shoes."

Airmen surrounded them. His crew, Edson and Klein and their crew, and more friends than he'd realized had come. They slapped his back, punched his arms, and shook his hand until his shoulder felt loose.

"Hey, let's go to the beach and have a party. The Red Cross gals should be there." Klein paused. "That is, if you can bear to shed your uniform and DFC."

Daniel raised his fist. "To the beach."

They raced back to Parnamirim and exchanged their formal wear for beach attire. Daniel and Isabel claimed the back seat of a jeep. He clasped her hand. "Wrong time of day for the tides to wash any shells up on the shore."

"Doesn't matter. It's still the beach."

While some men immediately set up a volleyball game, others frolicked in the surf or flirted with the Red Cross girls. Still holding Isabel's hand, Daniel led her down the beach and allowed the waves to splash around their feet. After walking a short distance, they sat on the sand, close enough to keep their feet wet, but not the rest of them.

"I almost forgot. A letter came from my mom." Daniel pulled an envelope from his shirt pocket and pried it open. "Let's see. Huh. My little brother Gerrit is disappointed that the sand I sent from Algeria is the same as the sand from here. Imagine that. Sand is sand."

Isabel scooped up a handful of sand and let it run through her fingers. "Did he hope for a different color?"

"Probably. Our cousin Gloria sent black sand from Hawaii. Ah." He tapped the letter. "Elise got an A on her essay on ... guess who ... Mrs. Roosevelt. She's been telling everyone Mrs.

Roosevelt's coming to give me a medal. No one believes her. Mom says the First Lady wrote about her upcoming trip as the president's eyes and ears, and she asks if it will really happen." He raised his eyebrows. "I can confirm that rumor. I hope Kenny got at least one great photo."

"That will stop people from saying you're allergic to combat."

"We can hope." He scanned the letter. "Uh-oh. A nineteen-year-old neighbor is missing and presumed dead after his ship went down in the Pacific." He gazed across the waves. "Sharks get a lot of sailors floundering in the water. We hear stories. A guy is bobbing in his life vest. The guy next to him yells and is pulled under. The water turns red."

Isabel rubbed his back in soothing circles. "Lots of awful ways to die in war."

She twisted to face him. "You often speak of your mother. I've never heard you talk about your father."

"No?" He glanced at her before looking back to sea. "He's a bean counter."

"Excuse me?"

He laughed. "Sorry. A company bookkeeper. Actually, you and he are similar. He's clever with numbers too." His shoulders sagged. "Dad's stern. He wasn't always like that. He'd come home and play with us until supper was ready. Then some of his accountant friends decided to start their own business. They wanted him to join them. He declined. He had a steady, secure job. Then their business took off."

When he didn't continue, Isabel asked, "And he regrets still being a company bean counter?"

"Yeah, I think so. He knows he missed a great opportunity." With his heel, Daniel dug a trench in the sand. Water flowed up to them. "He failed to take risks like your dad did. Your dad came to South America with spare change in his pocket and started an air freight business. When war loomed, he read the writing on the wall and relocated away from the German community. He's happy with his choices, right? He would do the same things over again?"

"Yes, I believe he would. He misses his family in Germany. He doesn't know who may have died in the war. And he misses his friends in Florianópolis, although he sees them often. But he likes being his own boss."

"Yeah. A lot of joy went out of Dad when he realized his mistake. I fantasize that one of the partners will retire early or maybe the war will bring them so much work they'll need another partner, and they'll ask Dad again." He wagged a finger at Isabel. "Don't be afraid to take risks. You may miss out on a blessing if you don't."

A gust of wind brought a rogue wave over their feet, and they scrambled to stand before their clothes were drenched. He twined his fingers with hers and they walked some more.

"I've been yammering on about my family and telling you about my two buddies, but what about you? You must have left behind good friends in Florianópolis."

"Yes, but ..." She pursed her lips for a moment. "I've never had a best friend. When I started school, my favorite friend was Elsa, but I had to share her with Katya. Later, there was Anna and Marta and Paulina. And Amelia, although I think she was more interested in gaining access to my brother." Isabel rolled her eyes toward him. "Marcos wasn't appreciative."

She raised their hands to cup his within both of hers. "I never had a friend who wanted to spend all her time with me. Who knows all my secrets. Since moving north, well, Graziela has been a good friend. And Flora now. My Florianópolis friends and I stay in sporadic touch."

A hint of sadness surrounded her. Daniel squeezed her hand.

They stopped at a food vendor's booth. These guys were clever to come to the beach where large numbers of Americans hung out. Isabel didn't hesitate. "These are b*olinhos de becalhau*, cod cakes. Delicious."

"And these are those cheese bread balls, right?"

"Yes, p*ão de queijo*."

"All we need now is pineapple."

A voice boomed behind them. "Lambert."

Turning, he spotted Colonel Sanborn bearing down on him. "This can't be good."

"I'm sorry I didn't get to attend your meeting with Mrs. Roosevelt. Proud day for you, son."

Son? Maybe this wasn't bad news.

"We've learned that a plane is missing. It should have arrived here two days ago. Never received any distress calls. It has to have gone down in the Atlantic." The colonel paused and referred to a paper. "The navigator onboard was your old one."

"Nelson?" The news jarred him to his toes. They hadn't been friends. Daniel didn't miss him. But to go down at sea? The Atlantic had sharks too.

"The investigation has just started. They took off from Accra on the Gold Coast with a dozen passengers in a C-87 Liberator Express. We've heard they didn't plan to stop at Ascension to gas up because of a strong tailwind. If true, that was reckless."

The C-87 claimed four engines and bigger fuel tanks. "They may have encountered a headwind in mid-Atlantic. Nelson never volunteered where we'd find a tailwind. I had to ask. I thought it was because he didn't like me, but maybe he didn't like his next pilot either. Or he was unaware of their gas situation." Daniel blew out his breath. "I've heard Liberators don't do water landings very well."

"Bad situation all around. But I've got some good news for you too. You and your crew are due for some R&R. Go to Rio for a few days. Leave on Thursday and return on Monday. And you can go too, Miss Neumann. They'll need a translator to keep them out of trouble."

The colonel strode off before Daniel could catch his breath.

"Rio de Janiero. Wow. Have you been there?"

Isabel nodded. She didn't look too excited about the proposed trip.

Before he could question her, his crewmates ambled up. Kenny thumbed over his shoulder. "What'd the colonel want? Do we have to go back to Africa?"

"We're going to Rio for R&R."

"We are?" Kenny leaped two feet off the ground. "Wahoo." He wiggled around like he might be trying to dance. "Copacabana."

Even Isabel laughed. "It is a nice beach."

One of the Red Cross girls wandered over. "Isabel? There are two guys, one there and one over there. Every time we look at them, they seem to be watching you."

Uwe. And Pelican too.

Isabel blanched. Daniel slipped his arm around her and pulled her close. "Good time to disappear to Rio."

Chapter Twenty-Two

The sun glared down on them as they stepped down from their transport plane. Isabel shaded her eyes. The airport resembled a beehive with planes buzzing and servicemen scurrying around. Despite the busyness, it was a peaceful tableau. She'd heard the widely held opinion among the Americans that Rio was the best duty post outside the U.S. Eager excitement described the men's mood.

She forced herself to relax. Nothing scary was going to happen here.

"Where do we go first?" Kenny's wide eyes swiveled all over. "Which way to the beach?"

Daniel knocked his cap forward on his head. "We have a great beach in Natal. What's different about Rio's?"

"Are you kidding? They've got Copacabana here. Girls from all over probably come here."

Isabel nodded. "It is more like a resort than Natal."

Mike hefted his duffel. "First thing, shouldn't we find our accommodations and change into civvies?"

Unlike in Natal, the servicemen were advised to wear

civilian clothes in Rio. Their bulging bags indicated they'd brought along plenty of changes. This should be interesting. Except for beachwear, she'd never seen them out of uniform. Her lips quirked upward. She doubted any of them owned a white suit.

"Okay, the Luxor Hotel is where we're to stay." Reggie handed Mike a page of military-issued recommendations. "You're the navigator. You can get us there."

"When's the best time to go to that statue?" Hal stared at the mountains surrounding Rio. "I don't see it. Isn't it supposed to be huge?"

"You're looking at Sugarloaf Mountain." Isabel pointed to another peak. "*Cristo Redentor* is on Corcovado."

"Whoa." Kenny planted his hands on his hips. "Look at that big guy. We can go up there?"

"Yes. There's a visitor's platform."

"Imagine the views from up there. How about going there tomorrow morning while it's cooler?" Daniel glanced around at them. "We can spend the afternoon at the beach. After that, whatever strikes our fancy. How does that sound?"

"Beach time." Kenny clenched a fist. "Yes."

The crew chief displayed a side of himself that Isabel had been unaware of. She hated to dampen his enthusiasm. "Brazilians tend to spend morning hours on the beach. You'll find fewer people there in the afternoons."

His shoulders sagged, but only for a moment. "Tomorrow will give us a chance to get the lay of the land."

Reggie took him by the neck. "Don't do anything your mother wouldn't approve of."

The Luxor proved to be a ten-story hotel fronting Copacabana. All the rooms featured balconies. What a view, if Isabel had an oceanside room. Jittery nerves fluttered as she accepted a key to a room on the third floor. Flora had set her up with a roommate from USED. No reason to expect they would not get along. She'd probably be more like Flora than Sandra. Of course, Isabel didn't plan on spending much time in the room. Chin up, she headed for an elevator with Daniel.

He tilted her hand to read the room number on her key. "Hmm. We're way up on the ninth floor. I wonder if they try to keep men and women separate." He held open the elevator door. "How about we ditch our gear and head for the beach? I'll come to your door in fifteen minutes?"

A short while later, they strolled along the beach hand in hand. Isabel never tired of watching the waves and gazing toward the horizon. After a while, she realized Daniel watched her more than the sea.

She ran a hand over her hair, caught up in a loose knot on the back of her head, but pulling loose in the ocean breeze. "Is something out of place?"

His quick smile appeared lopsided. "Everything's exactly in place. Are you happy to be here?"

At first, his question seemed ridiculous. He had to know the beach was her favorite place.

"How could I not be happy at the seashore?"

His lips pursed as he nodded once. "Let me rephrase that. Are you happy to be in Rio?"

Foiled. The man was too perceptive. Saying she was happy to be anywhere with him would sound trite. And evasive. She recalled his admonishment to be honest with each other. She squared her shoulders.

"My family came to Rio for Carnival when Marcos and I were five or six. I guess you have Mardi Gras in the United States?"

"Yes, in Louisiana. I've never been there."

"I've heard it described as an explosion of revelry and hedonism before the beginning of Lent, when it is time to be sober. That is a good description." She stopped walking and faced the sea. Daniel waited patiently as she gathered her thoughts.

"In Brazil's northeast, much of the population is African, and their culture came with them. They have a religion that is like voodoo, based on black magic."

She stepped into the surf, imagining the waves washing away the memories. With her arms wrapped tightly around herself, she turned to Daniel.

"It was evening. Getting dark. The streets were crowded. Most people wore masks. A group bumped into us and I was separated from my family. Pushed along in the crowd. A man grabbed my arm. He said something like, 'Look what we have here.'"

She hadn't realized she was gasping for air until Daniel began massaging the back of her neck. Her lightheadedness receded.

"In kindergarten in Florianópolis, we heard about Hansel and Gretel and the wicked witch who planned to eat them. We learned about the evil of black magic and voodoo. Somewhere, I'd seen a cartoon about missionaries captured by natives and put in a pot of boiling water. I was sure those revelers were going to put me in a cooking pot and eat me."

"Oh, Isabel." He enclosed her within his arms, pressing her head to his shoulder. They swayed, matching the rhythm of the waves. "Obviously, they didn't do so."

"No." Her voice quavered. She took a deep breath. Another. "After what seemed like forever, Papai reached in and pulled me out. The revelers tried to prevent him. They raised their arms like they were casting a spell. I had nightmares for months. Years, really. This is the first time I have been back to Rio."

His hand stroked her back, and she snuggled closer.

"When you left Florianópolis and moved to Recife, did that resurrect the memory?"

"It did. Recife seemed like it was in a foreign country. Like going from a German town to an old Mediterranean city near the equator." Memories of her first look at Recife surfaced. Portugal had influenced the architecture, but the people were an ethnic mix. Brazil's racial tolerance was much higher than what she'd heard was practiced in the United States, with intermarriage between the races common. Still, knowing these northern Brazilians might favor voodoo and practice black arts worried her.

"My parents thought I might like to go to a secretarial school or some such, but I preferred to stay close to home. I made a few friends at church, but not like my friends in Florianópolis. I felt like I was waiting for something, like going back to Florianópolis."

Daniel nodded. "Which, because of the war, was being de-Germanized and becoming an unfamiliar place."

De-Germanized? A grin threatened.

Daniel's hand stilled. "Was any consideration given to sending you to Germany with Marcos?"

"Yes. The invitation was for both of us. But what would I have studied? Visiting Papai's homeland held appeal, except we were already hearing about the Nazis. Through the years, I exchanged letters with a cousin who's a couple years older than us. I think she favors the Nazis and maybe looks down on us for not living in Germany. I wasn't interested in meeting her."

"If you had gone, the Germans may have refused to let you leave as a way of making Marcos do their bidding."

"That thought has occurred to us."

Daniel's chest expanded with his inhalation. "You know, I never realized I had such an uneventful life."

Isabel laughed, then jumped when a dog barked close by. The sun had disappeared behind the mountains in the west. In the fading light, three people watched them. Their hefty dog's tail didn't wag. She shivered, imagining them wanting to assault them, their dog sinking its teeth into her leg.

"It's getting late. We have an early start in the morning." Daniel surveyed the beachfront and nodded in the direction of the Luxor. He offered his arm. "Shall we?"

In the morning, she met the crew for breakfast. The officers appeared wide-eyed and rested. Too bad she couldn't say the same for Kenny and Hal. They must have been out carousing last night.

"Maybe we should leave them behind," Reggie said.

"I heard that." Kenny snapped to attention and raised his camera. "You need a photographer."

Photos of their excursion would be nice mementos. If he stayed awake. Sitting in front of her and Daniel on the tour bus, Kenny promptly dozed off, his head bumping against the window as they wound up the mountain.

Under a crystalline sky, Rio de Janeiro grew smaller. The sprawling city took on an ethereal quality. The sparkling turquoise water of the bay heightened the enchantment. Or maybe Isabel's mood had something to do with the man beside her.

Yesterday's talk had reopened a ghastly memory but may also have been cathartic. She hadn't dreamed at all last night. Maybe they should have returned to Rio all those years ago. As she'd heard an airman say, get back in the saddle after the horse bucks you off. They had simply been in the wrong place at the wrong time. Most people attended Carnival to have fun.

The city certainly looked peaceful and inviting now.

They left the bus and trekked up zigzagging stairs, finally arriving at the platform.

"Would you look at that?" A note of reverence tinted Daniel's voice. Rio had cast its spell on him.

They could see for miles. An oceangoing vessel looked like a bathtub toy. To their right, on a spit of land, Sugarloaf Mountain rose.

Kenny squatted down in front of them. He peered through his viewfinder, leaned back, and looked again. "No good. Too big."

Distracted, Daniel asked, "What are you muttering about?"

Kenny propped his elbows on his knees. "Have you even looked at the statue?"

They turned around.

Arms spread wide, Christ loomed over them.

"Impressive." Daniel didn't sound impressed. "Would it be disrespectful to say it's more impressive from a distance?"

Mike stood beside them. "I agree. Here, all I feel is overwhelmed by the size. How tall is that?"

Reggie had picked up a fact sheet. "Nearly one hundred feet high, not counting the pedestal. The arm span is ninety-two feet. Completed in 1931. So it wasn't here when you visited, Isabel?"

"No, I've only seen it in pictures."

"The organizers were motivated by what they saw as the godlessness of society." Reggie continued reading. "Brazilians designed it, and a Frenchman sculpted it. Huh. It's not pure Brazilian."

"The French had much influence in Brazil in the nineteenth century," Isabel said. "I've heard that more people here know French than English."

"Really?" Mike rocked back on his heels. "I'll have to try speaking French while we're here."

Daniel draped his arm around Isabel. "Why? Why not put all of our Portuguese lessons to work?"

203

Mike snorted. "Fat lot of good that will do me." He affected a high girlish voice. "*O tempo está bom hoje.*" The weather is nice today. He dropped his voice. "*Que horas são?*" Do you have the time?

Hal stood looking out over the city. "That's more than I can say."

As Isabel laughed with them, she gazed around the visitors' platform. A brief glimpse halted her gaze. Was that Uwe?

It couldn't be. Could it? He couldn't know she'd come to Rio. And follow her here to Cristo Redentor? Shivers raised goose bumps on her arms.

Whoever she'd seen had disappeared. It had to have been someone who resembled him. Still, her gaze shifted up to the statue's face.

Lord, have mercy.

Chapter Twenty-Three

Daniel dug his heels into the sand at Ipanema Beach. This was the life. No military officers scrutinizing their every move. No late night or before dawn flying assignments. No planes roaring overhead.

He tilted his head back and closed his eyes. What did he hear? Surf splashing onto shore, birds twittering somewhere behind him to his right, conversations increasing and fading as people walked by, a breeze ruffling the palm fronds.

He filled his lungs with the sea air. It would be hard to scrunch himself back into a cockpit for another nine-hour flight to Ascension.

His eyes popped open. Why spoil the moment when he still had today and tomorrow?

Isabel trudged across the sand, her cupped hands dribbling water. Her turquoise bathing suit was soaked. The water was much too cold for swimming in the late southern autumn, but that didn't stop her from plunging in to snag a potential treasure.

He chuckled, remembering her reluctance to remove the

long-sleeved shirt she'd worn to cover her modest suit on their first day at the beach. He'd admired her alluring figure, but so did a lot of other males. The wolf whistles hadn't been appreciated by either of them.

Dropping to her knees, she displayed her cache. "Mostly common scallops, but here's a prize." She thumbed an inch-long spiraled shell in a vivid carroty shade. "It's a conasprella with a little hole here. But that's fine for me. I'll attach it to a design on this side and the flaw will be hidden."

She plopped down beside him on his towel and sorted her collection. He smiled as she examined her finds with a huge grin. Her delight in simple things tickled him.

He picked up her shirt. "Looks like you either need to go inside or wear long sleeves. You're pinkening."

"Pinkening? You mean burning?" She shoved her sleeves up to her shoulders. "I don't want that. I vote for returning to the hotel for clean clothes, and then we can go to Copacabana."

He pushed to his feet and offered her a hand. "Are you sure you don't want to visit any sites here?"

"Like what? Go to the capital building and tell President Vargas how to run the country? No, thank you."

He pointed beyond her. "How about tomorrow we ride the cable car up to Sugarloaf Mountain?"

She followed his gaze. "All right. I've never been on a cable car." She slid her hand into his as they walked across the mosaic tile sidewalk. "I remember in school, a teacher asked what best symbolized different countries, like the Eiffel Tower for France or a red phone booth for England. Sugarloaf and Copacabana were the choices for Brazil. Is that what you think of when you picture Brazil?"

Daniel rubbed the back of his neck, tender from too much sun. "No. My first thought would be the Mardi Gras carnival, or the Amazon jungle. I heard about the Amazon in school, and probably the carnival too, although that may be from movies. And that singer. Carmen."

"Carmen Miranda, who wears fruit on her hats," Isabel said. "She received much criticism a few years ago when she returned from the U.S. after making several movies. Mostly from the upper class. She'd become too American, or she sang black sambas, or she portrayed the stereotype of a Latina bimbo. She left Brazil and hasn't been back since."

"You can never please everyone all the time. Although maybe some of it is sour grapes." When Isabel's eyes widened, he added, "You develop a negative attitude because someone else has something that you can't acquire for yourself. Like fame. However, if all her movies are like the one we saw, *Down Argentine Way,* she will have trouble finding other roles."

"I think my old housemate, Sandra, has sour grapes."

"How so?"

"She wanted you."

Daniel came to an abrupt halt in the middle of the intersection. Isabel urged him on. He suppressed a shudder. "Her sentiment is not reciprocated."

A row of vendors offered souvenirs. One man sold colorful multi-lingual parrots. Daniel imagined a bird squawking something inappropriate in a polite setting. He grinned, picturing his mother's indignation.

He paused by a display of homemade dolls. His sister Elise collected dolls and might like one from Brazil. Most of these were ugly, but one was rather cute. He heard Isabel catch her breath.

"Those are voodoo dolls."

Daniel didn't know much about voodoo, but he believed it involved satanic influences. Even if the doll was harmless, it was an affront to Isabel. He clasped her hand and continued on.

Mike joined them on their excursion to the Sugarloaf peak. At thirteen hundred feet high, the steep granite rock didn't resemble any mountains Daniel had seen. Granted, most of those he'd seen, like the Rockies or the Appalachians, had only been photographs.

"So, Isabel, as the native expert, what does sugar have to do with Sugarloaf?" Mike adjusted his Ray Bans as they boarded the first of two cable cars.

"Expert? You are assuming I remember my school lessons." Isabel laughed but tapped her chin in thought. "This goes back to the sixteenth century when the Portuguese had a thriving sugarcane trade here. Sugar was formed into blocks with conical molds for transporting to Portugal. The mountain resembles the shape of those sugarloaves." She inclined her head. "I think my teacher would approve of my explanation."

The cable car delivered them to the shorter Morro da Urca peak, where they transferred to the next car that whisked them to Sugarloaf. The view stole Daniel's breath. Now that they'd spent a few days in Rio, he recognized landmarks that hadn't meant anything during their visit to Corcovado. There lay Copacabana Beach, curving into the spit of land that jutted out into the bay. On the other side was Ipanema. Three miles away in the other direction, the Christ the Redeemer statue rose even higher.

"Interesting how the city grew up around all these rocky outcroppings. They remind me of giant ant hills," he said.

"And the people on the beach are ants." Mike wandered to the other side of the platform.

Daniel slid his arm around Isabel. "I don't know what I expected Rio to look like, but I'm surprised by how many high-rise buildings are here. Hollywood movies don't show this. Where does the carnival take place?"

Isabel gazed around the city spread out below them. "I'm not sure. Everywhere, maybe." Her brow puckered. "The streets must be closed, because I think that's where we were, on a street, like there was a parade."

The mountains continued to fascinate Daniel with their sheer rock faces, yet with trees growing on their tops. Even a long-armed cactus reached skyward beside the platform. A bird with a turquoise plumage, bronze chest, and long beak flew out of the nearby branches and over their heads. Daniel smiled. A natural habitat for wildlife in the middle of a huge city.

Mike had borrowed Kenny's camera. "Time for a photo shoot. Face me, cuddle up, and smile."

Daniel laughed at Mike's Groucho Marx impersonation, but a photo would be a nice souvenir of their visit.

Over an hour had elapsed when they finally headed for the cable car for the ride back down.

"All good things must come to an end. Time to return to the real world." Daniel took a last look around as they waited to board. "Hard to believe a war is tearing the world apart in Europe and Asia."

Isabel's hand slipped around his arm as they walked down the incline from the last cable car, so he knew the moment she tensed.

"Look. That's Pelican." She gasped in a breath. "He must be following us."

The person who caught Daniel's eye couldn't be Pelican. He looked like an Amazon jungle dweller with a pierced nose and big disks in his ear lobes. He raised a long pipe to his mouth.

Before Daniel could ask where Pelican was, sudden pain stabbed his right arm. He jerked to the side, bumping into

Isabel. He should apologize, but the words stalled in his throat.

A thin stick poked out of his arm, a trickle of blood dripping down. He wanted to pull it out, but Isabel hung onto his left arm.

Except … no … she'd stepped away. His arm hung limp. "What …"

The Indian. The pipe. A poison blow gun. He'd been shot.

He stumbled. His legs weren't working too well either.

"Daniel?" Isabel sounded farther away than two feet.

Mike gripped his right arm. "What's the matter?" He spotted the dart. "What is this?"

"Oh, no. Oh, no." Isabel clutched his hand. "Get him to this bench." She tugged out the dart. "We need to get to a hospital. This must be curare. It's paralyzing him. He won't be able to breathe." She talked about him like he was no longer there.

"You mean he'll suffocate?" Incredulity filled Mike's voice, even while it sounded like he spoke into a tube. "How did this happen?"

"I saw my enemy's partner." Isabel sounded breathless, like she verged on tears. She patted his cheek. "Daniel? Stay with us."

Daniel wanted to reassure her. This wasn't the Stone Age, after all. His mind still worked, but his body refused its commands. The world seemed to spin around him. Weariness swept over him, and his vision blurred and darkened.

A shrill whistle roused him. Mike waved his arms, full of energy, yelling at someone.

Daniel's eyes closed. Just let him rest. He'd be good as new.

A man in uniform loomed over him, speaking loudly in a foreign language.

Leave me alone. So tired.

A STRANGE HISSING WOKE DANIEL. Like a snake, but snakes wouldn't hiss so long and steadily. Or maybe he heard humming. His nose twitched as he recognized the sharp smell of antiseptic. A hospital? He tried to turn his head. A flat, hard pillow failed to cushion his head.

"Daniel." Isabel was beside him. Her hands roved over him, touching his arm, his chest, his face. He turned so her hand cupped his cheek. She allowed the contact to linger for only a moment before her fingers combed into his hair. "Daniel?"

He tried to speak, but his mouth was dry, his tongue swollen.

Isabel held a glass to his lips. Cool liquid dribbled into his mouth. Water never tasted so good. He wanted more, but she set the glass aside. She eased back and studied him.

He stared back. "What happened? I seem to remember ..." What did he remember? He reached for his right arm. Bandages. "Something in my arm. Then nothing worked. What was that?"

"An Amazon blow dart. I saw Pelican and an Indian right before he shot you. Apparently Uwe doesn't appreciate me spending time with you and tried to eliminate you." Her voice caught and tears spilled over. "I'm so sorry."

"Hey, it's not your fault." He tried to sit up and spotted the intravenous bag overhead, connected to his arm by a needle. Lovely. "Um, what is this for? What was on that dart?"

"Mostly curare."

"Curare? Isn't that poison? Mostly? What else?"

She glanced aside. "Snake venom, maybe some ..."

He flicked his fingers. "I don't think I want to know." He nodded to the needle. "This stuff is purging me?"

She grabbed his hand. "Yes."

The door burst open, and Mike and Reggie strode in.

"Oh, good. You're still alive." Reggie nodded to Mike. "He made it sound like you were at death's door."

"He was," Mike said. "He'd be dead if Isabel hadn't given him mouth-to-mouth resuscitation."

Daniel jerked his gaze to Isabel. She played with his hand, intertwining their fingers, sandwiching his hand between hers, rubbing her thumb across his palm.

She finally looked up. "Curare causes paralysis, which will cause asphyxiation."

He twisted his hand so he could catch her fingers. "So you breathed for me until we arrived here."

"Just like in the movies. Our heroine." Reggie gave Isabel a dramatic bow before pointing at Daniel. "Ready to go? We still have a plane to catch tomorrow, so this is our last night in Rio."

His crewmates' words buzzed past him. Yes, they had to return to their war duties, but only one thing really registered. Isabel had saved his life with her breath.

Chapter Twenty-Four

Mrs. Becker, the general's wife, sat at a table in the mess hall. Good. Isabel didn't feel like fending off the men eager to talk to a woman.

She hesitated at the table. "Would you like company?"

"Isabel. Of course. Have a seat. I haven't seen you in a while."

The effusive greeting buoyed her, and she plopped into a chair. "I've been in Rio for a few days. I think they call it R and R?"

"My dear, you don't look rested."

Isabel fiddled with the utensils. "I went with Daniel and his crew. Rio isn't my favorite place, but it was fun, at first. But then, on our last day, Daniel was shot with a poison dart."

Mrs. Becker gasped. "Shot? Poison? You mean like in the Amazon jungle?"

Isabel's lips twitched. The elegant lady was so flustered. She clasped her hand to her chest, where her fingers tangled with the silky ribbon bow at her throat. When she lowered her hand, one tail of the bow stuck to her fingers and pulled loose.

"My goodness. I've never heard of such an occurrence on base. Is ... oh my dear, is Daniel ..."

"He's here, in his barracks. The doctors have done all they can. He's out of danger and just needs rest. They won't let him fly until they're sure he's fine."

"Of course. They don't want him to relapse on those long flights."

Isabel leaned back as a server brought bowls of mangoes and melon slices. Her cheeks burned when she spotted her spoon lying perpendicular to the knife. She whisked it back to its correct position. "There is no concern of relapse. The poison is flushed out. It can't flare up again."

"Oh, goodness." Mrs. Becker noticed her untied bow and, with a furtive glance around, retied it. She patted her updo, where every hair was in place. "But how did this happen? Jungle weapons in the big city? Was Daniel simply in the wrong place at the time or—Goodness, he wasn't the intended target, was he?"

"Yes, he was. I told you of the German's obsession, yes? He thinks I'm his woman, so Daniel must be competition." The very idea that two men would fight over her was preposterous, except the bad man was the only one fighting and the good man was in danger. "Any time we go off base now, he could be attacked again. And using blow guns, or real guns, means we won't have any warning."

"Hmm." The other woman set down her fork and regarded her. "And how are you doing?"

"Me?" Isabel wanted to protest. She hadn't been injured. She understood, though, what Mrs. Becker was asking. Daniel's admonition rang in her mind. *Don't say you're fine when you're not.*

"I want to scream and wail and crawl onto Papai's lap like I did as a little girl. That Uwe wants Daniel dead and will do anything to achieve his death, and what he has planned for me once Daniel is gone ..." Her breathing quickened, like she had run a long distance. "He terrifies me, but I'm supposed to be a tough cookie. Captain Carter always says that. And tough cookies don't cry."

With a gentle laugh, Mrs. Becker patted her hand. She allowed her hand to linger. "I believe you mean tough cookies don't crumble." She squeezed Isabel's hand. "What you're feeling is shock. Give yourself grace. You're a human being with a full range of emotions. Don't bottle up the negative ones. They'll fester and cause more problems later on."

She spoke as if she had experience with troubled feelings. Isabel wanted to ask what had happened, but the older woman's life was none of her business.

"Daniel has become quite special to you, hasn't he?"

Isabel couldn't hide the truth as her face heated. She had to clear the quaver from her voice. "Yes."

"Have you made any plans for after the war?"

Did she mean marriage?

"Nooo. But I know he does not mind that I am not American."

Steaming bowls of fragrant soup were set in front of them, and Mrs. Becker dipped in her soup spoon, giving it a cooling stir. "Can you imagine yourself raising babies with him?"

Isabel nearly dropped her own spoon. Babies?

Drawing in a deep breath, she considered the question. It made sense. Most girls in the bloom of love became starry eyed, dreaming of moonbeams and wedding clothes. After the wedding, though, came a life together. Raising children required hard work and sacrifice. Parents might not agree, but they had to find middle ground to provide stability.

When the first blooms faded, did they have enough love for the long haul?

Long after they finished lunch and parted, she continued visualizing spending her life with Daniel. He loved his family. He might joke about having too many sisters, but he adored them. That would carry over to a family of his own. His father's example made him determined to live life to the full. To take risks to achieve the best.

As she sat on a bench outside the chapel, a distant memory tickled Isabel's thoughts and she latched onto it. She'd gone home with her friend Ella when they were in primary school. Ella's father sat on their sofa wearing shorts and a sleeveless tee shirt, which didn't hide his large belly. He held a smoldering cigarette in one hand and a stein of beer in the other, and he yelled for his wife to bring him something. Ella led Isabel to her room, unsurprised by his behavior. When she returned home and told her mother, Mamãe said he lacked ambition.

She couldn't imagine Daniel ever being like that.

"Isabel."

She jumped up and gaped at the man she'd been thinking about. "Daniel, what are you doing out here? You're supposed to be resting."

"All I've been doing is resting." He paused as a plane thundered overhead. "How about going to the beach?"

Surely her jaw dropped. "Go to the beach?"

"It's not a hard question. Don't you want to go?"

"Always, but, what about Uwe?"

Daniel took her arm and steered her back to the bench. "As long as we need to discuss this, we may as well sit down."

She huffed. "What's to stop him from trying to kill you again?"

A shudder rippled through her. She'd come so close to losing him.

Drawing her close, he rubbed her arm. "He's likely to lie

low for a while. He may not know we're back here and I survived. But we can't live in fear. We'll take precautions, of course, but consider this. Our lives are in God's hands. If it's our time to go to our heavenly home, we will. If not, we won't, no matter how much anyone here wants to help us on our way."

Take risks. Daniel didn't shy away from life, and he was right. God was greater than Uwe. Bad things did happen to godly people, but that was a theological debate for another time.

"All right. Let's go to the beach. Let's stay near the beach watcher, though, okay?"

They'd spent lots of time on Copacabana and Ipanema, but those beaches were at the heart of a cosmopolitan city. Here in Natal, broad expanses of open beaches greeted the eye. Instead of high-rise buildings, Natal boasted sand dunes. Palm trees bent inland, thanks to the prevailing ocean breezes that blessed them with a favorable climate.

In this area, south of the USO beach club, small windowless thatched-roof houses made beachfront living affordable for lower classes. Uwe probably wouldn't think to look for them here.

They strolled the beach, letting the waves tumble about their feet. Small shells glistened in the surf. Isabel picked up one, then another. Most were common scallops, nothing that would excite a collector, but they served a useful purpose. She held up a variegated purple shell. "I need at least five more like this."

Daniel plucked the shell from her grasp and examined it. "Pretty colors. Why do you need six?"

"Scallops make lovely flower petals. Larger ones make nice wreaths. All sorts of purposes."

"All righty then." He handed it back. "On the lookout for purple shells. Like that one there?"

She snatched the shell tumbling in the surf before it could be dragged back into the ocean. "Perfect." She slipped the seashells into her pocket.

Overhead, a flock of sea birds soared, dipping down and fluttering about. Something was out there. The coast watcher and another man stared into the distance. The soldier adjusted binoculars and murmured a few words.

Isabel translated for Daniel. "He sees a small boat."

"The way those birds are circling, someone must be dead."

They watched the boat drift closer.

Daniel's hand tensed on her shoulder. "It's a life raft."

The yellow rubber raft bobbed in the waves, and a stench wafted toward shore. The soldier waded out and grabbed it. He stopped abruptly and turned away, fighting for control.

"It ain't pretty." Only Isabel heard Daniel's quiet words.

With the raft beached, she saw the gruesome sight. The remains of one man lay inside. She glimpsed sunburned skin and damage from birds before the odor of decay drove her back several feet.

Daniel moved upwind and studied the raft. He pointed to a bent insignia amidst scattered fish bones. "A fishhook made from a colonel's eagle."

A small sack lay alongside the body. He retrieved it and opened the neck. His shoulders slumped as he pulled out something. "He wasn't the only survivor at first." He opened his fingers to display several disks. "Dog tags."

When a soldier queried her, Isabel nodded. "Military identification tags of six other men."

Daniel read each one. "They weren't all American." He froze. His head dropped back, and he stared heavenward. His gaze dropped to the sea. Then he held one up. "William Nelson."

Isabel stifled a gasp. "Your former navigator."

He pointed to the raft. "They evacuated the aircraft, but it doesn't look like they brought their survival gear. Their plane was a Liberator, which is a notoriously poor ditcher. They must not have had time to gather their supplies. It's been over three weeks that they disappeared. No drinking water, no food except a few raw fish they may have caught. One by one, they died and were pushed off the raft until only he was left."

"I'm sorry," Isabel whispered.

Daniel stared at the corpse. Using a stick, he pointed to the man's collar. "He was a major. Probably died just two or three days ago. Must have drifted over a thousand miles."

Isabel translated his comments for the coast watcher. "He says the air base has been notified of this, uh, arrival."

Daniel nodded. "Good. Nothing we can do here. Shall we continue on?"

They walked in silence for ten minutes. She watched him. His eyes held a far-away look. "Are you thinking of Bill Nelson?" she asked.

A small smile appeared and quickly vanished. "I should feel sorrow for him, but his whining is filling my head. I wouldn't be surprised if he spent the last few days of his life blaming me for his presence on the doomed plane."

"Daniel." She tugged his hand. "Really?"

"I can't recall a single time he said something nice." He chuckled and shook his head at the same time. "I'm glad I don't have to write to his family. I couldn't find anything positive to say."

They walked ten paces before he stopped and faced the ocean. "I'm thinking of our forced landing in the Sahara. Having Mike Green as our navigator was a godsend. His good humor, his willingness to pitch in, his knowledge of French. What would have happened if we still had Billy Boy?"

"You would now have an Arab wife?"

Daniel surprised her by pulling her close in a tight hug. "Bill's transfer saved my bacon."

Chapter Twenty-Five

He should have taken more sick leave.

Daniel stared at the eager beaver young pilot bouncing on his toes. Was he tall enough to see out the cockpit window and work the rudders at the same time? Why was he here?

Ignoring him, Daniel spun to face the jeep wheeling into their staging area. Mike hopped off.

"Where's Reggie?"

Mike grimaced. "He broke a tooth and has to have a root canal. Right away, the dentist said."

"When? At dinner? What was he eating? Rocks?"

"I don't know what it was, but I heard the crack from across the table."

Daniel rubbed his jaw, feeling the pain, and sighed. "Great. Well, okay. Let's get on with it. That's why we have a new pilot here. What's your name?"

The stripling snapped to attention and saluted. "Lieutenant Jim Blake."

Mike glanced at Daniel but returned the salute. "How old are you?"

Blake stretched taller. "Twenty, sir."

Mike waved away the salutation. "Don't *sir* me. Do you have any experience?"

Daniel should be asking these questions, but he was content to let Mike play the heavy.

"I just got my wings." Blake beamed his pleasure. "This is my first assignment."

"Imagine that." Mike glanced around before turning to Daniel. "More bad news. I heard that Hal is, uh, under the weather."

"What?" Daniel whipped his gaze around. No sign of Hal, but a stranger with radio insignia loitered by the plane. And Kenny slumped on the bench by the check-in shack, looking miserable.

"Is Kenny sick too?

"No, but we supposedly don't need him for this flight."

"Is that right?" Daniel blew out his breath. "Make these guys useful while I straighten this out."

He marched to the shack. "Kenny, grab your gear," he said, jerking his thumb toward the plane.

Woebegone face instantly transformed, Kenny catapulted off the bench and dashed for the aircraft.

"Lieutenant." The captain in charge of this section of planes hailed him. "You don't need a crew chief with your load."

"Yes, I do, sir." He stepped up close so no one else could hear his words, which could be considered insubordination. "I'm not flying over open water for nine hours with half of a rookie crew. We need Kenny."

The captain eyed Daniel for a long moment, but he refused to squirm. He really should have taken another day off.

"Are you sure *you* should be flying?"

Had Daniel voiced his thoughts out loud?

"I'm fine, sir. It's just that the new guys don't inspire me with confidence. Have you checked whether that new pilot doesn't need a booster seat?"

The captain gave a bark of laughter, but he waved Daniel off. "Take your chief."

Daniel wasted no time in getting airborne.

An hour into the flight, he realized that while he felt fine, his injured arm ached while holding the plane on course. He tried stretching out his arm and rotating his shoulders, but the ache persisted. Finally, he pried himself out of his seat. "I'm checking out the cargo hold. Are you ready to hold the course?"

The kid's eyes brightened. "Yes, sir."

Before leaving the cockpit, Daniel watched Blake position his feet on the rudders. His lack of view out the window didn't matter much now, but no way would Daniel let the kid try to land. The fact that the kid had won his wings boggled his mind.

The radio guy appeared to be listening to whomever might be out there, twisting the dial in small increments. Daniel glanced at Mike. The navigator raised both hands. The replacement seemed to know his stuff.

Kenny had his nose to a window. "Look here, Lieutenant. There's a small convoy down there."

Sure enough, under a full moon, Daniel made out five freighters and two destroyers. Maybe that's what the radio guy was listening to.

He pointed to the radio compartment. "Do you know what his name is?"

"Heard someone call him Smitty. Hey, check out this cargo." Among crates of radio equipment, Kenny had found a suit of evening attire. "Someone's going formal."

Daniel couldn't begin to guess why it was needed. Returning to the cockpit, he made a mental note to ask Isabel if she knew of other tuxedoes.

They'd reached the halfway point of their flight when Mike announced, "We're going the wrong way."

Daniel's eyes shot to the compasses. "We're east southeast."

"No, we're not. The compasses are wrong. The constellations that used to be on our right are now in front of us. We're heading south."

A wave of heat flushed through Daniel. Off course. In the middle of the Atlantic. An image of the desiccated corpse in the raft filled his mind. That would be them if they couldn't find land before they ran out of gas.

"Do you think there's a German U-boat down there jamming our radio compass to lure us off course?" Kenny stood behind them.

"I don't know." Daniel switched on his flashlight and scanned their instruments. Something flashed in the light. "What is this?" He grabbed a medal swaying at eye level and yanked hard. Its chain snapped. Lettering surrounded the etching of a man. St. Christopher. He aimed the light toward the copilot. "Did you put this here?"

The kid's mouth opened and closed. "Y-yeah. He's the patron s-saint of t-travelers. He'll p-protect us on our j-journey."

Kenny snorted. Or maybe it was Mike. Or maybe Daniel did.

"This is a worthless piece of metal. It demagnetized our compass. We're lost in the middle of nowhere."

Mike said they were heading south, so Daniel banked left. But how far to the left? They required pinpoint accuracy to hit Ascension.

"Hold on. I'm doing celestial navigation." Mike muttered under his breath, trying to plot their position. "Okay, left five degrees more. Yeah, that trio of stars is back in position now, but I don't know how far south of our path we are. We may have been flying in circles instead of due south. We need to contact another plane."

With all aircraft blacked out to avoid detection by the Germans, spotting another plane was impossible. If they were just a few miles away from their route, they might spot Ascension, but not if they were too far away ...

"Hal, uh, Smitty? Do you hear any chatter?"

"Not at the moment." His reply came instantly. He was on the ball. "I'll try other frequencies." A moment passed. "There's someone far off and growing fainter."

"Would he be able to hear you? Or Mike?" An idea latched onto Daniel. "Mike, if you lay on the Southern accent real thick, the Germans won't be able to interfere."

Minutes dragged by before Mike said, "No dice. They're too far away."

"All right. Divide and conquer. Smitty, I'll monitor the radio from here on the Command Set. You use the Liaison Set on other frequencies. What about the VHS Set? Can Kenny connect with anyone there?"

"Leave no stone unturned." The emergency didn't seem to faze Smitty.

"I'll keep doing periodic call-outs on both radios." Mike came forward and borrowed Blake's headset.

The kid sat shriveled in his seat. Daniel should probably reassure him, but his patience was frayed. The rookie's carelessness caused their dangerous situation, and they weren't out of it. Not by a long shot.

Two hours later, Smitty let out a yell. "I hear someone."

In moments, Daniel heard Mike's heavy drawl. "Georgia

bulldog looking for a touchdown. Who's going to clear the field for me?"

A cautious but curious voice responded. Sending Kenny up into the astrodome, Mike asked the contact to flash his lights. Kenny's "Wahoo" nearly broke Daniel's ear drums. The other plane's lights appeared to their south, at least a dozen miles off.

They had been flying in circles. Now they were too far north.

"We are demagged. Can you point us to the hump?"

Daniel laughed under his breath at Mike's veiled query. He relaxed after adjusting course. Fuel would be tight, but they just might make it.

He laughed out loud when Smitty announced he had found Ascension's radio beacon. "We have a homing lock. How's our fuel?"

"We ran out five minutes ago." Kenny sounded like his usual cheery self. "Can you swim?"

Dawn streaked the eastern horizon when Blake finally spoke up. "There's a cloud formation directly ahead. Are we heading for a storm?"

"That's the cloud cap of Ascension's mountain," Daniel said. "We'll be heading straight in because we're down to fumes. Kenny, everything secure back there?"

"Snug as a bug in a Persian rug."

The plane made a beautiful landing even as the right engine coughed. Halfway through their roll down the runway, Blake jerked. "We're going to go off the runway."

His legs extended, reaching for the rudders, but he'd stretched too far upward.

"Don't touch a thing, kid. As soon as we're over the hump, you'll see the rest of the runway."

"The hump?" The plane went up and over. "They have a hump in the middle of the runway?"

"Yeah." Daniel took pity on the kid. He'd had a rough flight. "Lots of guys don't pay attention in their briefing or they forget, first time they come here. They think they're about to run off the end, and they stomp on the rudder, throw out the anchor, the whole works. All they do is blow out their tires and ruin their brakes. Or they swerve off the runway. One pilot on takeoff, thinking he was airborne, retracted his wheels and, splat, down he went. Lots of red faces on the first timers here."

"Huh. A hump in the middle of the runway."

After seeing to the cargo, Daniel grabbed a towel and headed for the beach. He needed a bath.

The next day, Daniel met Kenny at their aircraft for the return flight. A few small crates waited at the cargo door. "That's all we're taking back?"

"Oh, no, sir." Kenny squirmed. "We'll haul a full load."

Alarm bells chimed in Daniel's head. "What exactly are we hauling?"

"People."

"Wounded?" The hold hadn't been fitted out with stretchers.

"Them." Kenny jerked his thumb in the direction of a group of nattily attired civilians, including two women and a few children.

Daniel kept his voice down with effort. "We're not a passenger plane."

"Apparently the Nazis want to grab them. They were whisked out of southern France and have been high tailing it around the Med for a while. Now they're heading for the States." He tapped a crate with his foot. "There's supposed to be a picnic lunch for them in one of these."

If these were high class folks, they might expect to be

waited on. The folding seats along the fuselage weren't comfortable for one hour, much less nine.

"Rig a few stretchers on the lowest racks so those kids can nap. Maybe add two more, so the ladies can rest too."

"Good idea. I heard the guy who brought them here tell 'em it would be primitive, but we would roll out the red carpet for them."

Daniel snorted. "I hope he brought the carpet."

He approached the group. The men stepped forward, effusive with their gratitude for the ride. Their accents jolted him. These people were German. Two Christian pastors, who refused to kowtow to the Nazis, and their families, fleeing from the Gestapo.

A little girl, perhaps four years old, gazed up at him with worried eyes. He grinned at her and crouched to her level. *"Wie geht es Ihnen?"*

Her pinched brow relaxed when he asked how she was. *"Ich habe ein Buch."* She held up her treasure. *"Auch Hansel und Gretel sind der Nazi-Hexe geflohen."*

Her book consisted of fairy tales from the Brothers Grimm. The tyke equated herself with Gretel, fleeing from the Nazi witch. Daniel tried to keep his smile in place as he patted her head. Turning his attention to the men, he had to clear his throat. "We'll be taking off shortly."

He had a hard time swallowing the lump in his throat as he settled in the cockpit.

Chapter Twenty-Six

L eaning back against the picnic table outside the officers' barracks, Isabel watched a flock of gulls overhead play a rousing game of tag. Or maybe it was keep away. A small gull with a brown streak across his left wing sounded increasingly frustrated. She was about to point him out to Daniel when he dropped his feet off the picnic table bench.

"I don't understand this war."

She rubbed her hands across her legs, waiting for something more. He'd been distracted since returning three hours earlier. She hadn't wanted to press him. Reggie, his copilot, hadn't flown with him. Maybe the replacement had been difficult to fly with. Or something else.

When he remained silent, she ventured a guess. "Did someone accuse you of a combat allergy again?"

His startled expression gave her a negative response before he did.

"What? No. We didn't see any combat crews."

Okay. She tried again. "Did the new copilot know his business?"

A snort of laughter.

"Sort of. Mostly. He did pull a real boner on the way out."

Isabel wrapped a lock of hair around her finger. The new man had been a problem, but not what caused Daniel's pensiveness.

He exhaled, swung one leg over the bench to straddle it, and faced her. "We flew in two German refugee families. They're on their way to Washington, or somewhere in the States. I spoke with the men briefly. The story they told ..."

She twisted sideways and reached for his hand. "What did they say?"

"Did you know the Gestapo is terrorizing the German population? If you don't agree with the Nazis, you're liable to be arrested, tortured, murdered. These men are Christian ministers who refuse to endorse the Nazi agenda, so they've been harassed, thrown in jail, denied ration cards. They'd been tipped off it was about to get worse, like their whole families being sent to concentration camps, which they say are actually slaughterhouses. So they fled. Wives, little kids. With only what they could carry."

Isabel stroked her thumb back and forth across his palm and waited.

"I guess I always thought the war was because Germany invaded everybody. Took over all their neighbors, made life miserable for them, executed resisters. Stole their crops to send to Germany." He gripped her hand. "Did you know what it's like for the German people? Your relatives, did they ever write about it?"

"The last letter we received from Huberto's mother came two years ago. Papai thought her writing was stilted, like she suspected the letter would be censored. She mentioned a few neighbors had suddenly moved away. She gave one name, Marguerite, and Marcos remembered meeting them. They're Jewish. After Kristallnacht, it's no secret the Jews have been persecuted."

Now Daniel played with her fingers.

"One of the little kids had a book of Grimm's fairy tales. She likes Hansel and Gretel. Like those storybook characters fleeing the wicked witch, these families are fleeing the Nazis. What kind of a life is that? If the Nazis aren't stopped, they'll conquer the whole world and take pleasure in making life miserable for everyone."

He interlaced their fingers. "We read about their dastardly deeds and feel sorry for the people in occupied countries, but those families, that little girl, put faces on the victims for me."

"We know Huberto is against the Nazis, but Marcos says the family he stayed with in Heidelberg thought Hitler was doing so much good to get Germany back on its feet," Isabel said. "The reparations from the last war and inflation were so bad, but suddenly everything improved. Huberto said everything was tidied up during the Olympics in 1936, but after the foreigners left, the Nazis tightened their control. That's when he realized they were in trouble."

"So when the *Graf Spee* went down in Montevideo, he saw his opportunity to escape."

She nodded. "It was a terrible choice. His family and everything familiar or freedom. He has no idea if his parents and sisters are still alive."

Daniel stood and pulled her up with him. They walked along the paths, passing barracks, administration offices, machine shops, and a photo lab. The tantalizing scent of fresh baked bread wafted to them. The bakery must be nearby. Overhead, the roar of engines continued unabated as planes flew in and out.

He cocked his head. "Your brother told me about the expeditionary force Brazil is raising to fight in Europe. One reason Brazil wants a strong military is to keep control of the German population. Marcos figures that's why he wasn't drafted."

"We're relieved he won't be involved. Papai doesn't think the Allies need Brazil to send men, but the government hopes to gain favor in the postwar world."

"It's a war of attrition, but that won't hurt the Allies. Germany can't replicate a base like this. They'll run out of oil, parts, men. We may have lost the trail of breadcrumbs that would lead to early victory, but we'll shove the Nazi witch into the oven and find our way home victorious."

A frown flickered across Isabel's brow, but then she smiled. "Hansel first collected pebbles to find their way home. I would keep seashells in my pocket."

They paused at a bulletin board and scanned the notices.

Daniel pointed to one. "Tonight's movie is *Action in the North Atlantic*. The merchant marine versus the U-boats. I much prefer hauling cargo through the air."

"My guess is you much prefer action movies rather than musicals." She nudged him with her elbow. "I thought you might fall asleep last month when we watched *I Married an Angel*."

"Not possible. It was too loud." He looked so cute when he made that disgruntled face. "I know it's a movie, but seriously, how often do people sing to each other like that?"

"They do in the movies, because movies portray things that only happen in movies."

He narrowed his eyes. "R-right."

"That movie was a fantasy meant to entertain. Did it entertain you?"

"Let's see. A secretary has been in love with her boss for

years, but he believes the only woman good enough for him would be an angel from heaven. When an angel shows up, they marry, but he soon learns, be careful what you wish for." He spread his hands and offered a melodramatic sigh. Then he clasped his hands beneath his chin and tilted his head to the left. "Oooh, aren't they divine?" He tilted the other way and ramped up his falsetto voice. "Oooh, why won't any man sing to me like that?"

Isabel burst out laughing. An idea popped up. "Why don't we test the movie method? Tomorrow night—will you be here? —we'll go to the mess and sing to each other."

She stepped back, one hand on her chest, her other arm outstretched to him. "I'll be seeing you in all ..."

He grabbed her hand and pulled her against him. His lips covered hers, cutting off her song.

She forgot the words anyway.

He raised his head and gazed into her eyes, just like in the movies.

She caught her breath. "Okay. No more musicals. Only action movies."

"Thank you."

"Humphrey Bogart stars in your merchant marines. He won't start singing, right? And look." Isabel pointed to another notice. "He'll be here on Wednesday for a USO show."

"How about that." Daniel rocked back on his heels. "I can't imagine him doing a soft shoe dance, and I don't know that he sings. Wednesday. I should be here. Want to go? See a famous movie star?"

"Yes, let's. And we'll see this movie tonight so he's fresh in mind."

"I'll have to bring my short-snorter for him to sign."

"Your what?"

"A dollar bill that's already been signed by Nelson Eddy and Paulette Goddard, and even Mrs. Roosevelt."

"Why do you call it, what you called it?"

"A short snorter. It's what they're called. Lots of servicemen collect autographs on dollars. When Paulette passed through here, I was inspired to start my own short snorter and asked her to sign it. I think she was tickled pink to do so. My little sister would call it my autograph book."

"I don't remember her being here." Isabel would have enjoyed seeing Paulette Goddard.

"She just passed through with no time for a show for us."

"Hmm. When did you get Mrs. Roosevelt to sign it?"

"Just before she left. I couldn't believe my nerve. I thought her handlers would tell me to get lost. She saw Paulette's signature. Said she was in good company."

Too bad Kenny wasn't aware of it. A photograph would have made a remarkable keepsake of a more casual moment with the First Lady.

Wednesday evening offered glorious weather to be outside. The USO show was held in the same outdoor theater where they watched movies. Daniel and Isabel took one of their walks around the base before, approaching it from the rear. They were about to pass a small group of people when Daniel grabbed her arm.

"That's him." He pulled out his dollar. "Now or never."

Daniel approached the movie star and politely asked for his autograph. He looked like a shy little schoolboy.

A woman with Bogart also signed the dollar. His wife? She wore a fancy red dress that glittered. Stage clothes, no doubt.

Isabel ran a hand down her simple dress of deep orchid with a print of tiny white flowers and a lacy white collar. She straightened her shoulders. She hadn't planned on mingling with celebrities, and she wasn't trying to impress anyone except Daniel, who said she looked great. She drifted closer.

The woman took a closer look at the bill. "Is that Eleanor Roosevelt's signature?

"Yes, ma'am."

Isabel refused to let him get away with the brief answer. "Mrs. Roosevelt pinned on Daniel's Distinguished Flying Cross."

The couple regarded him with newfound respect. "Are you the pilot who bombed a German U-boat?" the woman asked. "I read about that in the newspaper."

Humphrey Bogart shook Daniel's hand. "That was quite an accomplishment, young man."

A nervous stagehand prompted them to move along. "You'll want to find seats before the place fills up."

As they walked around to the front, Isabel asked, "Was she his wife?"

"I guess so." Daniel studied the dollar. "May?"

"Mayo Methot." Another stagehand crossed their path. "She's a Broadway star and will sing tonight."

"Never heard of her." Daniel carefully tucked his short snorter into his pocket.

They found seats. Mayo did sing. Bogart recited speeches from his films. It was a pleasant evening made more special because they had interacted with the famous actor.

On the way out of the theater, Isabel suddenly felt a chill.

Clarence Berelli stared at her. His eyes shifted from her to Daniel and back again. He frowned. His lips firmed. He was up to no good.

Chapter Twenty-Seven

Daniel ran down the preflight checklist with Blake. Squelching a sigh, he had to admit the kid knew how to fly. His lack of stature remained a concern, but at least he kept his good luck medal out of sight. Still, Daniel would be glad to have Reggie return. Hal was already back at the radio.

Catching the eye of a ground crewman, Daniel twirled a finger. Time to rotate the propellers through three revolutions. When the man completed his task, Daniel opened his side window and called, "Clear." When the crewman moved away, he engaged the starter.

Once the engines were running, he checked in with Kenny. "Are our passengers secure?"

"You betcha, Lieutenant. There's a corporal here who seems to be the jittery sort. I'm having a hard time seeing him as a paratrooper who's going to jump behind enemy lines. Are you sure that's what they're going to do?"

Daniel chuckled. "The fact that we were told they're a

sabotage unit makes the possibility suspect. That kind of intel should be secret."

Their taxi clearance came, and they trundled to the end of the runway. The engines whined as he increased power. After a last check of his instruments, he released the brakes. "Here's to another routine nine hours of flight."

Blake glanced his way with a grin. "You mean boring."

"The only way to fly."

They reached their cruising altitude of ten thousand feet, flying at one hundred eight-five miles per hour. For six hours, the only thing to break up the flight was Kenny serving their now traditional bottles of Coke and visits to the lavatory.

"Looks like we're in for a bit of weather. I'd say there's seven tenths cloud cover down there. Not much view of the waves." Daniel gripped his throttles when the plane jerked.

Through the headphones, he heard Kenny. "Not to worry. We just hit a pothole." After a pause, he said, "Don't pull your hair out, Corporal. These are tough birds that can fly on one engine."

The aircraft hopped all over the sky. A loud crack suggested flexing in the fuselage.

Kenny couldn't resist. "Huh. They can also fly on one wing."

A shrill, "What?" traveled from Kenny's headset to Daniel's. Daniel didn't know if the loud *thunk* he heard also came through the headset or if he felt it through the structure of the plane.

"Careful, Corporal. Breaking the glass isn't going to do us any good."

That raised Daniel's eyebrows. He keyed his mike. "What's going on back there?"

"Nothing too serious." Suppressed amusement filled Kenny's drawl. "The jittery corporal just about knocked himself out trying to look out the window. I think he'll be quite docile now."

The plane continued to bounce around.

Daniel pushed the throttle forward. "We're heading down to find calmer air."

They dropped down to six thousand feet before he leveled off. While their flight smoothed out, the ocean remained elusive beneath fluffs of cloud.

"Hal, how far out are we from Ascension?"

His reply came promptly. "About four hundred miles to go."

As Daniel pressed his mike to acknowledge him, he spotted something flying up in front of them.

Before he could ask if Blake had seen it, Kenny hollered. "We're taking fire. Bullets going through the fuselage."

Daniel nearly bumped his head on the window as he tried to spot their foe. Still too cloudy. "There must be a U-boat on the surface, and they got a lucky shot. Brazen of them. What's the damage?"

"Three holes exiting the roof. One round pierced a barrel of that high octane gasoline. It's spewing out. I don't have anything to plug it with. A rag will soak it up right away. The bullet went in low on one side and out high on the other, so I can't lay it down."

A fifty-five-gallon barrel spilling its fuel. Heat surged through Daniel. It was a miracle that barrel hadn't exploded. "That's bad."

"It ain't good." Kenny paused for ten seconds. "We need to remove the panel in the cargo door and give this the heave-ho, don't you think?"

Daniel glanced at Blake, who stared back wide-eyed. Mike remained silent. The joys of command. He stared out the window and considered the problem. Since it hadn't exploded immediately, it didn't seem likely it would later. No guarantees though. Any little thing might spark it off. He cleared his throat. "How close to the door is it?"

"Close enough. We can put it on this little wheeled platform to move it over."

"Do it. Get the paratroopers to help you."

He put the plane into a shallow descent and throttled down to one hundred thirty miles per hour. The lower, slower flight might make only a psychological difference, but that was enough for him.

Kenny's mike must be stuck open. Disbelief flooded Daniel at what he heard.

"Should we jump?" The high-pitched voice must belong to the jittery guy.

A barely audible voice replied. "Perkins, we're over the ocean. Only thing nearby is the submarine. You hoping to join them? Or maybe you want to provide a meal for a shark."

Daniel could only shake his head.

"On three." A bit of grunting. "It's out of here. Too bad that U-boat's not right below us. I'd like to conk 'em on the head with that."

Trust Kenny to maintain his sense of humor.

"Hey. Stop that right now." Kenny's bellow nearly blew off Daniel's headphones.

He reflexively tightened his grip on the control column, causing the plane to shimmy. He trimmed their flight and fumbled for his own mike. "Now what's happening?"

"Einstein here tried to light a Coleman burner." Kenny yelled his next words at the hapless paratrooper. "Don't you see all this gasoline on the floor? And these rubber containers? They hold highly flammable aviation fuel necessary for our long-range flight. Are you trying to blow us up? Whose side are you on?"

Daniel heard a timid voice say, "I need some coffee."

He unbuckled his safety belt. "Blake, you have control. I need to get back there."

Kenny and all the paratroopers were on their feet. Kenny held an old towel saturated with gas. He'd been trying to sop up the spill and wring it out in a bucket. One of the troopers boxed up the burner and returned it to their supplies.

The ranking trooper forcefully told Perkins to stay in his seat for the rest of the flight. He turned and acknowledged Daniel's presence. "I'm Captain Jameson." He glanced back at his delinquent team member. "Sorry about him."

"Are you sure you want him on your team? I always thought you guys required nerves of steel to jump behind enemy lines. If he's caught, he'll jabber like a parrot." At the captain's raised brows, Daniel added, "He'll repeat everything he's heard."

Jameson sighed. "I'm having doubts. We've trained for months to be a tight unit, anticipating each other's actions and needs. If he can't cut it ..."

A replacement could be found, but the team's cohesiveness would be lost. If he were sneaking into German territory, Daniel would want one hundred percentage confidence that his mission could succeed. Questioning a teammate's ability might cause fatal caution.

"Maybe he'll step up to the plate when you go into action. Like nerves before the big game, but then cool steadiness when the action starts."

"Maybe." Jameson didn't look convinced.

Daniel decided not to mention Blake's mistake with the St. Christopher medal. Demagnetizing their compass and nearly being lost at sea didn't seem quite as dramatic as blowing a mission in enemy territory.

He indicated another team member. "What's his story? I

detect a German accent." When Jameson did a double take, Daniel said, "My mother grew up in Germany. I'm fluent."

"He's a Jew from Alsace-Lorraine, fluent in German and French. Until now, he's been my main concern. I worry that his desire for revenge may make him do something rash."

Daniel studied the man. He didn't appear foolhardy, but in the heat of the moment, who knew?

Kenny tapped his shoulder. "We've got more problems. I found the entry holes from the bullets. One of 'em cut a cable."

Chapter Twenty-Eight

Isabel hurried to the PX. She'd discovered only that morning that Flora's birthday was tomorrow. A little shell arrangement would make a nice gift, but Flora already had one and she was almost out of her favorite perfume.

She pulled open the door and paused to get her bearings. Perfume, perfume. Likely over there. Did all PX stores on U.S. bases stock perfume? It seemed an unlikely souvenir for men to buy for their ladies, since it came from the military rather than the host country. Wouldn't the ladies prefer a native gift?

If Huberto sent her anything from Washington, what would she like? Postcards were a wonderful gift, allowing her to glimpse what he saw. That is, if he actually saw the scenes. Ever since Daniel suggested Huberto hadn't been to Cypress Gardens, his cards were suspect. She still enjoyed viewing the American scenes, of course. And Huberto was her cousin, not a sweetheart.

Daniel had brought her a book about Cypress Gardens. She grinned. She could practically recite it now.

Four selections of perfume sat on the shelf. None were Flora's preferred scent. A gap amongst them must have been Elizabeth Arden's Blue Grass essence. Isabel debated on the others. A bottle of John Frum *eau de parfum* caught her eye. The fancily cut bottle had a picture featuring a pilot giving it a thumbs up. Did that mean it was a men's cologne?

Offering five options must be generous. Her lips quirked as she recalled Cynthia's pique that cold cream and face powder were not stocked. Catering to women was not a priority at the PX.

"Oh, there you are. Good."

Isabel stiffened at the familiar throaty voice. She kept her own tone flat. "Hello, Sandra."

"I was afraid I'd have to run all over the base to find you. Come for dinner tonight. Six thirty. Be prompt." Her former housemate took a step away.

"No, I won't."

Sandra spun back. "Of course you will. I'm having a little do, and your presence was specifically requested. I won't take no for an answer."

Isabel's eyes narrowed. What was she up to? Specifically requested? None of her friends would plan a get-together with Sandra. Spending time with her was definitely not on her list of fun things to do.

"I have plans for this evening."

She turned away, but Sandra grabbed her arm. "Dallying with the cargo pilot? He's an American. Leave him alone and stick to your own kind."

Isabel wanted to laugh. Her own kind? Sandra believed she was better than Brazilians. She sucked in her breath. Did she mean Uwe Schneider?

She shook off Sandra's hand. "May I remind you that you are a guest in my country? Mind your manners."

"Oh, come off your high horse. *Your* country should be grateful we're helping you out. And don't think your little friend Grazella is on a par with me. She isn't well educated. Even you don't have a degree. And Graz, well ..."

"What? She's not lily white? Only Aryans are good enough for you?" Isabel grabbed a bottle of Coco's perfume extract with its vanilla pineapple scent off the shelf. "I won't socialize with you or Schneider. *I* refuse to collaborate with the enemy."

Sandra's face puckered like she'd discovered a leech on her arm. Not a flattering look.

"Oh, and by the way, my dear friend's name is *Graziela*." She spun on her heel and marched to the checkout. She looked at the bottle clenched in her fist. Maybe she should try the French product. Daniel might like the pineapple scent.

Her lunch hour was nearly over, but she would be late. First, she had to find Major Herdman and report Sandra's words. Uwe Schneider was still trying to weave his web around her.

When she finally returned to the staging office, Daniel rose from her desk chair to greet her. He frowned. "I'm guessing you're not having the best day."

She didn't care who might see. She launched herself at him and hugged him for all she was worth. His arms came around her and he patted her back like she was a little girl. A smile teased her lips, and she managed a laugh. "My day just became one hundred percent better."

He eased her back and studied her. "What happened?"

"Sandra happened." She filled him in on her former housemate's demand and her own suspicions. "Major Herdman took me seriously, I think. He's going to have her followed, and also send someone to watch her house. Uwe's smart, though. He'll probably watch the house, too, and when I

245

don't arrive, he won't approach. Once security sees how things unfold, they'll interrogate Sandra."

Daniel whistled softly. "The guy doesn't quit." He pulled her close and gave her arm a brisk rubbing. "I'm glad Herdman's in your camp now. He probably still wants you under surveillance to watch for Uwe."

She jerked away from him. "I'm under surveillance? Someone is spying on me?"

"Not spying. Just staying close." A grin spread across his face. "Me."

Isabel's blood pooled in her feet. "You've been keeping me under surveillance?"

His grin faded, like he realized he'd said too much.

"The morning after you found those radio parts under your bed, Herdman called me in. I thought I would hear that Uwe had been captured. Instead, he interrogated me about you and your family." He pursed his lips and stared into the distance. "He suggested your father might be a sleeper agent, waiting for the Nazis to activate him on a mission. I told him that was a lot of rot, although not in those words."

"Why didn't you tell me?"

He placed his hands on her shoulders, his thumbs circling in his soothing, magical touch. "How would you have acted around Herdman if you knew? A little stiff? Unnatural? He might have decided you were acting guilty. And I didn't take his surveillance as a negative. I thought he was going to tell me to avoid you. Instead, we have official blessing. I was pleased as punch."

She relaxed with a sigh and leaned against him, wrapping her arms around him. He hugged her close as if he would never let her go. She felt his chest rumble before hearing his laugh.

"And here I thought I had an exciting day yesterday," he said.

"Why? What happened?"

"The ignominy of being shot up by a U-boat, despite a cloud cover that prevented them from seeing us. Actually, it was the flight out two days ago. Today's return flight was as boring as can be."

Shot by a U-boat. The C-47s were unarmed and couldn't shoot back.

"What is ignom …?"

"Ignominy. Embarrassment. Humiliation. We weren't at our usual altitude because of turbulence and a nervous passenger. Still, it makes me wonder if the subs now have some form of radar. A lucky shot doesn't seem plausible." He shrugged. "At least they didn't bring us down."

She gaped at him. His former navigator's fate came to mind. The mystery of that plane's ditching might never be solved. They might have been the recipients of another lucky shot. The cargo planes and their crews might be noncombatants, but that didn't mean they weren't in danger every time they took off.

"You made it safely back, so obviously, you didn't have serious damage."

"We had to pitch a leaking fifty-five-gallon barrel of high-octane gasoline overboard. And Kenny had to scrounge through our spare parts compartment for a replacement cable so we could land. Fortunately, we had a paratrooper team onboard, and they were able to help him install the new cable. That's usually something you want to do while on the ground."

"But they did a good job, and you landed safely."

"Yep." He chuckled. "The nervous paratrooper wanted to jump when we arrived over Ascension. His teammates were quite insulted that he thought they wouldn't have done a satisfactory repair job. I told them we'd circle over a barren part of the island if he really wanted to practice a jump. Since the island is made up of volcanic rock, and there are rocks all over the place, there was a good chance he'd break a leg. The team leader ordered him to stay put."

Not for the first time, Isabel wished she could visit Ascension Island. It was so much a part of Daniel's job. Of his life. Kenny had shared a few photos, but that didn't compare to being there.

Her own job here was important. An unbalanced or overweight plane led to tragedy. Staying at the airfield didn't allow for adventures though. Not that being shot at or tossed around in turbulence were desirable adventures.

Maybe it was Daniel's ability to travel that she envied. He was seeing a bit of the world. Her brother had lived in Germany for a couple of years. Papai had grown up in Germany and visited several European countries. She'd visited Uruguay, Paraguay, and Chile, but only because Papai was a pilot and had his own planes. They'd visited German communities that weren't much different from Florianópolis.

"I'd really like to go along to Ascension one of these days."

"It's a nine-hour flight of sitting on uncomfortable seats."

"I'll bring seashells and create arrangements. Or bring a book that I haven't had time to read. And a pillow to sit on."

Daniel laughed and gave her a hug. He looked over the cargo slips strewn across her desk. "What's this? Chocolate bars? We're hauling chocolate by air?"

"Shh. If anyone knows what they're carrying, they might land on Ascension with empty crates." She glanced around the room. "Captain Carter heard a cargo ship carrying chocolate was torpedoed. He doesn't know the particulars of who is to receive it and why, but it needs to be replaced in a hurry."

He gave her puppy dog eyes. "I'll be flying again in two days."

"By then, this will all be dispersed and on its way."

He scowled. "Killjoy." With a melodramatic sigh, he propped hands on his hips. "Think of all the sick fish who gorged themselves on the sweet treats that sank down on them."

A cartoon vision of eager fish exploring sunken cargo ships caused her to giggle. The image dissolved into a cargo plane, and she shuddered. "That could have been you."

Daniel rolled his head and rotated his shoulders, as though stiff from his flight. "Hal, my radioman, suggested the Krauts were retaliating for sinking the milk cow." He shook his head. "Nope. Impossible. It had to be totally random. Uwe may have heard I sank a sub, but he can't know when I'm flying or the exact time I take off, to notify a U-boat to shoot me down."

Chills passed through her. Would Uwe really do something like that? She bit her lip. Of course he would. He'd had Daniel shot with poison in Rio. Downing a cargo plane would hurt the Allies more than eliminating a single pilot. They'd thought he targeted Daniel because of her friendship with him. That was probably right, but Uwe would be more than glad to do something more spectacular.

Plotting his course and time would be easy for a navigator. All he needed to know was the time of takeoff. For that, he'd need someone on base.

She thought of Sandra. She'd tried to attract Daniel, but he hadn't been interested. Would Sandra betray him to the enemy? For spite, because he wasn't interested in her?

Surely not.

☆�※☉☼※☽☉☉☀☉☉☼☉

Two days later, Isabel and Daniel met for an early dinner before his flight. His buoyant mood infected her.

"I hit the jackpot in mail today. Eight, count 'em, eight letters."

She offered an innocent smile. "How many were from delinquent bill collectors?"

He drew back and pretended offense. "Puh-lease. Every single one of them was a fond, newsy missive from friends or family."

"One from your mother?"

"Indeed. She now teaches Sunday school for second and third graders and fears for her sanity. She's a mother of five, but we were such angels, she's ill prepared for the antics of her students." He folded his hands and might have looked angelic if not for the devilish gleam in his eyes.

"Angels? I seem to remember you offering me one of your sisters. That doesn't sound angelic."

He scowled. "Ah, yes. Theresa's behavior has resembled a fallen angel's."

Isabel took a sip of water. "I meant your willingness to give her away."

"Psh. That indicates my generous nature. I also heard from her cohort in crime. Our cousin Gloria, who's the navy nurse on the *Serenity*." He pulled the letters from his jacket pocket. "She wrote, 'Dear old Dad may need to change his opinion that his war produced the most gruesome wounds. We have two sailors with the worst burns from head to toe, yet they still live. Not for long, we suspect. When I gave one a morphine shot, his eyes pleaded with me to let him go. The morphine is only to ease his departure. I feel so bad for them. I've never forgotten the pain when my hand was burned at the church picnic.'"

He set the letter aside. "Neither have I. A careless boy barreled into the coffee table, knocking over the pot, and piping hot brew spilled on Gloria. She screamed in a perfect high *C*. I remember that every time I hear opera singing."

Isabel sputtered on a mouthful of soup and quickly lowered her spoon. "Did that prompt her nursing career?"

"No, she was always finding hurt birds and chipmunks and such." He waved another letter at her. "My little brother Gerrit wants me to send him money. I'm in the military. Why would he think I have spare change? Who in the military is rich?"

"Generals?"

"Do I look like a general?"

"With proper insignia, you would look like a fine general."

Daniel leaned over and kissed her.

She accompanied him to the airstrip and watched the crew make final preparations for departure. Daniel stepped off the plane as Kenny approached, yawning wide enough to crack his jaw.

"What's with the stretcher mounted on the top rack?"

Kenny yawned again. "I'm gonna take a nap."

Shaking his head, Daniel came over to her. They'd said their goodbyes in private. Now his eyes gleamed. "Would you like me to bring you something from Ascension?"

Isabel tried to keep their time light to avoid a maudlin parting. "How about one of those wide awake birds the airfield was named for?"

"A tern?" Daniel's nose scrunched. "It would make an awful mess in the plane."

"I suppose." She brightened. "How about some little volcanic rocks that will work well in my shell arrangements?

He grinned and gave her a quick kiss. "It doesn't take much to please you."

She waited until his plane taxied into first place on the runway. The engines revved up, and the aircraft raced down the strip and lifted smoothly into the air.

She pivoted away, missing him already. Catching sight of

Clarence Berelli, she stiffened her spine. The loader would not see her looking weepy.

"Good evening, Isabel."

Surprise filled her when she recognized Daniel's bomber friends, Klein and Edson. "Hello, boys. You are not flying this evening?"

"Nope. We just returned today. Want to go flying with us tomorrow?" Klein nodded to his copilot. "Eloise is taking Ed's back seat. Care to ride in my bomber?"

Isabel stepped closer and dropped her voice to a whisper. "Is that allowed?"

"Who's going to stop us? Those planes are for fun. You'll be wearing your uniforms. No one will look too closely."

She'd rather fly with Daniel, of course, but it would be fun. She was used to flying in small planes with Papai. And Eloise? She must have met Edson at the USO club.

"I think I'd like that."

They'd made plans to meet the next morning and walked to the pilots' jeep when Edson asked, "When will Daniel return? On Thursday?"

Isabel nodded. "Yes, he'll be back late Thursday."

Behind them, an authoritative voice caught her attention. "What do you mean by that?" She turned to see Captain Carter glowering at Berelli. "Why won't Lieutenant Lambert be back on Thursday?"

Isabel's heart skipped a beat. What had Berelli said that the captain had overheard? What could a loader possibly know? Unless—fear swept through her—was he Uwe's inside man? Did Berelli plan to notify Uwe that Daniel had taken off?

Berelli looked scared but defiant. "It's just a guess." He sent a sneer her way. "Everyone knows she's a Hun lover."

"What have you done?" Carter had lost patience and his mild voice roared.

"I didn't do anything. She did."

"What did you do?"

Berelli's face glistened with sweat.

An officer unfamiliar to Isabel lifted the loader's tool satchel. "Is this yours?" He rifled through it.

"Hey, you can't do that." Berelli took a step toward him, but Carter grabbed his arm.

"What's this?" The officer removed a small object.

"Put that back," Berelli shrieked.

The officer opened the item. "This held explosives."

Someone must have summoned the military police. They snapped handcuffs on Berelli and took him away. Captain Carter and his companion hopped into their jeep to follow. He paused by Isabel. "We'll get to the bottom of this."

She felt faint. Daniel was flying out over open ocean.

And there was a bomb on his plane.

Chapter Twenty-Nine

Isabel paced in the control tower. Four steps across the front, two steps along the right side, seven steps to skirt the corporal seated at the radio table, back to the front, and around again.

Please, God. Please, God. Keep Daniel safe. Please.

The demolitions guy whom Captain Carter consulted had confirmed the explosives they'd found in a search of Berelli's barracks could bring down a C-47. And Berelli had the nerve to insist he hadn't known he was planting a bomb onboard.

"Her real boyfriend doesn't appreciate her fooling around with that pilot. He just wants to make a little stink so he'll leave that dame alone."

How absurd. How was a bomb supposed to make a little stink? Why would Daniel think it had anything to do with her? Could Berelli really be so stupid?

He seemed to realize the folly of his claim when Major Herdman grilled him about why he had explosives under his bunk. He sweated enough to have been out in a rainstorm. And still he had the gall to make excuses in his whiny voice.

"I didn't look inside the box. I didn't know it would … it would …"

Isabel clenched her fists as she made another circuit. Her stomach ached, like a batch of popcorn was popping against her insides, bloating her stomach.

Why was she thinking about food? She was likely to throw up.

Why weren't they contacting Daniel's plane?

In answer to her unspoken plea, a newly arrived officer shooed the corporal aside and donned headphones. "Niner triple six, Natal. Come in."

Nine-six-six-six was Daniel's call sign. Finally.

"Some people are superstitious about six-six-six." Captain Carter stepped up beside Isabel, forcing her to stop pacing.

"Why? What's wrong with sixes?"

"It signifies evil or the devil. Something about the mark of the beast in the Bible, I guess."

She eyed him. He didn't seem fazed by the number. The only beast in the Bible she could think of was in the last book, Revelation. The end times. These could be the end times for Daniel.

"Niner triple six, Natal. Come in."

Why didn't they answer? Had the bomb already gone off?

"Could the bomb have exploded when they reached a certain altitude?"

"I doubt it." The captain nodded to the demolitions guy standing by. "He believes that would be too sophisticated for Berelli or the German. More likely it's on a timer or it will explode on contact. If it's on a timer, it's likely set to go off when they're at the midpoint."

In the middle of the Atlantic, where debris or survivors were less likely to be found. If they managed to ditch and get into their life raft, they could end up like Bill Nelson or the body on the beach.

"Natal, niner triple six."

Isabel's breath swooshed out of her. Hal Busch's voice came in clear, but distant.

"Niner triple six, Natal. Search your aircraft for a small tin container, probably along the fuselage near a wing. Do not touch it. We need a description first. Use extreme caution."

A long silence followed. Then a slow drawl. "Roger."

Now Hal would be alerting the rest of the crew. What did Daniel think? Surely he would take this seriously. They'd just spoken about Sandra and her effort to lure Isabel off base, about Uwe needing an inside man. Would Daniel immediately realize Uwe had succeeded in a horrifying way?

Minutes ticked by. The officer kept Hal talking about their speed, their altitude. She glanced at her watch. They'd been flying for ninety minutes. They still had most of their fuel. Was that good or bad?

✦ ● ◈ ✦ ● ◈ ✦ ● ◈ ✦ ●

"We received an odd message from Natal." Hal's voice sounded strange over the headset. "They want us to look for a small tin container, probably along the fuselage near a wing."

Daniel glanced at Reggie, relieved to have him back in the cockpit. "What's special about this container?"

At first, Hal didn't reply. Then Daniel heard him take a breath.

"It could be a bomb."

"A bomb?" Kenny's voice jumped an octave.

"We're not supposed to touch it. They're still trying to figure out how it might explode."

257

"Are you kidding me?" All color drained from Reggie's face.

Queasiness invaded Daniel's stomach. Is this what the bomber pilots experienced when they flew toward enemy territory? He unfastened his seat belt. "Mind the controls. I'm going back for a look."

Mike waited beside his office. "You want to take one side, I'll take the other?"

Daniel nodded and took the right side. He paused alongside Kenny, standing rigid. "You remind me of the jittery paratroop." He laughed at Kenny's scowl. "Want to help us look?"

The three men examined every inch of the fuselage. Since cargo wasn't placed against the side of the plane, it wasn't hard to determine nothing was out of place.

"No dice." Mike propped his fists on his hips. "What about the fuel tanks? A bomb going off by one of those rubber containers would really put a hole in the sky."

Nothing.

Maybe it was just a scare. Except Daniel didn't believe it. He and Isabel had spoken of the possibility of Uwe having an inside man to report when he took off. The chances of a U-boat deliberately shooting at his plane seemed too remote to succeed, but placing a bomb aboard the aircraft was a whole new ballgame.

"The equipment bay." He had Mike's and Kenny's attention. "Everything here is too neat. Something that doesn't belong here would stand out. But not among the spare parts."

"And there it can blow off the horizontal stabilizers," Mike added.

Kenny dashed to the rear. The tight space allowed only one man.

"A-ha. Here it is." Once more, Kenny sounded cheerful in spite of the emergency.

Daniel peered over his shoulder. "It's not a tin box. It's a cardboard box that should hold candy bars." It didn't appear to be large enough to hold a bomb, but what did he know of ordnance? "Hal, tell Parnamirim we've located the device. Now what?"

✶⬢⬡✶⬢⬡⬡✶⬢⬡✶⬢

"Natal, niner triple six. We have a candy bar box in the spare parts compartment that doesn't belong there."

A collective sigh rose in the control room. They'd found a bomb, but now what?

"Niner triple six, Natal. Someone needs to very gently place a finger on its side to feel if it's vibrating. That would mean it's ticking."

Would Kenny do that? Or would Daniel take it upon himself? Did it matter if the bomb exploded?

"It's ticking." Hal didn't bother with call signs.

Neither did the officer. "That's good. If it's ticking, it's a time bomb rather than a contact or altitude bomb. Throw it out the window. Carefully. Shaking it may disrupt the timer."

"Ri-ight."

Isabel had never heard Hal on the radio. Her best memory of him was when he'd lost his immunization card. He'd been almost frantic about having to repeat all the injections. He'd been so relieved when she presented him with the recovered dirty card.

Now, in an emergency, he sounded almost laidback.

His next words shattered her composure.

"Exploded. Out of control. Going down."

Chapter Thirty

Busted.

Throw it out the window, they said. Nothing to it. Except something went wrong. Daniel had flipped the box out of the window and watched it sail over the wing. Then the plane lurched. The bomb had exploded.

The aircraft's nose dropped.

Daniel scrambled into his seat and yanked on the control column. The plane wobbled and continued losing altitude. He took a deep breath. Another.

The C-47 might be a mundane, unexciting airplane to fly, but it was rugged. The bomber boys delighted in the B-17s' ability to take punishment and bring them home, but so could the C-47.

He reduced power and airspeed. Gradually he regained control, but the controls were sluggish. The rudder didn't respond at all.

"Kenny, can you see what the damage is?"

"I don't see any holes, but I hear clanking noises like things are loose and sometimes falling off." After a pause he added, "I think I can make out the tips of the horizontal stabilizers, but it's getting too dark to see."

Daniel thought fast. They needed to know what was damaged and how badly. "Hal, call in. There should be another plane a few minutes behind us. We need them to catch up and have a look. We're down to one hundred miles per hour. Reggie, make sure all our lights are on so they can find us."

Their landing lights on the leading edge of the wings, the navigation lights—red on the left wing tip, green on the right—and recognition lights on the top and bottom of the fuselage would help an aircrew find them, but—he hoped—not any observant submarines. The taillight below the rudder at the very back of the plane would be helpful, but he suspected theirs wouldn't be working.

Hal and Mike pinpointed their location, and then Hal switched over to his liaison radio.

The airplane wanted to porpoise, and the up-and-down movement was pushing Daniel's heart into his throat. He moved the elevators up, which should force the tail down and raise the nose. The plane responded grudgingly. And then the nose rose too high. He dropped the elevators. Ever so slowly, the nose came down.

"We're turning around. We'll never make it to Ascension. We might be able to hang on for two hours to get back to Natal."

He wished for daylight. If they had to ditch, he wanted to see the ocean's surface.

Hal offered a positive note. "A Liberator sees us. He'll match our speed and fly around us."

Daniel spotted their visitor as a dark shape against the fading light in the western sky. Its rapid approach tightened his gut. He had to trust the other pilot's skill to avoid a collision. Reggie waved, but the other men were unlikely to see in their darkened cockpit.

Hal's voice in his ear startled Daniel. "They say to look away from them. They're going to turn on a spotlight. Switch to the command radio so you can hear them."

The Liberator eased in close and Daniel turned his face away. Bright light bounced into the cockpit. That must be some light they carried.

"Whoa, look at that." Awe filled their observer's voice. "Most of the vertical tail section is gone. The whole rudder, it appears. The horizontal looks a little shredded too."

Daniel's blood turned to ice in his veins. What hope did they have of returning to Natal?

The light shifted to the other side as the Liberator looped around. "Looks better on this side." The remark sounded dubious, as though it hardly mattered with a missing rudder. Their passing travelers could do nothing for them. "Good luck, fellas." the observer said.

The Liberator turned away and resumed its course.

The plane was losing its fight. Daniel found it increasingly harder to maintain any control. He descended to five thousand feet. If they went into a sudden nosedive, they might have a chance to survive if the drop wasn't so severe. He almost laughed. He was grasping at straws.

"What are you doing?" Hal sounded like the strain was getting to him. Daniel could relate.

"Getting the life rafts ready, just in case." Kenny sounded irritated. "I don't aim to be shark bait."

Daniel thought out loud. "We can't lighten up the plane by tossing cargo overboard."

"No kidding." Kenny almost laughed. "We need a forklift to hoist the engines off the floor. Those babies must weigh a ton."

On into the night they flew, jockeying the elevators to keep the plane level. Reggie spelled Daniel when his arms grew shaky. Kenny brought him a Coke. The fizzy soda tickled his throat and brightened his outlook. He recalled a billboard advertisement showing a beautiful girl wearing a pilot's helmet with goggles and holding a bottle of Coke. He doubted she actually flew the racing plane behind her, but yes, Daniel appreciated the refreshing drink she enjoyed.

The plane was taking longer to achieve steady flight after each adjustment. The time between elevator manipulations grew less. He scanned the instruments.

In Mom's last letter, she'd mentioned that one of his old classmates now flew bombing missions as a B-17 navigator. His mother reported that, before takeoff, men so inclined gathered together to pray. That didn't happen in Natal. Planes flew individually rather than in groups, and they didn't fly into combat. Still, that would be good.

The Lord is my shepherd, I shall not want. He maketh me to lie down in green pastures, he leadeth me beside the still waters. Daniel filled his lungs. Exhaled. *Yea, though I walk through the valley of the shadow of death, I will fear no evil: for thou art with me.* He stretched his fingers. *Surely goodness and mercy shall follow me all the days of my life, and I will dwell in the house of the Lord forever.*

Not a prayer *per se*, but it did his heart good.

Mike broke into his ruminations. "As things are now, we'll arrive in Natal in just under an hour."

An hour. A lot could happen in an hour. An hour could really drag, like Mr. Menzel's English classes. Daniel smothered a laugh. He hadn't minded reading literature, or even a poetry selection, but all that nonsense about conjugating verbs and prepositional phrases? Who cared if he could diagram a sentence?

Eventually, a hint of light appeared and steadily grew. The

coast of Brazil. The plane had been holding itself together so well, but now it relaxed, too soon, or maybe he had. The Gooney Bird wobbled over the shoreline, and he fought it for all he was worth.

He spotted the runway, shining bright. If he could just stay lined up ...

Chapter Thirty-One

"There it is."

Isabel followed the man's finger. Two landing lights appeared in the east. She frowned. They weren't holding steady.

"Niner triple six, Natal. You are cleared for priority landing."

"Roger. The plane's barely holding itself together now."

She closed her eyes and imagined Daniel in the cockpit. The picture refused to form. Her brow furrowed. He'd said it was a tight squeeze to get into his seat. Instruments surrounded him. He kept his hands on the control column and his feet on the rudders. That was easy enough for a pilot's daughter to know.

The lights were brighter now, closer. Still bouncing.

Her gaze strayed to the runway. Lights lit it up like noontime. And along the runway stood fire trucks. They didn't normally park there. They were there for a disaster. They didn't expect Daniel to be able to land his crippled plane.

Isabel's breath shuddered out of her, and she covered her mouth.

"They're coming in awfully heavy." An officer scowled at the plane.

What did he expect? They'd had a full fuel load and used only about a third of that. They carried four Pratt and Whitney engines weighing over twelve hundred pounds each. Of course they were heavy. The only way to lighten the plane would be to have the five crewmen bail out.

Not a bad idea, really. Would Daniel have a better chance in a parachute?

The landing gear came down.

She wanted to grab Captain Carter's binoculars and take a closer look for herself.

The plane smacked down hard on the runway. Part of the tail broke off and skidded straight at a fire truck. They'd come in fast and needed to race down the runway while dissipating speed, but the aircraft refused to travel in a straight line. It veered to the left, away from the missing tail piece. Dust flew up as it left the runway. The plane whipped around in a half circle. Did a wing scrape the ground? It shuddered to a stop.

The fire trucks closed in on it. They must expect the fuel to burn.

Isabel wasn't breathing. She couldn't. Captain Carter slapped her on the back. Her lungs deflated.

"That was one for the books." He sounded like a proud papa.

"They're far enough off the runway that we can reopen it soon." Someone ordered a squad of men to clean and inspect the runway so circling planes could land. Parnamirim was too busy to have one of its two runways out of service. Business as usual.

Isabel took a deep breath. Her heart settled into its normal rhythm. "I need to go out there."

Captain Carter led her down from the tower and commandeered a jeep. Sticking to perimeter roads, he parked away from the activity. Already, a forklift pulled out the engines from the cargo compartment. They'd be loaded onto another plane and arrive only a little late at their destination. The war didn't pause for saboteurs.

Daniel sat slumped on a fire truck's running board. First aid men buzzed around, but he waved them away. His face lit up when he spotted Isabel. Lurching to his feet, he draped his arms around her. She staggered under his weight.

"Are you all right?"

He straightened, and his head dropped back as he looked up at the sky. The extra lights had been doused, and he was shadowed. "I feel like my mother should hang me out on her clothesline."

A plane roared past, causing a rush of hot air to envelop them. She'd never been so close to the runway.

Daniel was watching her. "It's the middle of the night. You're still up?"

Well, of course she was.

"We found out you were in trouble before you even took off. The loader who tried to take advantage of me, Clarence Berelli?" At Daniel's nod, she squeezed her eyes shut at a sudden press of tears. "He did it. He's Uwe's man."

Daniel pulled her against him. His hand stroked her back. His hold was so different than Berelli's had been. She could stay here for the rest of the night.

"We need to go to the beach. Watch the sun come up."

Her favorite thing to do.

"But, what about Uwe?"

"He's unlikely to know what happened. What are the chances he'll be looking for you on the beach in a few hours?"

They could do this. Sunrise on the beach with Daniel, alive and well. A yawn escaped her. As long as they could stay awake. They'd have to stick close to the coast watcher. If their guard was down and they fell asleep, Uwe could find them.

Chapter Thirty-Two

The eastern sky lightened in tiny increments. Waves splashed onto their feet, chilling Daniel, but he had no urge to step away from them. A seagull strutted close by, its beady eyes focused on them.

Sorry, buddy. No handout today.

An orange speck appeared on the horizon.

"Here comes the sun."

Beside him, Isabel sighed. "Is this where we're supposed to say, 'all's right with the world'?"

He tightened his arm around her. She didn't sound like all was right with her.

"I remember studying that in a high school English class. A poem by Robert Brown. No, Browning. 'The lark's on the wing, the snail's on the thorn. God's in his heaven, all's right with the world.' Or in our case, the gull's on the wing and the snail's in his shell."

She squinted up at him. "Then why do I know that phrase?" She tilted her head. "We did have a segment on international literature. Maybe it was there. I remember his

271

wife wrote, 'How do I love thee? Let me count the ways.' The class clown knelt before his girlfriend and recited the line about loving to the height and depth and breadth he could reach, and the teacher told him to put the words in their proper order."

Daniel glanced around. The beach was deserted. He could make a fool of himself. He dropped to one knee and took her hand.

"Isabel, how do I love thee? Let me count the ways. I love the concern you show for your friends. I love your intelligence, even if it comes from having swallowed a calculator."

Despite the raucous caw of a gull, he was pretty sure he heard a soft snort.

"I love how your eyes out-twinkle the stars. I love your enjoyment of sand between your toes."

She laughed outright and tugged on his hand until he stood on both feet. A rogue wave smacked them, sending water swooshing up to slap them in their faces. She laughed again. "And sea water in my ears?"

"We could have done without that."

A complete orange ball balanced on the horizon, still low enough that he could stare at it without hurting his eyes.

Beside him, Isabel's shoulders rose and fell with another sigh. "He's becoming bolder."

No need to question who she meant. A sudden thought chilled him more than the waves.

"Don't ask me to stay away from you. I won't. I don't want to, and besides, that would allow him a victory."

"Even if he kills you?" She swung to face him and gripped his hand. "In Rio, the poison dart was meant just for you. And now this. All the men on your crew would have died with you if … if …"

"But we didn't." He stroked a thumb over the back of her hand. "Do you want me to stay away?"

"No." The inflection in her answer told him she meant it.

Her head dropped to his chest and her arms wound around him, holding him tight. They stood together, swaying in the surf while the sun crept two inches above the horizon.

"I don't understand why the police haven't arrested him," she said. "Are they even looking for him? A year or two ago, most German sympathizers or those with saboteur ability were swept up when complaints about complacency were made. Now, I don't hear anything about arrests." She shrugged. "Of course, I'm isolated on the base."

"They'll search for him now. The base will see to that. They don't look too kindly on people who try to bring down their airplanes."

He nudged her to start walking. "Funny thing about facing the very real possibility of dying. My life didn't exactly flash before my eyes, but I did recall incidents. Some that I haven't thought of in years."

Isabel rubbed the backs of her hands across her eyes. Evidence of tears lingered on her damp, clumped eyelashes. "What kinds of incidents?"

"Mostly with my buddies, John and Stefan."

"The unholy trio."

"Ah, yes. Compliments of Mrs. Lester." He chuckled. "I wonder what became of the old biddy. Anyway, the three of us wanted to climb a tree. We decided one of us should go first to make sure it was safe. Guess who?"

She grinned, the sparkle back in her eyes.

"I got up pretty high. At least, they looked mighty small down on the ground. Somehow, a branch went up under my shorts and out at the waist. I must have slipped down a bit for that to happen. So there I was with a branch inside my shorts with me. I could not figure out how to get it out. It was too thick to break. Those were new shorts. I worried what Mom would say if they ripped."

The day replayed in his mind like a motion picture. All those branches seemed bent on scratching him, like creatures from an animated movie, where they came to life and captured him. The wind sighing through the boughs of the evergreen sounded as if the branches were muttering and bemoaning his unwanted presence among them.

"So, what happened? How'd you get down?" Isabel stood before him, fists on hips.

"John flagged down a fire truck. Attracted quite a crowd with their ladder. My mom was down there. She said, 'Forget the shorts.' She just wanted me down safe in one piece. The firemen pulled down my shorts to get me out of them so they could get the shorts off the branch. Then they had to get me back into them, because, you know, I was seven. No way did I want to be seen in public in my underwear."

He loved the sound of her laughter spilling out.

"I suppose a lot of girls were watching."

"You better believe it. Including Theresa and Gloria. I don't know why we didn't go to the park to climb trees instead of picking one on our street." He scoffed. "At least the girls were properly impressed with all my bloody scratches."

Isabel splashed into the surf and snatched up a seashell. After rinsing it in a wave, she inspected it and dropped it into her net bag. "Did you think of that incident because the bomb threatened to bloody you?"

"Maybe I did. Or, because it's a memory of doing something stupid, like throwing a bomb into the wind."

A seagull stood four feet away, watching them. It had a red spot on its lower beak. So had the bird he'd noticed when they arrived at the beach. The silly gull was keeping pace with them.

"Why do you think it was stupid to throw the bomb out?"

"Not just out. I threw it into the wind. I threw it out my cockpit window. It should have gone out Reggie's window." He held his left arm straight out. "As we flew west, we had a crosswind from the south, like this." He moved his left hand toward his right. "I saw the bomb go over the wing. But by throwing the bomb out that window, the wind pushed it back. I'm sure it exploded because it hit the tail and mangled it."

Isabel stood still. "Daniel, it's not your fault." She took his arm and gave it a little shake. "It's not your fault. Did anyone suggest they're blaming you?"

"No, but there'll be an investigation. The fact is, the airplane was severely damaged. If it's not scrapped, it'll need a whole new tail assembly. Wiring, cables, maybe the landing struts."

His only thought while holding the bomb was to get rid of it. Only after it exploded did he remember the crosswind. No one had commented on checking wind direction. Would the investigators grill him about that?

"You saved five lives. I think your mother would say, 'Forget the airplane.' She wants you back safe in one piece."

Yeah, Mom wanted him home. Even if he was disgraced. No one need know that. The investigators wouldn't court-martial him. At most, he'd probably receive an official reprimand. He'd still be a pilot rather than being knocked down to copilot. No one would blame him for the outcome more than he did.

Isabel hopped into a fighting stance and raised her fists, the right one inches from his chin. "If anyone dares to criticize you, I'll punch their lights out."

Chuckling, he took her face between his hands. She was so

precious. He pressed his lips to hers. Her hands moved up his arms and around his neck. Her fingers combed his hair.

He pulled her close in an embrace. All was right with the world.

A loud squawk jerked them apart. The seagull stood at their feet, glaring at them.

He sighed. "Our chaperone doesn't approve."

Isabel eyed the sun. "Looks like it's around seven o'clock. I should return to base. It's a workday for me."

And time for him to face the music.

"Lambert, what am I to do with you?"

Daniel gulped. He hadn't expected General Becker to preside over the investigation.

The general leaned back in his chair. "You already have one fancy medal, and now I've got people saying you should receive another."

Daniel's first thought was, *why*? But asking why would be stupid. The general must mean his feat of bringing back and landing a damaged aircraft. It had been stressful, but the flight through the electrical storm had been worse.

"I don't see that happening, sir."

A colonel whose name he hadn't caught asked, "Why do you say that?"

"Every day, pilots land planes that have been so shot up it's a wonder they stay in the air. This was no different."

"I'm glad you think so, because I can't in good conscience recommend you for another DFC. We expect our pilots to utilize their training and skill." General Becker tapped an open file in front of him. "You were shot with a poison dart not so long ago. Now a saboteur targets your plane. What did you do to grab the enemy's attention, lieutenant?"

They would blame Isabel.

"I believe Uwe Schneider, a German native, is behind both incidents, sir. He wants my girl."

"Isabel Neumann, Carter's human calculator." The general scanned a paper. "Major Herdman, why hasn't this man been picked up?"

"He's a ghost, sir. Every time the Brazilian police think they have him cornered, he disappears."

"Very well. Have copies of that artist's sketch posted all over the base. I don't want any more of our men committing treason for that scoundrel. Dismissed."

Once outside, Daniel slumped against the building. The crosswind hadn't even been mentioned.

Chapter Thirty-Three

Isabel slipped into her daring new two-piece swimsuit. Was she brave enough to wear it to the Red Cross beach party? Only about three inches of skin showed between the two pieces. The thin stripes in two tones of maroon flattered her figure, but goodness, she felt so exposed. Maybe she should stick with her blue one-piece. After all, this was a Fourth of July party, and maroon wasn't an American color.

The door burst open and Flora rushed in. "Ooh, Isabel. That suit is darling." She circled around her. "I should have gotten a new suit. I really like this floral pattern, but look here. This seam looks like it's about to separate. I've gained too much weight."

Isabel pursed her lips to keep from laughing. Flora's hourglass figure was the envy of most of the women in their barracks. "I'd offer a safety pin, but I'm not sure it would help or hurt that rayon fabric."

Flora reached for her beach cover-up, a long-sleeved, short-skirted affair in a red and white check that reminded

Isabel of a picnic tablecloth. "I guess I won't be playing volleyball today."

Someone in the hallway called out, "Time to go, ladies. Hurry if you want to ride in the truck."

Isabel scrambled into rose polka-dotted culottes and a matching blouse. Her wardrobe choices were final. She grabbed her bag filled with beach necessities and rushed out the door on Flora's heels.

In spite of the early hour, the beach was already crowded. Isabel headed immediately for the shore. A cool breeze blew off the ocean. Cotton candy clouds filled the sky. Small birds chased the waves. A seashell tumbled at her feet, and she scooped it up.

Daniel joined her, draping his arm around her shoulders. "Lovely flying weather."

She laughed. "Wishing you were on the way to Ascension Island?"

He looked delectable in his unbuttoned tan shirt and black swim trunks. Her face heated when she realized she was staring at his chest.

"Nope. This is the best place in the world to be today." He took a deep breath of sea air. "I thought you might have come out early with Eloise and the other Red Cross gals."

"I heard them leave. They tried to be quiet, but someone dropped what sounded like a sack full of coins that clattered all over the hall." And uttered some very choice, unladylike words. "I didn't know if they'd want anyone getting in their way."

"They would have put you to work. Eloise recruited Edson to help with setup, and he recruited me. We brought enough gear to last a week."

"Klein didn't come too?"

"He's flying today. Edson was promoted and now commands his own crew."

"Good for him, but it's a pity Klein has to miss this."

"Not really." Daniel's arm tightened around her. "Edson told me Klein made a move on my girl."

Isabel frowned. Made a move on?

"Oh, because he asked me to fly with him? I forgot about that. Oh, dear. Is that what you call standing him up? I thought we'd have a great story about how we found a submarine of our own."

Daniel gave her a squeeze, then reached for her hand. "Let's go get one of those pineapples."

Besides the Red Cross food, vendors hawked their produce. They strolled through the clean white sand to what looked like a farmers' market at the beach. She recognized the seller Daniel had purchased a pineapple from in town.

Daniel approached him now. "*Olá, meu amigo. Qual é o abacaxi mais saboroso que você tem?*"

Isabel smothered a laugh. The tastiest pineapple?

The man made a show of inspecting his fruit. "*Ah, este é o melhor que você vai encontrar.*"

Isabel grinned as the vendor held one up. The pineapples looked the same to her. Daniel handed over a quarter, and the man did rapid work of slicing and coring the pineapple and handing it over on a plastic tray with knives and forks. Daniel cut a bite and popped it into his mouth. He raised his right fingers and thumb to his lips, kissed the tips, and tossed his fingers into the air. The gesture seemed very Italian to her, but the seller loved it.

They returned to the water's edge to eat. The fruit truly was scrumptious. Surrounded by shouts and laughter, Daniel surprised her by turning serious.

"You mentioned you don't feel at home in Recife, and probably no longer would in Florianópolis. What about your father? Is he happy in Brazil?"

Isabel licked the juice from her lips. "I think he's content. He misses the Germany of his youth, although he realizes he remembers mostly the good. He didn't foresee the present war and is relieved not to be under the Nazis. Brazil welcomed him. Or at least, the German community did. Whether he's as happy in Recife as he was in Florianópolis, I don't know. My parents don't socialize as much."

"Having a rootless feeling isn't all bad. Did you know the chapel minister has been leading a Bible study about heaven with the airmen? That's where our citizenship is, and we should look forward to going there and being with God. That made me think of your situation."

She'd heard a verse about that. Maybe in the chapter of Bible heroes in Hebrews. She'd have to look it up when she returned to her room.

Mike Green called to them. "We're going to explore that fort. Want to come?"

Daniel raised his brows at her. "What do you know about it?"

"*The Forte dos Reis Magos*, or the three wise men," Isabel said. "I haven't been there, but I've heard you can see them."

Daniel stood and offered her a hand. "Well, by all means, let's go see them."

He jogged to the vendors to return their tray and utensils, and they joined the group of explorers. Isabel tried to recall what she'd heard about the fort. The Portuguese began construction on the sixth of January, 1598, the day of Epiphany of the Three Kings, hence the name. Its purpose was to deter French pirates from entering the river, but the Dutch captured the fort some thirty years later. Twenty years after that, the Portuguese reclaimed it.

"It could only be built during low tide. During high tide, the sandbar is underwater."

"So we have to watch the time, or we'll have to swim back."

At the entrance were three statues. Melchior, Gaspar, and Baltazar.

"Hmm." Daniel studied Melchior's hands. "Looks like at one time, Gaspar and Melchior held gifts for the Christ child, but someone swiped them."

They wandered around the nooks and crannies of the structure. As befitting a fort, it offered spectacular views. At one point, Isabel turned around and glimpsed someone ducking out of sight. Her blood chilled.

"Isabel?" Daniel touched her arm. "What's wrong? You've turned white as a ghost."

"I thought I saw Pelican." She gulped in air. "I must be getting paranoid."

His thumb stroked her hand. Usually, it was a soothing touch, but now it didn't affect her. Tears pressed against the back of her eyes. Uwe Schneider was ruining her day, whether in fact or because he had gotten into her head.

They returned to the party and joined a volleyball game. Usually she played well, but not today. After only one game, Daniel grabbed her hand. "Time for a dip."

They waded into the shallows. Here she was in her element. The water had warmed in the sun, and they swam farther out. Her mood brightened.

"We should have goggles." Daniel treaded water. "I think there's a lovely big shell down there, but I'm not volunteering to dive for it."

"Aw, that's not very gallant of you." Trying to speak without laughing proved impossible. She attempted to spot what he'd seen, but the restless water obscured it. "Maybe the tide will wash it up. We'll have to come back early in the morning."

He saluted. "Yes, ma'am. Then I'll have to hit the sack. I fly tomorrow night."

And Isabel worked during the day. Getting their schedules in sync proved to be a challenge. For today, she mustn't think of that. They were together now.

Beyond the breakwater, they lay back and floated on the undulating salty water cushion. The sun offered a bright, warm caress, and she became sleepy. She reached for Daniel's hand. "If we fall asleep, we'll float out to sea and eventually wash up in Africa."

"Nah. We'll be shark bait long before then."

She rolled over to look around. "They won't come this close to shore, will they?"

He twisted them around so they pointed toward shore and began a lazy kick. "If they do, punch them in the snoot."

Was that possible without her hand going down its throat? She joined him in kicking.

He interlaced their fingers. "You've always lived near the shore, right? Even in Florianópolis?"

She turned her head to face him, and her ear filled with water. "Yes. In Florianópolis, the beach was half an hour away."

"Would you miss not living near a shore?"

His voice sounded casual, but she detected a note of concern. Was he asking if she could be happy living in Milwaukee? Was he going to propose?

"Probably. At first, anyway. Don't you live near a shore?"

"Lake Michigan, yes. The Great Lakes are huge. You can't see the opposite shore, so you have the illusion of an ocean. They don't have the seashells of the ocean though. Or the salt. Or the sharks. And it's usually cold all the time."

She tried to picture it. A tame ocean? "No sharks is good."

Through his hand, she felt the vibration of laughter.

Splat. Seawater splashed in her face. A volleyball floated between them. Daniel stood, the water up to his neck, and flung the ball back.

A crowd gathered around the Red Cross grills. He nodded toward them. "If we want a burger, we'd better head for shore."

Before joining them, Isabel ducked into a changing booth to dry off and dress in her street clothes. She longed for a shower to rinse away the salty residue.

Eloise waved her over to the serving table. "We're running out of condiments. There's another bin in that truck with the balloons. Would you mind fetching it, please?"

Isabel scurried up the beach, waving to the pineapple seller. At the truck, she pulled back a tarp and found two bins. Which held the condiments?

Arms came around her and yanked her back.

"Hey ..."

A large hand slapped over her mouth, causing her to bite her tongue. A sour odor wafted over her. Pelican's bad breath. Her heart racing, she struggled against his hold, trying to kick his legs. He half carried, half dragged her away.

As though from a long distance, she heard someone call, "What are you doing?"

Someone saw her troubles. Help would soon be here.

Pelican lifted her up and dumped her into a dark place. Her head bounced on something hard. A lid slammed down. A car trunk. The engine started and swerved away. She tumbled about, banging her elbow on the funny bone.

God, help me.

Chapter Thirty-Four

"Help! Help! Someone's been kidnapped."

A momentary hush settled on the beach. Then a dozen men converged on the petite brunette wringing her hands on the edge of the dune.

Daniel searched through the crowd as he and Mike joined the group. Where had Isabel disappeared to?

The girl, her hair wrapped around the top of her head like a crown, was practically hyperventilating. "A blonde. Wearing a red dress, I think. With polka dots. Maybe it was pink. Or in between. I don't know."

Daniel's breath whooshed out of him as if he'd been kicked in his stomach. Isabel. The saboteur's henchman. She thought she'd seen him in the fort. He looked frantically in all directions but failed to locate her.

"What happened after he grabbed her?" A captain Daniel didn't recognize led the questioning.

"He threw her into a car trunk and roared off." The brunette pointed south.

"Why would anyone kidnap an American girl?"

Daniel vaguely recognized the airman who spoke as one of Edson's pals. "She's Brazilian," he said. "Isabel Neumann. She works in weights and balances. The German saboteur who bombed my plane is obsessed with her. She thought she spotted his sidekick at the fort."

"A German saboteur?" A radioman who had been showing off a small battery-operated set stepped forward. "I was listening to a frequency the German navy likes to transmit on, band four at ten megahertz. There's been a lot of hot noise." He gulped as Daniel glowered at his prattle. "There may be a U-boat nearby."

A wave of nausea swept over Daniel. "Schneider may expect to be picked up. He means to take Isabel to Germany."

The captain spun back to the petite girl. "What kind of car did he have?"

"I don't know. It was cream colored. A coupe?" She reached out to her boyfriend. "We passed it when we arrived, remember?"

"Yes." The man stabbed the air with his finger. "It has painted-on whitewalls. A rear one was smeared, and the fender was dented."

The captain took charge. "All right then. A cream car ought to stand out. Let's head south." He pointed to the radioman. "Call the navy. Give them all the info you have, and tell them to find that sub."

Daniel turned toward the parking lot. Eloise stood there, her hands over her mouth, tears welling in her eyes. "I asked her to get more ketchup. It's all my fault."

He touched her shoulder. It wasn't her fault any more than it was his for letting Isabel out of his sight. He would have told her so, but his throat was too tight. Instead, he hopped into the nearest jeep.

Mike jumped into the back. "We'll find her."

Daniel nodded. Folks uttered trite comments meant to comfort, but they had no guarantee. Oh, they might find Isabel, all right. They might find her dead. He pictured Uwe's hands around her neck, squeezing the life out of her because she refused him.

Father in heaven, You see her. Keep her safe. Bring her back. Help us find her.

His prayer stalled. He'd heard the frequent admonishment against telling God what to do. God knew best, even if that meant taking Isabel to heaven now.

No. Not yet.

The jeep bounced across a rutted, unpaved road. This area was too open. No U-boat commander in his right mind would surface around here. Unless he waited until dark. That would be after six, hours away. What was Uwe doing to her?

To their left, the ocean glistened in the sunlight. Such a tranquil scene, but who knew what hid beneath its surface? Would a submarine really heed a summons from Uwe Schneider? Was he that important to Germany? The guy seemed clumsy for an enemy saboteur. He had his cruel streak, though. That was what worried Daniel. Poison darts, bombs on airplanes, yanking Isabel around in front of her parents. Was he likely to change now that he had her in his grasp?

The road veered inland and wound through scrub brush, palm trees, and jungle-type growth. The taillights of the vehicle ahead of them flashed on. Several yards down a turnoff stood a cream car. The men jumped out and ran to the car. A two-door coupe, dented fender, smeared paint on the corresponding tire. The getaway car.

Someone knocked on the trunk lid. No one knocked back. Another man grabbed a crowbar from a toolbox in one of the jeeps and wrenched open the lid. Daniel sagged when he saw the empty void. Expecting to find her so quickly had been a forlorn hope.

But wait. The trunk wasn't empty. He picked up a small white object and turned it over on his palm. A clean, shiny seashell.

"Isabel likely has seashells in her pocket."

The captain surveyed the area. Hills rose to the east. Nestled in the valley stood a lower-class neighborhood of one- or two-room houses with thatched roofs. "Someone around here should know something about a foreigner in their midst. You say the Kraut's blond?"

"He's the stereotype of a perfect Nazi."

The turnoff where the car was parked dead-ended, surrounded by brush.

"Let's go back to the road. We'll start canvassing the homes."

Another airman held up a crumpled cigarette package wrapped in a handkerchief. "I found this in the car. I didn't touch it in case there are fingerprints on it."

"Good thinking." The captain took a close look and stopped. He looked at Daniel with raised brows. "Chesterfield. Readily available on base."

"Clarence Berelli collaborated with Schneider to place the bomb on my plane. He may have given them to Schneider."

They continued down the road to a fork, where the captain said, "Some of you go that way. We'll go this way."

"Wait." Daniel stooped down on the left side. "It's another of Isabel's seashells." He swallowed hard as his voice quavered. "She's leaving a trail."

One of the men poised to head down the right side frowned. "How can you be sure?"

Mike stepped up and gripped Daniel's shoulder. "This

shell's clean and hasn't been ground into the dirt. It's been dropped recently."

"And she's familiar with Hansel and Gretel." Daniel was sure Isabel had dropped it.

"Everyone to the left," the captain said. "We're on the right track. Keep an eye out for seashells."

Daniel's mind settled on one thought. She'd kept her wits about her.

Attagirl, Isabel.

Chapter Thirty-Five

Every bounce over the rutted road added more bruises. Isabel attempted to brace herself, but too many items in the trunk were no more secure than she was. Her fingers explored her black prison. Nothing felt clean. Grit coated the floor. Even small stones.

Good thing she'd changed out of her swimsuit. Hysterical laughter bubbled up as she imagined Pelican's paws on her bare midriff. The wet swimsuit would have been a magnet for all this dirt.

Her chest heaved as she sought to gather her composure. She must be strong. Confident.

Or maybe not. There was that king in the Bible who feigned madness and was told to leave. Wise old Solomon? No, his father. David, a man after God's own heart.

Would Uwe be disgusted if she whimpered and wailed?

She must be a woman after God's heart. What would such a woman do? She prayed. She accepted the tough assignments, like Mary agreeing to be the mother of Christ. But did Isabel have the right to expect God's help? Her prayers consisted mostly of mealtime grace and bedtime good-nights. Now she was in trouble, and she wanted help.

He would offer help. He loved to welcome the prodigal.

"Our Father which art in heaven ... My Father in heaven, hallowed You are. May Your will be done on earth as it is in heaven."

The car slowed and turned off the road.

She swallowed a sob. "Deliver me from evil. Yours is the kingdom, the power, and glory forever."

Pelican raised the lid and leered at her. Thinning dark hair that needed a trim lay matted on his forehead, like he'd been sweating. A dueling scar marred his left cheek. Of course, he probably saw it as a badge of courage. Marcos had told her the university fraternity students who fought the Mensur duels practiced in Germany's academic fencing classes believed girls favored scars. Pelican's made him look uglier.

She drew back as he reached for her, but there was nowhere to hide. He grabbed her arm and pulled her forward. Sore from the ride, she wasn't fast enough to climb out of the car, and he dragged her over the bumper. Her knee scraped the edge and blood immediately trickled.

"*En tut mir leid, meine Dame.*" His smirk rendered his words of apology false. He was not sorry. And his foul breath hadn't improved. It would offend a jaguar.

His high voice transported her back to the church. If only Graziela was here and they could escape again. Her thoughts must have been evident, for he glared at her and yanked her through the brush surrounding the car to a road consisting of more ruts than flat surface. No wonder she was so battered.

As she stumbled along, her hand bumped her pocket. It was bumpy. She slid in her hand and discovered her seashells. Such comforting little things.

When Pelican shoved her down a fork in the road, she slipped out a shell and dropped it.

Find me, Daniel.

He must be searching for her. That girl with the coil of braids had witnessed Pelican hauling her to the car. Isabel had seen her wide eyes, her dangling jaw. Surely she told someone.

They entered a neighborhood of little houses close together. No cars were parked near any of them. This was far from a well-to-do area, but the residents took pride in their humble homes. From what she could see, their tiny yards were free of clutter. She dropped seashells until she ran out.

Pelican pushed open the door to a house set a bit apart from the rest and thrust her inside. She stumbled against an open-ended packing crate serving as an end table. As she struggled to keep her balance, Pelican tossed his keys on the crate.

Uwe Schneider rose from a rickety-looking table. A satisfied smirk spread across his face. "Well, well, Isabel. You have finally seen fit to join me."

White hot rage flared within her. After all the frustration and grief he'd caused, the implication that she chose to be here infuriated her.

He stalked closer and placed his palm on her cheek.

She jerked away. "Keep your filthy hands off me."

"Foolish, foolish girl. You cannot thwart me." He spoke in German.

"I am nothing to you and never will be. I despise you. You are nothing but a criminal."

He slapped her face hard enough to snap her head back. Her vision blurred and white noise roared in her ears.

"You will speak to me in our mother tongue, *Mädchen*. And you will show me respect." Grasping her shoulders, he shook her. With her head already spinning, dizziness threatened to upend her stomach.

"I will never respect you."

He pushed her into a chair so hard she expected it to topple. At least his hands were off her. She suspected he didn't understand enough Portuguese to recognize *respect, despise,* or *criminal,* but her tone gave away their meanings.

He stood over her, breathing hard. "Why are you bleeding?"

She bit back a snort. He didn't mind trying to break her neck, but a little blood bothered him?

Marcos had said he understood English. While she refused to speak German, a little communication might be to her advantage. "Ask Pelican." When his eyebrows rose, she clarified. "Your henchman."

"Why do you call him Pelican?" Uwe readily switched to English, an enemy language.

Seriously?

"Because the stench of his foul breath must match the collection of dead fish a pelican saves in its beak."

Uwe uttered a laugh, and he stood tall. "Our führer has bad breath. Nothing to be ashamed of."

Isabel couldn't help it. She rolled her eyes.

Uwe glowered at her, but he kept his hands to himself.

He turned to Pelican. "Time to make the call."

The two men hauled a crate to the table and pulled out a radio with cables, a headset, microphone, and antenna. She stared at it all in confusion. Uwe had left a boxful of radio parts under her bed. The police thought he wanted to implicate her. Maybe he meant to involve her in his schemes, informing him of flight schedules or cargo lists, and she'd located his stash before he completed the setup.

As they warmed up the tubes, her gaze roamed the single

room. Furniture was sparse. A mattress hugged a corner. Did they both sleep there? Four wooden chairs didn't offer comfortable seating. The house lacked electricity and a bathroom. A table shoved under the lone window held assorted foodstuffs.

A distant sound registered in her mind. Waves on a beach. They had traveled south and not too far inland. Closing her eyes, she listened to the beloved song of the surf. Funny how the sound of crashing waves calmed her scattered wits.

Uwe spoke of an *Unterseeboot*. Her eyes snapped open. A U-boat? Why would he contact a submarine?

Heat flushed through her, followed by an icy chill.

He called the U-boat to pick them up. To take them to Germany.

She swallowed hard against the bile that rose in her throat. If he managed to get her out of Brazil ... if they managed to reach Germany ... her life would be forfeited. Who would believe she had been kidnapped? Who would care? For sure, he wouldn't allow her to contact her relatives.

What did he intend to do with her there? He didn't know her. All he knew about her were her looks, her pure Aryan looks. Blue eyes and blonde hair. Big deal. Why hadn't he grabbed a girl in Germany? Maybe all the girls in Germany rejected him because he was such a creep.

Understandable.

And Germany was hardly a healthy place to be now, not with the Allies bombing it into a rubbish heap.

Why was Uwe so determined to have her? Why would the Germans accommodate his desire? Committing sabotage in an out-of-the-way place like Brazil couldn't grant him much clout. Was he Hitler's nephew that they would cater to his whims?

She reached for the comfort of the surf and breathed deeply to calm her frantic heartbeat. Where was Daniel?

Father in heaven, I need Your help. Don't let him take me to Germany. I love Daniel. I do. Will I see him again? And Mamãe and Papai. And Marcos. He'll blame himself for bringing Uwe home.

She struggled to inflate her lungs.

I'm sorry I haven't accomplished anything with my life.

Seashell art. Had she wasted her life? What else could she have done? Her arrangements did give people happiness. A bit of brightness to enjoy on cloudy days.

All the Bible stories she'd heard since childhood agreed that Jesus always welcomed people. He would welcome her. Snatches of a hymn—a German hymn—spooled through her mind.

A mighty fortress is our God, a bulwark never failing. ... And though this world, with devils filled, should threaten to undo us, we will not fear, for God has willed his truth to triumph through us ... the body they may kill ...

Uwe might yet kill her. Or she could die under the bombs. But she wasn't dead yet. She wouldn't go meekly off to Germany with him.

Uwe strutted toward her with a triumphant tilt to his head. "We leave tonight. It will do you good to be away from all these degenerative people."

No. She felt the color leach from her face. "I'm not going anywhere with you."

Crack. Lights danced in her head as her cheek burned with pain from his slap. She ran her tongue around her teeth, making sure they were still attached.

He loomed over her. "You will do as I say. You belong to me, and you will behave."

"Never." He had to be insane. She screamed when he grabbed her hair and yanked her up.

Chapter Thirty-Six

One by one, the men found seven seashells. The last one left them in the vicinity of half a dozen small homes. A woman peered at them from the doorway of the nearest house. Definitely a Brazilian woman.

Daniel nodded toward her. "I'll ask if she's seen any blond men around here."

The captain accompanied him. The woman eyed them with suspicion that morphed into amusement. Maybe Daniel's Portuguese wasn't as good as he thought. What was the word for blond? Were any Germans nearby?

The woman pointed to the cabin set off by itself before stepping inside her home and closing the door.

"I take that to mean we didn't hear anything from her," the captain said in a dry tone.

"Nope. Didn't hear a word out of her."

They hurried back to the others. A man with a walkie talkie waved them over. "The navy spotted a sub thirty miles due east. They're dropping depth charges."

The captain caught Daniel's eye. "That means no getaway." He pointed out the indicated house. "They're likely in there."

As they converged on the house, they heard a scream. The captain pounded on the door.

"Dan—" Isabel's voice.

The captain kicked in the door, and they rushed in.

Uwe Schneider held Isabel by her hair, his other hand clamped over her mouth. He threw her at a spindly chair, which promptly collapsed. Daniel shoved a hulking figure out of the way and knelt beside her. Her left cheek glowed red from where she'd been struck. Cuts and bruises covered her arms and legs. Rage built within him as he carefully lifted her.

"You came." He barely heard her whisper.

He swallowed hard. "We followed your seashells, sweetheart."

She attempted a smile. Her eyes weren't focusing. "I knew you would."

One of the men joined them. "I'm a medic. Why don't I give you a quick checkup, miss?" To Daniel, he said, "How about you lay her on the bed?"

Isabel raised a shoulder and pressed into him. "No, I will not lie on his bed."

"Of course not." The medic looked around.

Three men held Uwe in place on another spindly chair. One of them shoved him off and swung the chair around to them. "Will this do?"

Her eyes blinked rapidly without fully opening. She continued to lean against Daniel after he lowered her onto the chair. Her hands trembled.

The medic flashed a light in her eyes and touched her wrist, taking her pulse. "I imagine your ears are ringing."

She nodded once.

"We need to get her back to base and the hospital for a thorough exam. She's in shock."

The radioman announced the Brazilian police were on their way to arrest Schneider and Pelican, and base security wanted a look at Uwe's setup.

This was Daniel's first time to see Schneider in person. He gave an involuntary shiver as Uwe glared at them, his face twisted in hatred. Twice he'd tried—and failed—to kill Daniel. No more. A weight Daniel hadn't realized he carried dropped away.

One of the men asked, "Can't we just shoot him?"

Laughter rang out in the tiny house.

Daniel lifted Isabel and carried her out. A breeze fanned their faces.

She gingerly snuggled into his grasp. "I hear the ocean."

Chapter Thirty-Seven

T hey sat close enough to the water that the waves
washed their feet. Isabel raised her toes, sending a
spray of salty mist in their faces.

Daniel hugged her tight and kissed her. "Mmm, seasoned
just right."

Her shoulders shook in silent laughter, and she rested her
head on his shoulder. "I slept through the night, which
surprises me. So many thoughts have been whirling in my
head."

Most of them started with *why*. Why did Uwe target her?
Why did a submarine respond to him? Why was he so
important? Why had he been allowed to roam freely in Brazil?
Her head ached with the effort to understand.

Daniel yawned. "You were fortunate. I hardly slept at all.
Most of my thoughts entertained visions of Uwe Schneider
dangling from a rope."

She poked his ribs. "He may wish for that. I heard he's on
his way to Rio and a notorious prison where people tend to
disappear."

Daniel's thumb stroked her arm. "He caused a lot of German deaths. The navy hit that U-boat hard. It managed to pop to the surface, and many bailed out before it sank, but many more went down with it."

She closed her eyes against the images of being forced aboard the sub. The smell of diesel and unwashed bodies would have been overwhelming. The crewmen had to share bunks by turns, while one was on duty, then the other. Only one toilet for fifty or more men. Trapped beneath the surface, unable to see the sun or sky for days or weeks. How would they have treated her?

"Would they really have taken me? Just because Uwe wanted me? It makes no sense."

Daniel remained silent.

She shifted to better see his face. "Do you know something?"

He exhaled hard. "The navy interrogated the survivors. One was quite talkative. He said Schneider came from a prominent Nazi family, but he got into big trouble. Assaulting women, stealing credit he wasn't due."

He spilled sand between his fingers. "His bigwig daddy exiled him until the dust settled. Ordered him to do something remarkable to gain favor. Apparently, Uwe and the U-boat captain were pals."

Isabel stared at the waves washing her toes. "Why was he going back now? What remarkable thing did he do?"

"The police found some harbor charts and something about the Brazilian Expeditionary Force. Nothing that would aid Germany." Daniel shrugged. "Maybe Schneider realized he needed to get out of Brazil in a hurry. He may have deluded himself into believing his little gleanings would be game changers."

"And me?"

He played with her fingers. "My guess? He came here instead of the German communities in the south. He didn't find many Aryan women here. Maybe he wanted to return to Germany appearing as a respectable family man. He needed you to complete the picture."

Her stomach hollowed. Uwe never treated her respectfully. She took a deep breath. Another. The queasy feeling subsided. "My guardian angel was watching over me." She gave Daniel a sidelong glance. "Or at least an angel with a slightly tarnished halo."

"Hey, now." A chuckle escaped him. "My halo's shiny."

A strong wave swished up the beach, and they scrambled to their feet before it drenched their clothing. They began to walk.

"Captain Carter came to see me at my barracks last night," Isabel said. "He wanted to be sure I'm okay and asked if I wanted the day off." Maybe his visit had enabled her to sleep soundly. Her job was secure. She looked up at Daniel. "They had every reason to terminate me. I've been nothing but trouble."

"Whoa." Daniel pulled her to a halt. "You've been nothing but a valuable asset. You're the girl who swallowed the calculator, remember? You were the victim of the troublemakers. Uwe and Pelican and Berelli." He squeezed her hand. "You're a heroine who contributed to the capture of a Nazi saboteur. Got that?"

She saluted. "Yes, sir. I'm a heroine. But isn't that a drug?"

His head dropped back and he laughed. Then he darted into the surf and grabbed a shell. "Here. Put this in your pocket. You may need it."

She gasped. This was no common scallop. The red-toned *bullata lilacina* rarely washed ashore, but this tiny specimen, no bigger than an American quarter, had been captured by the current. She tucked it in her pocket. "This is a keeper."

He smiled at her with a bright intensity gleaming in his eyes. "So are you."

He looked out to sea. "Did you contact your parents?"

"I did. They're coming to visit today. Marcos too."

"Good. What time will they arrive?"

She checked the sun's progress. "They'll probably take off in about an hour."

"Good."

"Why is that good?"

"I need to speak with your father, but I also need to hit the sack before long. I'm flying to Ascension this evening." He pointed east. "Just over the horizon."

She laughed. "Just nine hours over the horizon. Why do you need to talk to my father?"

Papai had no qualms about her staying at Parnamirim. Uwe was no longer a threat.

"I have a question for him. Or a request." He caressed her cheek, the one that wasn't bruised. "Maybe I should ask you first."

Her hand flew to her mouth when he dropped to one knee. Tingles skittered all over her.

"Isabel Carin Neumann, will you do me the honor of becoming my wife?"

A hint of uncertainty replaced some of the gleam in his eyes. He was nervous about her answer.

"How do you know my middle name?"

He gripped her hand and his brows pinched over his nose. "Isabel."

"Yes! Yes, yes, yes. I would be honored to be your wife."

A beautiful smile spread across his face as he rose and embraced her. With his face buried in her hair, he hesitated.

"Marrying me will mean leaving Brazil, living in the United States. In Milwaukee, far from the ocean, from your family. The winters are freezing."

"But I'll have you." A sudden doubt struck. "What about your family? Will they be upset you're marrying someone they haven't met?"

"They love you." He stepped back and grinned. "After all, you're putting up with me. Besides, they've already seen you. I sent them one of Kenny's photos of us in Rio. I received a quick letter back from Mom saying, *do tell.* I think her only disappointment will be the wedding taking place here instead of there."

Isabel would have three sisters. She'd always wanted a sister.

How soon could they marry? Surely Daniel was allowed to marry, but could his wife live on base with him? Did the base even have married officers' quarters?

Thoughts buzzed through her mind like a colony of bees.

"You said we'd be near the big lake."

"Right. We'll get a boat. A sailboat, maybe. Or a speedboat might be better if we ever have to outrace a sudden storm." He didn't stop smiling as he toyed with a lock of her hair.

She curled her hands up behind his neck and drew him down for a kiss. He was quick to oblige. His lips melded to hers, gentle at first, growing bolder. She imagined fireworks exploding. Salty kisses, indeed. Her favorite.

"I don't have a ring for you." Concern darkened his eyes. "Where can we find one here?"

"You gave me a seashell. That'll do for now." She pulled it out. "I'll make a necklace with it, and I'll wear it for our wedding."

Our wedding. She wanted to squeal, or dance, or … She reached up for another kiss.

Squawk.

In a moment of déjà vu, they jerked apart. Once more, the beady-eyed seagull glared at them.

Daniel's shoulders slumped. "We may have to invite him to the wedding."

Epilogue

Winter Haven, Florida
November, 1945

Cypress Gardens was a feast of beauty and color for the eyes, just as Isabel expected it would be. The postcards Huberto had sent six years ago hadn't done justice to the park. Too bad she couldn't relax and enjoy it.

When Daniel suggested they renew their marriage vows on their first anniversary, the idea thrilled her. What a lovely way to start their life together in America.

Then he added another thought. His parents might like to travel to Florida for the ceremony. Unlike Isabel's parents, they'd missed the wedding last year in Natal. Then they could enjoy a vacation at the beach. His mother hadn't seen the ocean since the Strieder family emigrated in 1908. With the war over, travel restrictions should be lifted.

As Daniel made plans, Isabel agreed with everything. Now the thought of meeting his parents caused her to quake. What if they didn't like her? Had Daniel disappointed them by marrying a foreigner?

His mother had once been a foreigner. And Daniel believed they would love her. If only they hadn't been delayed by weather in Puerto Rico and missed the chance to meet last night.

Arched wooden bridges linked the brick pathways winding around the gardens, and Daniel indicated the path between two azalea bushes. "This way."

Isabel pulled an azalea bloom close for a sniff. "Mmm. Each flower improves on the last."

They rounded a bend.

"Ooh, look. This was one of Huberto's cards."

Across a lagoon, a serpentine row of flowers led to a landing where electric boats waited for passengers to glide through the canals and visit reflecting pools. Isabel forced herself to maintain a steady pace as they found another bridge. Their leisurely walk allowed her to enjoy the fragrance of gardenias, roses, and camellias. The sight of hibiscus, orchids, and poinsettias thrilled her.

A southern belle seated on the ground beside a floral bed attempted to rise, but dropped back when she spotted them. Daniel hurried over to offer a hand. "Oh, thank you, kind sir." She offered a conspiratorial look to Isabel. "These dresses may look like the epitome of gracious living, but they're totally ungraceful for getting up."

"It's a beautiful gown." Ruffles circled the yellow skirt. Another row of ruffles topped the off-the-shoulder bodice. Isabel couldn't resist touching the wide skirt. "I've dreamed of coming here for years, ever since my cousin sent photos."

The belle quirked an eyebrow, probably wondering about her accent. She nodded at the garden behind her. "You can witness a wedding here soon."

"Actually, that will be us." Daniel beamed. "We're renewing our vows."

"What a pretty spot to be married." Isabel clasped her hands under her chin. Memories of their wedding last year filled her mind. Nothing could top a sunrise beach ceremony, but this was a close second. She glanced down at her dress. "I should have brought my wedding dress instead of packing it in the luggage to be sent straight to Milwaukee."

The belle eyed her up and down. "Would you like to try on one of these dresses? Come on."

She led Isabel back toward the park's entrance and into a changing room. She rifled through a rack of gowns. "This one should fit. Oh, I'm Martha, by the way."

Rosy pink confection settled around the hoops Isabel had donned first. She blinked at her reflection in the mirror and ran her fingers over the ruffle at her shoulders. So gorgeous. And so heavy. The skirt had seven tiers of ruffles. "Isn't this hot?"

"It can be. While we're standing, the hoops keep it off our legs. Each dress contains six to ten yards of fabric, mostly in the skirt's ruffles. And then there are the twenty yards of lace. Let's find a flower for your hair. We usually wear cameos on ribbons, but your necklace is so pretty."

Isabel touched the shell. "This is my engagement seashell. I made the necklace so I could wear it at our wedding." She offered Martha an abbreviated account of hers and Daniel's courtship.

"That's perfect. You'll have to pose on the citrus throne for a portrait. Your husband looks so dashing in his dress uniform. We'd better hurry back to the garden now."

Daniel did a double take when he beheld Isabel decked out in the finery. "Wow."

An older couple stood beside him. His parents.

The hoops prevented them from standing too close

together, but Daniel took her hand and led her to them. "Mom, Dad, meet my wife, Isabel." His smile outshone the sun.

His mother clasped Isabel's hand. "I am so pleased to finally meet you."

His father didn't try to press close with her wide skirt. "Charmed, my dear. You've certainly enchanted our son. His letters have been almost poetic."

Both parents were so friendly, so accepting. The last bit of tension dropped away from Isabel.

In quick order, they were standing before a minister for a brief ceremony.

"Daniel and Isabel, it is your wish to reaffirm your commitment to work together to make your marriage grow and blossom in the years to come. May this renewal of the vows you took on your wedding day to become husband and wife remind you that, despite the stresses inevitable in every life, your love, respect, trust, and understanding of each other will increase your contentment and heighten your joy in living."

They joined hands, and the minister spoke to Isabel.

"Isabel, do you reaffirm your love for Daniel, and will you love, honor, and cherish him in sickness and in health, for richer or poorer, for better for worse, and forsaking all others, be faithful to him as long as you both shall live?"

She gazed into Daniel's eyes, blue like the sea, shining with love. "I do."

The minister repeated the vows with Daniel, and concluded, "It is with pleasure that I conclude the ceremony of renewing the vows of marriage that joined you and bind you as husband and wife. Please celebrate this renewal of vows with a kiss."

Daniel didn't need to be prompted twice.

When the kiss ended, applause startled them. A large

crowd of park visitors had been attracted to the sight of a belle and an officer taking vows. The photographer snapped away, and they finally stepped away from the garden.

Martha whisked Isabel away to the changing room. "Oh, my goodness. If all those people find out you're not one of us who work here, every bride will be clamoring to wear one of these dresses." She giggled. "Maybe I should suggest to the Pope family that owns the park to have a few wedding gowns to rent."

Isabel grasped her hand. "Thank you for this … this dream. This has been a magical day."

Back outside wearing her own sundress, she joined Daniel and his parents where they waited at a boat landing. Daniel handed her into the boat. "A honeymoon cruise as we sail into our new life in America, my love."

His mother laughed. "After a wedding last year and this ceremony now, what will you do next year?"

Isabel placed her hand over her abdomen. "I'm ninety-nine percent sure we'll have a new family member next year."

The way Daniel's jaw dropped was immensely satisfying. So was his kiss.

Author's Note

Most World War II novels take place in Europe. The war, however, was worldwide, in places like Brazil, Iceland, and the South Pacific.

One of my favorite feel-good stories is that of Gail Halvorsen, known as the Candy Bomber of the Berlin Airlift. Before he dropped chocolate to the children of wartorn Berlin, he flew C-47 cargo planes out of Natal, Brazil, during the war. My interest was roused. What role did Americans play in World War II from Brazil?

That question wasn't easy to answer. Very little has been written about Brazil and the South Atlantic theater. Eleanor Roosevelt and Humphrey Bogart really did visit. Red Cross and United States Engineering Department ladies worked in Natal. A pilot commented on flying dive bombers for recreation. Especially insightful was an out-of-print book of photographs by a Navy photographer. With clues found here and there, *Seashells in My Pocket* came to be.

Without the American Christian Fiction Writers and its critique groups and conferences, I would never have succeeded in my writing. Special thanks to Connie Cortright, Teresa Haugh, Erin Stevenson, Nancy Radesovich, and Cindy Peter for reading and critiquing this book. Thank you to the Scrivenings team, including Linda Fulkerson, Amy Anguish, and Susan Page Davis. And thank you to Anne Prado for reviewing my Portuguese.

If you're on Pinterest, see my board for *Novel: Seashells in My Pocket* for views of Parnamirim air base, Natal, seashells, and C-47s: www.pinterest.com/terriwangard/

I hope you enjoyed *Seashells in My Pocket*! Would you help others enjoy this book too? Recommend it. Help other readers find this book by recommending it to friends in person and on social media. Review it. Reviews can be tough to come by these days. You, the reader, have the power to make or break a book.

Connect with me on Facebook: www.facebook.com/AuthorTerriWangard. Visit www.terriwangard.com and sign up for my newsletter.

Thank you so much for reading *Seashells in My Pocket* and for spending time with Daniel and Isabel.

In gratitude,

Terri Wangard

About the Author

Terri Wangard grew up in Green Bay, Wisconsin, during the Lombardi Glory Years, but she didn't appreciate the Packers until she moved away.

Libraries have always held a special place in her heart. She has fond memories of visiting Green Bay's North Branch library, and looking for Maj Lindman's *Flicka, Ricka, and Dicka* books. She scribbled stories in a notebook (fortunately, not saved) and her first Girl Scout badge was the Writer. No surprise, she has a master's degree in library science.

She has lived in Michigan, Utah, Southern California, and is now back in Wisconsin, where her research for her first WWII series included going for a ride in a B-17 Flying Fortress bomber. The series, published in 2016, features B-17 navigators and the women they fell in love with. Terri has also written a novel about the *Lusitania*, far more interesting than the *Titanic*, and a companion novel set in World War I.

She won the 2013 Writers on the Storm contest and 2013 First Impressions, as well as being a 2012 Genesis finalist. *Classic Boating* Magazine, a family business since 1984, keeps her busy as an associate editor. In her spare time, she enjoys bicycling, reading, photography, travel, and genealogy. She is a member of the American Christian Fiction Writers, has served as treasurer for her local chapter and as the First Impression contest coordinator, and is now the local chapter's secretary.

You may also like ...

Beyond These War-torn Lands By Cynthia Roemer

Wounded Hearts—Book One

While en route to aid Confederate soldiers injured in battle near her home, Southerner Caroline Dunbar stumbles across a wounded Union sergeant. Unable to ignore his plea for help, she tends his injuries and hides him away, only to find her attachment to him deepen with each passing day. But when her secret is discovered, Caroline incurs her father's wrath and, in turn, unlocks a dark secret from the past which she is determined to unravel.

After being forced to flee his place of refuge, Sergeant Andrew Gallagher fears he's seen the last of Caroline. Resolved not to let that happen, when the war ends, he seeks her out, only to discover she's been sent away. When word reaches him that President Lincoln has been shot, Drew is assigned the task of tracking down the assassin. A chance encounter with Caroline revives his hopes, until he learns she may be involved in a plot to aid the assassin.

Get your copy here:

https://scrivenings.link/beyondthesewartornlands

Strong Currents by Delores Topliff

Columbia River Undercurrents—Book Two

When German Christian, Erika Hofer, opposes Hitler, church leader
Dietrich Bonhoeffer helps her flee to her uncle John Hofer along the
Columbia River in America's Pacific Northwest. Erika finds
acceptance and support but also suspicion, hatred, and an attempt
on her life.

American pastor's son, Josh Vengeance, joins the US Navy to serve
his country, but is injured at Midway Island and invalided home.
While healing in body and spirit, he joins a network of colorful
individuals, including John Hofer and his niece, Erika, who defend
their homeland as volunteers.

Can two wounded young people move past betrayal and

disillusionment to find love and freedom during a world at war?

Get your copy here:

https://scrivenings.link/strongcurrents

★·◉·◎·❊·◉·◎·❊·◉·◎·❊·◉

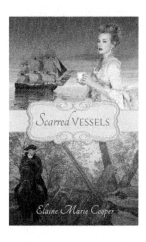

Scarred Vessels by Elaine Marie Cooper

In a time when America battles for freedom, a man and woman seek to fight the injustice of slavery while discovering love in the midst of tragedy.

In 1778 Rhode Island, the American Revolution rallies the Patriots to fight for freedom. But the slavery of black men and women from Africa, bartered for rum, is a travesty that many in America cannot ignore. The seeds of abolition are planted even as the laws allowing slavery in the north still exist.

Lydia Saunders, the daughter of a slave ship owner, grew up with the horror of slavery. It became more of a nightmare when, at a young age, she is confronted with the truth about her father's occupation. Burdened with the guilt of her family's sin, she struggles to make a difference in whatever way she can. When she loses her husband in the battle for freedom from England, she makes a difficult decision that will change her life forever.

Sergeant Micah Hughes is too dedicated to serving the fledgling country of America to consider falling in love. When he carries the tragic news to Lydia Saunders about her husband's death, he is appalled by his attraction to the young widow. Micah wrestles with his feelings for Lydia while he tries to focus on helping the cause of freedom. He trains a group of former slaves to become capable soldiers on the battlefield.

Tensions both on the battlefield and on the home front bring hardship and turmoil that threaten to endanger them all. When Lydia and Micah are faced with saving the life of a black infant in danger, can they survive this turning point in their lives?

A groundbreaking book, honest and inspiring, showcasing black soldiers in the American Revolution. *Scarred Vessels* is peopled with flesh and blood characters and true events that not only inspire and entertain but educate. Well done!

~ Laura Frantz, Christy Award-winning author

of *An Uncommon Woman*

Get your copy here:

https://scrivenings.link/scarredvessels

Stay up-to-date on your favorite books and authors with our free e-newsletters.

ScriveningsPress.com

Printed in Great Britain
by Amazon

45848347R00185